Michael Costello

Harold Effermere

A story of the Queensland bush

Michael Costello

Harold Effermere
A story of the Queensland bush

ISBN/EAN: 9783337323462

Printed in Europe, USA, Canada, Australia, Japan

Cover: Foto ©Andreas Hilbeck / pixelio.de

More available books at **www.hansebooks.com**

CONTENTS

CONTENTS

Chapter I

" The whining schoolboy with his satchel."
    —*As You Like It.*—SHAKESPEARE.

"IT is a strange life Harold has such a hankering for," said Mrs. Merton, as she sat at the breakfast table and poured out the coffee.

Mr. Merton was deeply interested in the columns of the morning paper, and in consequence his wife's remark did not come home to him very distinctly. He just muttered a vague, matter-of-form "Yes," and went on with his reading.

After a little while Mrs. Merton looked at him and said, " Really, George, I do not think you paid the slightest attention to what I said."

Mr. Merton instantly laid down the paper, and, turning to his wife, answered, with an apologetic air, " I beg your pardon, my dear ; I must admit I did not notice what you spoke about."

" It was about Harold," said Mrs. Merton, as she handed her husband a cup of coffee.

Mr. Merton stirred his cup in a meditative mood, and then suddenly looking up, said, "Yes ; his highest ambition is for the bush."

" And what will he get there ? "

B

"Ah, what will he not get there, in the way of things he did not bargain for! Well, among the items, a course of camping-out, watching cattle at night—often enough cold, wet nights too—getting pitched off 'buck jumpers,' and cursed by the 'boss' for falling off."

"What dreadfully rough people those bushmen must be!"

"My dear, they want to be rough; and, for the most part, they are ready too. They must have constitutions equal to any emergency. It is quite wonderful to see them eating salt beef—dry, hard, sapless, and, perhaps, weeks old; sodden 'damper,' that makes it a case of the survival of the fittest; black tea, that would shake the nerves of a giant; and, by way of a luxury, now and then, a 'brownie,' or dumplings with currants in them."

"It's a dreadful life!"

"Dreadful we might call it indeed, Rose; but I have only shown the bright side of the picture."

"The bright side?"

"Well, yes, to a certain extent. Salt junk and damper may not be luxuries, but there are times when the bushman has to do without them altogether."

"Altogether? My gracious! Then, of course, the poor fellows starve. But how does it come to that?"

"Well, from what I hear about it, they get what they call 'a bit of a doing for tucker'; but the fittest still keep surviving. As to how it comes to that, my dear, I can only put the statements of two persons before you, and let you judge for yourself. The squatter bitterly complains that his carrier has taken a notion of forming a cabbage garden on the road, and, becoming for the time interested in agriculture, does not like to leave his pumpkin patch till the vegetables are ripe. On the other hand, the carrier says that heavy rains prevented him from travelling, and that he had to camp for the wet season. He also says that the pastoralists should not leave the ordering of their supplies till the last moment, and then expect the carrier to come along like an electric telegram. At any rate, between the two the bush-man comes to pigweed and sun-dried beef."

"I cannot imagine why Harold should have any wish for such a life as that," said Mrs. Merton, adding, after a pause, "and you were expecting that he would be fit to take a place in the office now."

"I was, Rose," replied Mr. Merton ; "but the fact of it is, he hasn't education enough to address envelopes for a commission agent. I suppose it's the nature of his old wandering vagabond of a father, whoever he is, that's breaking out in the boy."

"I hope he'll be a very different man to his father," said Mrs. Merton warmly. "He must have been a most inhuman creature to desert his wife in that manner—leaving her in a perfectly destitute position." Then, after a pause, she added, "You should reason a little more with Harold, my dear, and get him to give up the notion of this bush folly."

"It would be no use," said Mr. Merton, shaking his head ; "boys like that have neither sense nor reason. The only way is to leave them to their own folly. By the way, I told you I had a letter from the head-master of the school ? No ? Well, then, I'll go and get it."

With these words Mr. Merton stood up, but suddenly remembering that he had the letter in his pocket, he took it out and sat down again, saying, "Well, my dear, this is what Mr. Wilson has to say about the boy ; and I suppose, being an apparently candid letter, it's the only thing he could say."

Mr. Merton with a little preliminary cough started to read the following letter :

DEAR SIR,—

"I very much regret that I am unable to send you a satisfactory report of Harold's studies. He has made but little progress in learning for the time he has been here. Not that he is by any means deficient in understanding or natural ability, but he is entirely lacking in application and interest in his studies. He takes a far greater interest in cricket and football than he does in his books, and, in fact, as a general athlete he is about the best in the school. I regret, moreover, to say that Harold appears to be a boy ready and willing to take a part in any mischief that may be going. But, at the same time, to do him justice, I have never known him to tell a lie, and when taxed with his misconduct he always openly confesses his misdoings. As an instance, the other day I was about to punish a boy for breaking one of the school windows, when at the last moment Harold came up and confessed himself to be the culprit. I asked him did he do it deliberately or by accident, but, to my astonishment, he replied that he did it on purpose. As may well be imagined, I was very angry at such wanton mischief, and was about to punish him severely for it, when the thought struck me to ask what prompted him to do such a thing. He replied that another boy dared him to do it, and said he wasn't game. The result was, that I flogged well the primary cause of the mischief, and let Harold off.

"Such, sir, is all I have to write concerning the boy You will, as I say, find him very deficient in book-learning for the time he has been here. But I hope, should you send him again to us next year, he will bring with him a deeper sense of the duty he owes to you, to the school, and, above all, to himself, and at the same time maintain that consistent regard for truth, which in my opinion is like charity covering a multitude of sins."

"That concludes the letter of the head-master," said Mr. Merton, "and it strikes me that our promising boy will make a good pedestrian, boxer, trundler —anything, in fact, where there is no mental exertion, but plenty of mischief and fun."

"And yet," said Mrs. Merton, "it is not altogether

a letter of woe. There are some bright spots in Harold's school career."

"Well, yes, well, yes," added Mr. Merton, "it might have been worse ; and I suppose as regards his wildness, there is some old saying about the wine that never ferments being never clear. It seems to me he has now made a little start in the way of sowing his wild oats, and as he is getting at it young, should have a nice, flourishing, full-grained crop of folly by the time he comes to reap it."

"I think you are getting absurd now, George. Harold is only a schoolboy, with a schoolboy's folly."

"It may be so, Rose, but the boy's folly often enough results in the deeper folly of the man."

"But men are different."

"Yes, being better developed fools. But it somehow has often seemed to me that, as the world is supposed to be growing wiser, boys also should show more sense."

"But about Harold ?"

"Yes ; the 'break-up' of the school takes place in a few days, and while he is here we must see what is the best we can do for him. In the meantime business is business."

With these words Mr. Merton swallowed the final cup of coffee and started out. About lunch-time he returned, accompanied by a gentleman of more than middle size, well past the prime of life—black and tanned by many fierce suns, and, in fact, unmistakably a bushman. Mr. Merton ushered the stranger into a room, saying, " You can go in there, Brownlow, if you want to wash your hands before lunch. The bell will shortly ring."

With these words he walked off to his own apartment, and meeting his wife there, remarked cheerfully, " Back again, Rose. We'll be able to settle the question of what to do with Harold now. I brought a bushman with me to lunch, and —— "

" My gracious! George," broke in Mrs. Merton. " Why did you not let me know of this sooner ? You could have sent a boy with a note."

" So I could, my dear, but, you see, it's only old Brownlow—a bushman, as I told you, and he never had much chance of being an epicure."

" George dear, these old bushmen are very fastidious when they come to town. They put up at the best hotel and think nothing is too dainty for them."

" Well, yes, perhaps so. But, still, it does not mark a man out as a high liver if he takes up his quarters at the best hotel after going through a course of salt junk and damper."

" Now, Brownlow," said Mr. Merton, as they all sat round the table, " you know the boy Harold Effermere, whom I adopted till my brother's children took his place. Well, I had hoped, when he had education enough, to take him into the office, and to try and do the best I could for him. He might have risen to an important clerkship in time, you see. Now what do you think—— "

"Dashed if I know!" said Mr. Brownlow gruffly, for that was the manner of the man. "I ain't an authority on that sort of thing. But if the boy is handy with the pen, and the screw is anything decent, why, be gosh! man, he couldn't have an easier time of it than sitting on a high stool, making a penholder of his ear, and when 'the boss' is not looking reading a 'shocker' to improve his mind."

Mrs. Merton smiled, but her husband, more serious, returned to the subject with, "You broke in before I came to the point, Brownlow. What I wanted to say is that the boy has no desire to be a clerk—his whole hobby is for the bush, and it is on that I wanted your opinion."

"Ah," grunted Mr. Brownlow, chewing away with great appetite, "just give him a trial of the bush, and I'll guarantee before many days he'll wish he was back at his desk, sitting nice and comfortable in the shade, paring his nails."

Mrs. Merton put in, "I would think so too, Mr. Brownlow, from what Mr. Merton has told me about the bush."

Mr. Brownlow, with a piece of meat poised on his fork, looked at her and said, "Be gosh! madam, and that's a fact. If you want to knock the nonsense out of a town boy, send him to the bush. He thinks all he has to do out there is riding nice little ponies and chasing kangaroos on a plain."

Mr. Brownlow gave vent to a loud, coarse laugh, and turning to Mr. Merton, continued, "Look here, sir, if you want to clear the boy's mind of all the nonsense he's got into it about the bush, just send him to me out on the station."

"By Jove!" exclaimed Mr. Merton, "there would be something in that. If Harold takes kindly to the bush, he might get along well there—for in what we like best we'll do best. But if he doesn't care for it, why, he can come back to me, and I would try and make him useful in the office. Will you take him, then, Brownlow?"

"I will, Merton," forcibly exclaimed Mr. Brownlow, with the air of a man resolving to do a desperate thing, "I will; though, be gosh! I know what town 'Jackeroos' are, to my cost—the greatest horse-killing wretches one ever launched a curse at."

Chapter II

"A progeny of learning."
  —*The Rivals*—R. B. SHERIDAN.

THE reader will probably be asking, "Who is this boy, Harold Effermere, whom Mr. Merton spoke of as the son of an 'old wandering vagabond of a father, whoever he is'?"

On that point we do not profess to be very clear, but can give what little we know in a few words.

Mrs. Merton was always a good, charitable woman—always doing little kindnesses for the poor, and cheering and helping the miserable and distressed, as far as lay in her power. In that respect she was somewhat different to her husband, being less discriminate and enquiring in her tributes to those in want, or apparently in need. One day, however, the news was brought to her of a poor woman, living at no great distance away, and who was in suffering and direst poverty. Straightway Mrs. Merton set off to the relief, and when she arrived at the miserable hovel, found indeed that all was only too true. There was a wretched woman, evidently suffering from starvation and want, and beside her a poor little crying infant that also felt the pangs of hunger. Day after day Mrs. Merton sent down food and drink to this poor woman and her child, and thus, in time, they got strong and well again.

But it did not end there, for Mr. and Mrs. Merton took a fancy to the bright-faced little boy, and as they had no children of their own, came partly to adopt it in time. The woman gave her name as Mrs. Effermere, yet said it was not her real one, but that some day she would tell it. Scraps of her history came out from time to time. She had married a drover—a reckless, improvident man—and he had deserted her. She was struggling to make an honest living, but it was a mere hand-to-mouth existence, and came to the verge of starvation when her child was born.

Mrs. Effermere proved to be handy at needlework, and her benefactress, seeing this, gave her all the sewing of the house to do, and, in fact, kept her employed profitably. After a while, too, Mrs. Merton brought the poor woman over to live in a little cottage on Mr. Merton's premises, and there Harold grew to be quite a big, strong, healthy boy, and in time was sent to a school in Melbourne. It was not that Mr. Merton considered the educational system any better there than where he lived in Sydney, but for the reason that he had a theory every boy should go through a sort of weaning process in order to make him more independent and self-helping. It may seem remarkable that the people who have no children of their own are generally the strongest and most dogmatic in their opinions of how youngsters

should be brought up.   At any rate, poor Mrs. Effermere cried a good deal when her boy was sent away,
but Mr. Merton consoled her by saying that we owed
a certain duty to our children by having them forget
us for a time in order that the final parting might be
less sorrowful for them.

But Mr. Merton had a younger brother—a wild,
careless sort of man, and who, like nearly all " ne'er-
do-weels," put the climax on his improvidence by, of
course, getting married.   It almost goes without
saying that the woman he chose was as gay, poor,
and handsome as himself—for it is strange that the
prodigal is nearly always a good-looking man.
Spendthrifts somehow have a point in common with
the good—they die young.   Somehow, also, they
have a talent for leaving behind them large families,
totally unprovided for.   These almost invariably fall
to the lot of those we are pleased to call the " miserly
relatives," who take them as security for the debts of
the deceased.   That was Mr. Merton's experience,
and thus it was that Harold, whom he might have
fully adopted in time, had to give place to those who
had a stronger claim.   Nevertheless, Mr. Merton tried
to do the best he could for the boy—sent him to a
good school, and would have given him a place in the
office when he became fit for it.   But Harold, as we
have seen, had little taste for learning, and, like not a
few town boys, a great desire to get away up into the
bush.

The "break-up" of the school had taken place, and now poor Mrs. Effermere was anxiously on the look-out for the arrival of her son. She was the first to see him coming up the pathway, and eagerly ran out to meet him. Harold was no less rejoiced to see his mother, and he laid down his little portmanteau and received her with the most affectionate greeting.

"Oh, mamie!" he exclaimed, "I think you ain't lookin' very well, but I bought yer such a pretty little shawl, that'll make yer feel nice and warm. Now won't it, mamie?"

"My dear boy, that was very kind and thoughtful of you," said Mrs. Effermere, patting the boy's cheek and looking at him through the tears of affection that stood in her poor, sunken eyes.

Next, all Mr. Merton's little nephews and nieces, seeing Harold, came running to welcome him and dangle about him, as little children will about an elder brother. Harold stooped down and kissed them all with the greatest affection, treating them to little packets of jujubes and lollies—the money for which he managed to spare from his scanty allowance. Mr. Merton did not believe in giving boys much pocket money, for he said they had no use for it, that they spent it foolishly, and, besides, it gave them extravagant notions as to the proper use of cash.

After Harold had been treated to some light refreshments in the way of tea and cake, Mr. Merton said to him, "Well, my lad, Mr. Wilson does not give a very glowing account of all the things you picked up at school, excepting cricket and football ; and I suppose you know they're not the main objects of a boy's education ? "

Harold muttered a dubious " No," which, under the circumstances, might mean anything.

" Well, so I understand," continued Mr. Merton ; " and, moreover, Mr Wilson's letter speaks of you being a wild character and ready to take a hand in all the mischief that was going."

" Did he say that, sir ? " asked Harold innocently.

" He did so ; and I must conclude that the natural inference is that a boy who is so successful in games must necessarily give a good deal of his attention to them, and that a boy who finds so much time for mischief and amusement must, in consequence, have so much less for study and improvement.   Does there not seem to be some truth in this ? "

" I don't know, sir, but ——"and Harold hesitated.

" But what, boy ?   Have you extenuating circumstances to offer ? "

" George Smithson got seven A's in the Junior Examination, and took two medals and one *prose. acct.* all in the same exam.   He's a rattlin' all-roun', sir, and made forty, not out, when we were playin' the opposition school—takin' three wickets for ' ducks' eggs ' in the same match.   He's 'bout the best Rugby player we have in the school, and can generally make a run for half the length of the field before he's ' collared.'   He makes the surest kick for a goal, and ——"

" Oh, well, there stop," said Mr. Merton. "I'll wager young Smithson doesn't allow his taste for games to interfere with his love for study, and that when he's engaged in the one he shuts out the other from his mind."

"Well, you see, sir," said Harold pleadingly, "he can't help but learn, and the rules of the school stops him from allus playin,' else——"

"My goodness! boy," interrupted Mr. Merton. "haven't they taught you better grammar than that? But go on, go on. Let us hear how young Smithson managed to learn in the school where you proved such a brilliant failure."

This interruption somewhat disconcerted Harold But he went on, scratching his ear, and a look in his face like a boy about to be caned : "I don't know what I was goin' to say ezactly, sir, but, accordin' to the rules, at 6 o'clock every boy has to muster into the study hall, to prepare his work an' lessons for nex' day, an' there he stays till the bell rings for tea, an' half an hour after that he goes to study agin till 9 o'clock, bedtime. And then when he gets up in the mornin', an' after prayers bin sed, he has another go at studies till breakfast-time——"

" You've got as many 'ands' in your discourse as if you had taken your text from the Bible," broke in Mr. Merton. "But go on. You have clearly shown that a boy must give a certain amount of time to study, or the pretence of study, whether his desires are that way or not. Therefore, unless he altogether lacks the capacity or inclination, he must succeed in learning to an average extent, anyhow.   Isn't that so?"

"Yes, sir," said Harold cheerfully, like a boy who has been prompted in a class; "and that is jus' what I was wantin' to explain about George Smithson."

"You stupid boy!   Then can't you see that what is applicable to George Smithson's case under the same circumstances applies to yours?"

"I wasn't thinkin' of that, sir," returned Harold, realizing that he had a somewhat peculiar and not altogether clear position to explain.

"How, then, do you account for it?"

"'Cause," said Harold slowly, and seeming to be musing, "'cause—— "

"Go on; we already have the result: what is the cause?"

Harold rubbed his hand up and down the leg of his trousers, as was his custom at school when he did not know the question given him, and had to prepare for cane.   Then he braced himself for a final effort, and returned to the attack, or rather to the defence, with "'Cause."   Then, after a few moments' silence, a brilliant idea struck him: "'Cause, sir, I don't know."

Mr. Merton on this was unable to suppress a laugh. But he excused himself by looking sternly at Harold and saying, "My lad, it's enough to make a dog giggle, if he had any sense of humour at all."

"Oh, you foolish boy!" exclaimed Mrs. Merton, who had listened patiently up to this time.   "You are a foolish boy, Harold. And, George, you shouldn't laugh at a thing like that."

"My dear," returned Mr. Merton, "there is often an element of the ludicrous even in the tragic. But I certainly endorse your remark that he is a foolish boy." Then, turning to Harold, he added, "Yes, sir, you are all that, indeed."

Harold hung his head, and two little tears glittered on his eyelashes. Then he wiped them away with the sleeve of his coat, and blubbered out, "I thought perhaps yer would be pleased to know I got these." He unlocked his little portmanteau with a trembling hand, and taking out two medals, presented them to Mr. and Mrs. Merton.

Harold was now very sad and downcast. He had hoped that his guardians would be greatly pleased with the degree of success he had attained in the cricket and football fields. But now these joyous hopes were fallen in the dust.

"I see," said Mrs. Merton, examining the inscription on the medal, "that this has been given you, Harold, for being the best 'all-round' cricketer in the school."

"Yes, ma'am," assented Harold, somewhat sadly.

"And this," said Mr. Merton, looking at his wife, "has been given him for general proficiency in the football club."

Harold looked at Mr. and Mrs. Merton with an almost beseeching expression, but no word came from them of approbation or pleasure for the boy's success

c

in games. A great void was in Harold's heart, and
tears of bitter disappointment poured freely down
his cheeks. What cared he now for the shouts of
hearty applause with which his schoolfellows greeted
him when he had been handed these medals at the
" break-up " of the school ? Nothing. What a dreary
mockery now the little stories which he had intended
to tell of his prowess and experiences in the field !
There was one great, heroic occasion which he fondly
imagined would have given his guardians the greatest
pleasure to have heard described. It was the school's
decisive match for the year, and Harold, by his own
single efforts, turned the whole tide of battle in a game
that seemed hopelessly lost. But now he truly
realized that he could never tell that story. Who
knows what pleasure it would have given him to have
told of his disappointments, his hopes, his fears, during
the course of that day ? To have told how he mas-
tered his nervousness at the outset of the game—
becoming cool, self-centred, self-governed, and patient;
why he thought this and how he judged that, exer-
cising a difficult caution at one time, and at another
being bold, and firm, and fearless. All the while, too,
bearing in mind that he was fighting for honour—the
honour of the school.

All that, and much more, he would like to have
told in his own simple, boyish way. But now he could
not. Ah, foolish old people ! you know not how much
perhaps, a man's great successes in later life are due
to his early education in the cricket ground.

Mr. and Mrs. Merton handed the medals back to Harold without one word of congratulation or approval. They only regarded such rewards as so much palpable evidence of the boy's neglect of study.

"Now, my lad," said Mr. Merton, "these things are very well in their way, but I do not count them sufficient compensation for your lack of knowledge in useful learning, for which I sent you to school. If you had brought home a prize for proficiency in book-keeping, I should be pleased with you. But as it is I'm far from being satisfied."

"They don't give prizes for book-keepin', sir," explained Harold.

"And why not? They would be encouraging something useful by offering premiums for such a branch of education. Book-keeping is all and everything to a business man, which I intended you to be. Do you think you would have gone anywhere near gaining such a prize if it had been offered?

"I don't know, sir."

"You should have some idea of how you compared with other boys in that respect. I suppose in nine cases out of ten it was generally known who were the likely boys to get prizes, even before the examinations for such took place?"

"Yes, the fellows who was well up in things could make a pretty good guess."

"Well, since there was no prize for it, I would rather have seen you with a little insignificant scrap of notepaper—certifying that you were the best in your class at accounts—than all the medals you could carry for cricket, and hockey, and marbles, and all such foolishness."

"*We* usen't to play marbles, sir," said Harold, with emphasis.

"It doesn't matter. You had other games, which occupied your attention just as much. Now tell me what advancement you made as an accountant, and what system you kept."

"I can't quite make out what yer mean, sir."

"Well, I simply asked what system you kept. Double entry, of course But I didn't mean that exactly. It's the particular system I enquired about. But you can, of course, better explain it on paper. Get those few sheets of 'foolscap' there and let me see how you worked."

Harold was perfectly bewildered, and blurted out, "We didn't do double entry, sir."

"I must say, then, that I'm surprised at that—very much surprised. Single entry is only fit for an apple shop or a basket hawker."

"We usen't to do single entry either, sir," said Harold, seeing that Mr. Merton expected further explanation as to his methods of accounts.

"Then, my goodness! what did you do? You kept a cash book, a journal and a ledger, did you not?"

"No, sir."

"Did you ever hear of such books?" said Mr. Merton at last, in utter desperation.

"No, I never heard on them, as I remember, sir,"

was Harold's answer, to the great astonishment of his inquisitor.

"In short, then," burst forth Mr. Merton, in an almost angry tone, "you were never taught to keep books. Did they teach it in the school at all?"

"I don't think they did, sir," replied Harold slowly, with his head down, seeming to be trying to recollect if such a branch of business education were taught in the school. Then looking up, he ventured with, "Some of the fellows well up might ha' been learnin' it, sir."

"Tut! nonsense! Do you think it was necessary to know quadratic equations and trigonometry before you could learn to keep accounts? The ordinary first principles of arithmetic are sufficient for the purpose. Now that's all I have to say. The fact is, they don't teach it, or you would have picked it up for the time you have been at school, unless you were absolutely a dunce. They evidently consider book-keeping beneath their notice. Well, after all this, the bush seems to be the only place you're suited for."

Mr. Merton's examination of the boy ended with that for the present, and Harold received respite from the trying ordeal. Mr. Merton turned to his wife after Harold had gone and said, "You see, Rose, the boy has received no business education in any way. I suppose he can manage to puzzle through passages of Thucydides or Virgil; but what's the use of that when he can't speak ten words of his own language without displaying the vilest grammatical errors ? "

"But, George, they assist one to get at the correct meaning of a word," pleaded Mrs. Merton in defence of the classics.

"Yes, I suppose they do. But a good dictionary does it much better. I prefer to leave those things to lexicographers and philologists, for it's their business to invent new words and trace to the root and stump the meaning of old ones. Well, I'm weary of all this, and as I have a few letters to write, I'll set about it at once."

Chapter III

"Seest thou a man diligent in his business? he shall stand before kings; he shall not stand before mean men."

—*Proverbs*—THE BIBLE.

MR. MERTON was a hard, practical, business man. He had none of that sentiment which passes for fine feeling in the world. He would kick a supplicant for sixpence from his door without the least compunction, and at the same time subscribe ten guineas to a charitable institution, when he had satisfied himself that the object was worthy of support. The cynical, we have no doubt, will smile at this and say, "Pooh! that sort of benevolence is only another form of selfishness. A man who puts his name down on a subscription list for a good sum only thinks of the good effect it will have in raising him in public estimation for his charity."

Good cynic, if this is what you think, what would you say if you saw Mr. Merton push the subscription list away, saying, "No. Put it down to a friend, for I can't have my name advertised to attract the attention of bogus charities"? He had a true appreciation of the value of money, for he knew what it was to want it; he knew what it was to work for it and to earn it, and therefore he wasn't a man to part with it easily. Raising himself from the humble place of a merchant's clerk, he—by perseverance, ability, and industry—was now in the position of a merchant himself. No man understood better the principles of business. He knew how to buy and when to sell, and none realized more clearly that a business to have security and stability must be based on sound financial rules, rigidly and systematically adhered to. He seemed to hold the pulse of trade in his hand—shrewd, calculating, a judge of human nature, watching the currents and the eddies, as it were, he made many a " lucky hit." Of course it was all put down to Dame Fortune ; people never attribute a series of successes to anything else. They are always pleased to exclaim, " What luck ! " " It is wonderful the chances that turn up for him." But the wise man smiles and passes on, and the good people who admired his "luck" continue their rule of thumb, and sink or swim, as the case may be.

Mr. Merton did not marry till he was a rich man. He was then rather well advanced in years, and, in fact, "a few grey hairs were mingling with the brown." Of course, it will then be said that he married for money—more money. If not, that he made a fool of himself by marrying a young and senseless girl, who accepted him only for *his* money. Well, strange as it may seem, inconsistent, incredible and all that, Mr. Merton married for love, a woman who had the same affection for him, and who was very nearly his own age. Mrs. Merton was governess in the old

merchant's family, and in the old merchant's office
at the same time struggled on George Merton—poor,
methodical, honest, yet ambitious.   Who knows, perhaps, what the influence of that early love might have
had on the poor, struggling clerk, who for *her* sake
persevered, economized, and battled with a hard,
relentless lot?   However that might be, George
Merton ultimately achieved success—such success,
too, as might have bought him the choicest youth
and beauty in the matrimonial market.

Harold Effermere was a tall, somewhat thin youth,
of perhaps about sixteen or seventeen years of age.
He had a very pleasing cast of countenance, and his
large dark brown eyes gave one the impression that
the boy had much fire and energy in his nature.
There was certainly very little of the student in his
appearance, and he did not look like one who was
likely to become a learned bookworm.   Yet he did
not give one the impression of stupidity by any
means, for in the broad, intellectual brow and well-
proportioned head no one could say that the boy
appeared to lack mental capacity, whatever his inclinations might be.   Such inclinations were not of a
studious turn, and if he came home with an amount
of erudition very little better than what he started
away with, it was not to be wondered at.   Book
knowledge does not come by intuition ; a hurried
glance at lessons just before entering the class-room
is not in itself, alone, a very certain method of
acquiring permanent information.   Harold proved

to be no remarkable and brilliant exception to the ill results of that cursory mode of study.

After Harold had been a month at home, Mr. Merton had ample opportunity of finding out that he was no more a classic than a mathematical scholar. The boy had a vague smattering of Latin, which he acquired from *Cæsaris Commentarii* by the aid of a translation, or rather, as he confessed it, a " cog." He also knew something of the Greek alphabet, and could decline the article ὁ, ἡ, τό through all its numbers, cases, and genders, with not more than a dozen inaccuracies. As for his knowledge of English, it was worse still; and with regard to spelling, he seemed to think that it hampered genius. His knowledge of arithmetic went as far as "the rule of three"; and in Euclid he knew as much as would enable him to describe a circle and give the definition of a straight line. It must not be forgotten that he also dipped into algebra, and could make the symbols *plus* and *minus* without always mistaking the one for the other. With this brilliant collection of knowledge Harold considered that he knew enough for all practical intents and purposes. It would seem as if he thought that a boy should not burden his intellect too much when in the plastic state, and that, like Cato and Alfieri, it would be time enough to learn Greek when he reached an advanced age.

Chapter IV

"And reach the far plains we are journeying to."
— *The Barcoo.*—HENRY C. KENDALL.

" By forest green embraided
The Western station lies."
—*Barwon Ballads.*—" C."

THE day arrived at last for Harold to take his departure with Mr. Brownlow for the bush. He felt a heavy sinking of the heart as he took an affectionate farewell of his mother at the railway station, and when the train left the shed, Mr. Brownlow saw that his *protégé* was in tears. Mr. Brownlow was by no means a man to feel much sympathy for such sort of grief. He was a hard, weather-beaten, rough-and-ready old bushman, whose environment made him little acquainted with the finer instincts of the heart, and who in this case considered Harold's weeping as only idle tears. " Pshaw! boy," said he unfeelingly, " what's all this blubbering about? Get out your handkerchief, wipe your eyes, and be a man."

This sort of kindly expression did not have the effect which was expected. Harold only answered by a pitiful sob, which struck no slumbering cord of sympathy in the stony heart of the seasoned old bushman. Mr. Brownlow emphatically pronounced him a soft youngster, and continued, "Why, confound it! lad, you got nothing at all to cry about yet. Wait till you get up to the station and get slung half a dozen times off of some of my colts, then you'll have something to make a row about."

"I can't help it," said Harold, making an heroic effort to recover tranquility; "I can't think of my mother at home without feelin' it might be I would never see her again."

"Foolishness!" said Mr. Brownlow impatiently. "It will be time enough for you to cry about it when you hear the news of such a thing happening. Why, boy, one would think you were going to a funeral."

Harold's emotion became at length subdued, and he amused himself looking out of the carriage window, and getting a fleeting glance of field and farmer as the train swept onward on its journey. They were bound for the prosperous inland town of Bourke, which is some five hundred miles distant from Sydney. We need not dwell on this journey; neither is it necessary to say much about the different stages and camps on the way to the northern cattle station, 150 miles from Bourke.

After leaving the train, Harold and his companion travelled by buggy, a little black boy driving the spare horses after them, and also doing the "horse-hunting" in the morning, whilst Harold was initiated in the mysteries of making "Johnny cakes."

Mr. Brownlow from the first showed no disposition to pamper his *protégé*. At daylight every morning he would call out in a voice a boatswain might have envied, " Get up there, now, you lad ; make a fire and rouse the nigger for the horses!"

After giving these instructions he would turn over and take another little nap, and after a while be called by Harold, when the billy was boiled and the breakfast ready. Mr. Brownlow would generally indulge in a good deal of grumbling during breakfast. He found fault with the tea for being too strong, and he would say that there was enough of sugar in it " to pass it off as treacle." He seldom, in fact, found anything to his satisfaction. The "Johnny cakes " had too much soda, or, as he used to express it, " too many eggs," making the bread yellow ; and he used to remark that there was more tea made than was necessary, though he used always to drink whatever was left over after breakfast. From the first night of their camping out Mr. Brownlow resolved to make Harold as useful' as possible, and determined that he should take full charge of the cookery department. He taught him how to make dampers, gave him instructions as to the making of tea and the boiling of beef, and then said, " There you are now, my lad ; I have shown you how the business is done, and you'll have to practise it on our trip up. Nothing like ' breaking in ' a youngster from the start and getting the town style out of him as soon as you can."

Mr. Brownlow kept his word, and seemed determined to make a good bush cook of Harold ; at the same time, he was neither liberal in praise nor miserly in abuse. "Do you want to poison a man?" he would exclaim on finding the damper heavy and sodden with acid. "Didn't I always tell you twice as much soda as acid? but never did I tell you twice as much acid as flour."

After five days' steady travelling, they arrived at the station, which was situated on a large permanent hole of water. The buildings were not remarkable for their great architectural design. On the whole, however, they might be accepted as a fair average of head-station improvements, where the owners were bachelors, and accepted the bush life as a temporary exile, to be quitted as soon as sufficient money was made to enable them to live in greater style and luxury in town.

A tall, healthy-looking stockman assisted to unharness the horses, at the same time giving all information about the condition of the stock, the state of the country, and such general items of local news as might be interesting to the owner of the station, While this operation was going on another individual came to the scene. He was a man of medium size, and wore a brown sealskin cap, which he tilted back on the poll of a most irregular, ill-shaped head. He wore strong cord breeches, which were supplemented by a well-wrinkled pair of leggings, and these fitted over his brightly polished boots to a critical nicety. But one of the most striking outward characteristics about him was the long-necked pair of spurs—nine

inches in length—which dangled and clinked along
the ground, at times very nearly tripping their wearer.
He was also dressed in coat and vest, collar and neck-
tie, and a large gold albert was very conspicuous on
the outside of his coat. His eyes were large, promi-
nent and excited-looking, and his moustache would
have been the pride of an Australian volunteer. This
gentleman's name was Ponsonby Oberon, but there
were people malicious enough to say they knew him
in Ireland, when his name was plain Paddy O'Brien.
Whatever truth there may have been in this, Ponsonby
Oberon did not look like a man who had delved in
potato fields or packed firkins of butter for the
country fairs. Although he was the station drover,
he did not appear to be a man who had driven many
pigs to market in his own country. He was certainly an Irishman ; but even if he had not confessed
to his nationality, his talk would have betrayed him.
Not that he had anything of the broad and hearty
brogue about him—for he spoke better English than
the average Briton—but he had at times, when it
suited him, that fawning *suaviter in modo* which in the
Erin Isle would be called " blarney," and an evidence
that he had kissed the celebrated stone of that name.
His manner was most effusive as he came forward
holding out his hand to Mr. Brownlow, and exclaiming, " My goodness gracious ! sir ; I'm surprised and
delighted at seeing you back again. As the poet
said, 'Welcome home, no more to roam.' But who's
the young gentleman you've got with you ? "

"Oh, that's young Effermere—a boy Mr. Merton gave me to have straightened out. So far I can commend him as a bad cook."

Mr. Brownlow did not trouble himself about introducing Harold to the worthy drover, but left him to cultivate that acquaintance for himself, which Mr. Ponsonby Oberon was not slow to commence.

"Master Effermere," said he, "I must make a drover of you. You must come with me when I am taking the next mob of cattle to market. I'll give you the proper 'breaking-in' on the road, for I'm, as you know, the king drover of Queensland—'My right there is none to dispute,' as the poet said."

Harold made no reply. He was greatly puzzled with the strange character before him, and did not know of anything particular to say to him at the moment. Mr. Brownlow, however, thought it necessary to say, "There is no mistake, Ponsonby, but most drovers can sound their own trumpets, but, by Jove! yours is a regular fog-horn booming away night and day about your droving—the same weary, cursed old tune that the old cow died on."

By this time they had reached the house, and were waiting in the dining-room till the cook brought in the refreshments. But Mr. Oberon thought that his dignity as a drover was slighted, and felt it his duty to exclaim, "Mr. Brownlow, I think that I have given you the fullest satisfaction on the road. I nursed my cattle all the trip, and I didn't care if I made sixpence by the contract, as long as I got my bullocks landed as I always do, in as good condition as when they started."

" Tut ! rot !" broke in Mr. Brownlow ; " one would think they were so many babies that you took on your knee. But, anyhow, I wasn't saying anything against your droving, man. You made a good trip, and your cattle brought a good price."

But Ponsonby Oberon was now started on his favourite subject, and was eager to make the most of his late success on the road, " Yes," said he slapping his chest proudly, " I did make a good trip and a draft of my cattle topped the Sydney market. And what's more to my credit, I did it with the worst mob of bullocks that left the station last year. I made the worse appear the better mob, as the poet said."

" You did it with no such thing," said his employer, warming also ; " you had the best mob in the paddocks."

"Now you know very well that I hadn't !" exclaimed Oberon, getting quite excited. " You gave me a mixed lot of culls, and that useless fellow Jackson got the best mob. And how did he get on with them ? Why, you could hang your hat on their hip bones after he was done with them. And that to your cost, you know full well, as the poet said."

" Curse the pote !" shouted Mr. Brownlow, " and you, for a natural born fool, Ponsonby. You had the first mob of the season ; and doesn't it stand to the common sense of any idiot that I'd pick the best and fattest bullocks, and not the culls and poor ones?"

"Another thing, Mr. Brownlow," pursued the drover, slapping his chest with great force, and now thoroughly excited, and intent only on his own ideas—"Jackson's mob, though twice as good as mine, only netted half as much, although he got in when the market had taken thirty shillings of a rise. By the hokey, sir, was ever such a combination against a man!"

"There you make an ass of yourself again," protested Mr. Brownlow. "Your mob was more likely twice as good as Jackson's; and as for the state of the market, allow me to tell you that it was thirty shillings of a drop it took, and not a rise. I had a letter from the agent at the time, and I can show it to you. He says the market had completely broken down and prices fell thirty shillings. By gosh! Ponsonby, but you got hold of the wrong end of the stick properly. As for what you say about your mob netting *twice* as much as Jackson's, I can show you the 'account sales,' which show a very different result."

"What! do you mean to compare me with that messer Jackson?" exclaimed Oberon, unable to control his excitement. "Do you mean to say there is any parallel between me and him, as the poet said?"

"I mean to say," retorted his bluff employer, "that if there is any comparison to be made, it's in favour of Jackson. He got in with every beast he started with, and you were a few short. At the same time, I admit that the percentage allowed you for losses covered all that."

" This is passing all understanding, as the poet said," exclaimed Ponsonby Oberon jumping from his seat and dashing his pipe against Harold's chair, to the boy's great fright and astonishment ; " you'd drive a man mad."

" That's impossible in your case," quickly returned Mr. Brownlow, " because you're a stark, staring lunatic already."

The drover was unable to wait for any more of such compliments, but rushed from the room in a frenzy of passion.

" Well, that fellow beats anything I ever heard of," remarked Mr. Brownlow. " He's a madman at large, be gosh ! "

" We used to say in our school books," said Harold modestly, " *Ira is brevis furor.*"

" Confound your little smatterings of French ! " broke out Mr. Brownlow in great annoyance. " Speak good common-sense English, and be dashed to you ! "

" See, he has broken his pipe," said Harold, picking up the fragments of an expensive meerschaum.

" Yes, and one that I made him a present of, for this very same trip we have been speaking of. But the next one I'll get for him I'll guarantee he'll take better care of. Be gosh ! boy, I should have got him a cast-iron pipe, and had an inscription on it, ' Proof against madness. To the king drover and blower—

Ponsonby Oberon.' How does that strike you for an idea? Be gosh! it tickles my fancy."

"What makes him like that?" asked Harold innocently.

"What makes him like that!" repeated Mr. Brownlow. "Potery boy, confounded potery. It leaks out of him at all points."

Mr. Brownlow was a man who had worked himself up from the ranks, and was, in consequence, of a very practical turn of mind, and, like many such people, hated "potery." Ponsonby Oberon, on the other hand, was anything but practical, and perhaps it was on that account that poetry had such charms for his soul. Yet Ponsonby and Mr. Brownlow had some small points in common. From living so much together, they got in a great measure to make common use of the same expressions and exclamations. Some of these might be considered good substitutes for swearing, and others might be thought curses in a novel and original form. Ponsonby Oberon put them down as "safety valves to the feelings, as the poet said."

However, Ponsonby Oberon paced up and down the gravel walk outside the house till his feelings reached their normal level. He then returned to the room and said, "Mr. Brownlow, let us say nothing more about it, old man. I'm so very impulsive, be gosh! that I say anything at the moment, and have vain regrets for it immediately after, as the poet said."

"Well, let us say no more about it," said Mr. Brownlow; "but, believe me, your confounded impulse will hang you yet. Dash my wig! Ponsonby, but you're a natural born fool."

At this the erratic Ponsonby slapped his chest, threw his cap on the floor and broke out as strong as ever. He was of that peculiar, excitable nature which blazes and flickers twenty to fifty times a day. He was a strange, complex personality, who could never prevent himself from exhibiting the extent of the good and evil in his system.

Harold found no amusement in being a witness to the display of such petty grievances, and he was glad to have an opportunity, after finishing his meal, to walk out and have a look at the general station surroundings. An hour afterwards, when he returned, he found master and man on the most friendly understanding imaginable. At least Mr. Brownlow was as agreeable as he would be under ordinary circumstances, whilst Ponsonby Oberon seemed pleased with all he said, and was ready to quote a poet or laugh on the smallest provocation.

Chapter V

"Some, for renown, on scraps of learning dote,
And think they grow immortal as they quote."
—YOUNG.

WHEN bedtime came, Mr. Brownlow told Harold to go with Oberon, who would show him a place to sleep. The drover led the way to a long, narrow, barrack-like room, where several hides were stretched on frames, and made to serve all the general purposes of beds. Harold looked around the room and remarked, —

"What a stock of old guns, muskets and bayonets you have here!"

"Yes," said his companion; "they belong to the days when my beard was black, as the poet said. Those rusty-looking old muzzle-loaders, I dare say, knocked over many a nigger, when they were pointed through those auger holes you see there in the slabs. The blacks used to come around here in the early days—long before my time—generally at night, and they would hang around for a chance to knock you in the head."

"That must have been awful!" exclaimed Harold. "Do they ever do that now?"

"No. They're all 'gone where the good niggers

go,' as the poet said ; or, rather, where the bad niggers go : for I believe they were about as lively a crowd as ever threw a spear."

Ponsonby Oberon slapped himself proudly on the chest, and said with an air of increasing excitement : " Ah ! if I were only here in those days, with that old bayonet there, I'd sally out at midnight and cry, ' Havock !' and let slip the dogs of war. I would spare nothing. My motto would be—' Slay all,' as the poet said."

As he spoke he seized the rusty bayonet and made some desperate thrusts at imaginary aborigines, calling out at the same time with convulsive fierceness : " Ha ! die, villain ! murderous reptile ! One, two, three ! Ho ! they run like chaff before the wind— the field is fought and won ! "

Harold gazed at the man in utter astonishment, and not without a certain terror—for which he had every reason, as the old bayonet now and then was thrust unpleasantly near.

" Please don't," he entreated. " You nearly ran it into me that time."

" If I did," exclaimed the dramatic Ponsonby, " I'd run it into myself next. Like King David, I'd perish by my own sword."

He laid the dangerous old weapon aside, saying with a laugh, " I suppose children and fools shouldn't play with edged tools. Now, Harold, stand up there and declaim a bit. Let me hear you recite " Mary Queen of Scots " or " Rienzi."

But before Harold had any time to confess his ignorance of the art of elocution the erratic Ponsonby had made a start on his own account. With much gesticulation and wild enthusiasm he waded into a long series of verse, which served as a "lullaby" to Harold, and sent him to sleep long before the reciter had come to the end of his efforts.

Ponsonby Oberon had—like most bushmen possessing a vague glimmering of literary taste—taken largely to poetry. Lindsay Gordon was his Bible, and the "Bush Ballads" and "Galloping Rhymes" were in his opinion the finest things on earth. After he had finished his recitation of "How We Beat the Favourite," he turned round to Harold to receive modestly that applause which he thought was his due. To his great disgust, he found his audience fast asleep. This poor appreciation of his performance forced the impulsive Ponsonby to exclaim :

"My goodness gracious! Is this the way you're rewarding me for trying my very best to amuse and entertain you? You, a stranger in a strange land, and I taking pity on you! Alas! ungrateful boy—wake up." Suiting the action to the word, Ponsonby Oberon gave Harold an enthusiastic slap on the back, which awoke him immediately from his impolite slumbers.

"Didn't you like my recitation?" demanded Oberon, with an offended air.

"Oh, yes!" replied Harold. "It was very nice. Did you make it up yourself?"

"No," said Oberon, slapping his chest and pointing to his forehead: "but I have whips of talent of my own, for all that; but I don't care to waste my sweetness in the desert air, as the poet said. Pshaw! boy; it's simply throwing pearls to swine—a man of my talent here in the bush."

"Yes; I see you are not like other men," assented Harold, making a clumsy effort at a compliment.

"Amen! I say, and may I ever be so. But you see the way I am treated: you witnessed the manner that old Brownlow got on to me to-day."

"I did, and felt sorry for you. I thought it was very bad of him calling you a madman."

Oberon threw his smoking-cap against the wall and exclaimed with a tragi-comic countenance, "If I am mad, then, and he is sane, I thank God there lies between us one difference plain."

Harold laughed and said: "You are, no mistake, a funny man. But what you said last sounds like poetry."

"Boy, know you not that it is poetry? My very soul is oozing with it. And then to call me mad! But, after all, great wits are sure to madness near allied, and thin partitions do their bounds divide ——"

Just then Mr. Brownlow appeared on the scene, dressed in his night gear and calling out in an angry voice: "Ponsonby, if there was ever such a partition in that confounded numskull of yours, it's been smashed to atoms long 'go. You fool! can't you go to sleep? and don't be howling like a hungry dingo on a winter's night."

He did not stay to say any more, but left Ponsonby in indignant astonishment standing in the middle of the floor. When that worthy recovered his self-possession, he said to Harold—in a cautious undertone —"Well, if that man isn't a brute! Now, this is how I'm rewarded for trying to amuse a guest. Harold, let my outraged dignity be upon your head? But enough; sleeping dogs may lie. *I* will not disturb his slumbers."

Ponsonby Oberon—like Captain Cuttle—had a passion for quoting; and, like that worthy old seaman also, his quotations were nearly all grossly incorrect. His ready extracts were so mixed up with his own garbled ideas that the authors from whom he essayed to quote—could they have heard him—would probably have never recognised what Ponsonby Oberon gave them all due credit for having written.

Oberon paced up and down the room, puffing great clouds of tobacco from a short-stemmed, wooden pipe, and muttering incoherent remarks, which fell almost unheeded on Harold's drowsy ear. At last, with calmer feelings, the drover came and sat down on the edge of Harold's bed, saying: "Wake up, boy! My gracious! what a lad you are to sleep. Blessed is he who invented sleep, said the poet; but, be gosh! Harold, you needn't have run away with the exclusive copyright. Get up out of those arms of Morpheus and tell a story or sing a song."

"You forget," said Harold, "that Mr. Brownlow was here a short time ago, and told you that he wanted to get to sleep, and that you were keeping him awake."

"Do you know what I have been thinking of, Harold?"

"No. I'm sure a lot of things must go through your mind."

"Ah, yes ; you're right there, lad. There are more things in my head than were dreamt of in your philosophy, as the poet said. Well, what I'm thinking of at present is that I'll give droving best. I'm full of the sweetly lowing cattle, stringing across the open with the bushman riding free. No ; I'll be a free lance once more ; I'll go and travel on the game."

"Travel on the game! What do you mean by that?"

"What do I mean! I mean simply to make a jolly living by my wits, to fatten on the talent which bountiful Nature has given me. Listen, boy ; I have two good horses—

"'Iron-sinew'd and satin-skinn'd,
Ribb'd like a drum and limb'd like a deer.'

Now with these two nags I'm going to travel about from race meeting to race meeting, win all before me, where it suits my book, and lose as often as the public fancy my own horses good enough to be favourites."

Enraptured and excited with his own ideas, Ponsonby Oberon got up and walked about the room, alternating lines of Lindsay Gordon with observations

of his own as to the scientific *modus operandi* of
"travelling on the game." Then he returned and sat
by Harold again, saying: "Yes, lad, that's where my
genius will shine like a meteorite. Not that I mean
that I'll 'go up like a rocket and come down like the
stick': no, my march through the country will be a
triumphal success."

"You expect then to do well," said Harold. "But
did you ever think that there might be other men
with better horses travellin' on the same game?"

"Ah, sonny," responded the enthusiastic Oberon;
"leave me alone for that. Yes, there are plenty of
other fellows going about on the same line, but what
sort of neddies do they have? Why, they're like
Goldsmith's poetry, that found him poor and kept him
so. Boy, I tell you that the crocks they have wouldn't
be able to win, *even* if all the other horses in the race
were public favourites and backed for hatfuls of
money."

"I don't understand it," said Harold, shaking his
head.

"No; I should think you wouldn't," returned Oberon,
with a contemptuous expression. "Do you think the
whole thing would come to you as easy as falling off
a log. No; it's an art, and like every other art it must
be cultivated, and besides, you must have your bump
of cunning well developed—standing out in fact like
a knot on a gum tree—before you're fit to think of
travelling on the game. Besides, you must be a
generally all-round, wide-awake sort of fellow, with

an eye to all the weak points in human nature, and the talent to take advantage of them."

"It does not seem to me a very honest way of makin' money," said Harold thoughtfully. At which Ponsonby Oberon laughed heartily, saying : "'Where innocence is bliss 'tis folly to be wise,' as the poet said. My gracious boy, don't you know what the poet said, 'Men of talent are the hunters, fools are the game ?' But all this smoking and talking have made me as thirsty as a fish in a dried water-hole, so I must go and get a drink."

Oberon went out to slake his thirst, and Harold, thinking how nearly he had been to forgetting his prayers, straightway knelt down and commenced his devotions. He had not been long at these pious duties, when his companion returned, and pushed in the door, saying : "I brought you a drink, Harold ; I thought your coppers might be a bit dry."

There was no response, and Ponsonby then looking up saw that Harold was in a kneeling attitude, and in profound meditation. The drover quietly left the quart of water down on a bench and seated himself on a stool, smoking hard and waiting patiently for Harold to make an end of his devotions. At last, when they were over, Ponsonby Oberon rushed over to his companion, slapped him heartily on the back, saying earnestly : "You're a good fellow ; you're a good young fellow."

"For what ?" asked Harold, looking with astonishment.

"Saying your prayers, my boy!" replied the enthusiastic Oberon. "Do you not know what the
poet says, 'He prayeth best who loveth best'; and I
know you're too young yet to be a real take-down
hypocrite."

"Why, do you never pray?" asked Harold, in some
surprise.

"Boy," exclaimed Oberon dramatically and striking
his chest, "you see before you a man who knocked
off praying twenty years ago, but who prayed once
since then and that earnestly."

"Ah!" exclaimed Harold, interested.

"Yes. It was a dark night, and I was on watch
with a mob of cattle I was taking down. A terrific
thunderstorm came on, and the lightning was flashing
and blazing all around me. At last a streak of lightning came and killed the horse I was riding; the
thunder which followed almost immediately boomed
like a thousand cannons, and nearly cracked the drums
in my ears. Boy, I thought it was my funeral knell,
and I prayed—there is no mistake, I did pray. They
were something like Dr. Johnson's prayers, made up
by myself, rough and ready at the moment, for I had
completely forgotten the prayers of my boyhood.
The lightning meanwhile seemed to ignite the atmosphere all around me, for there was flash after flash in
constant, quick succession. All this, Harold, you may
be sure, added to the earnestness of my prayers, for *I*
hadn't the courage of old mad King Lear to defy the
lightning, and tell it strike the fat rotundity of this

earth. The cattle rushed off camp, and my fellows, coming out to catch horses, ran across me, buried under a dead moke and praying like an anchorite. Well, I wasn't much hurt, and here I am to-day, as old and hardened a sinner as ever."

"Well, you had a narrow escape," said Harold, "but what time of the night is it now by your watch?"

Oberon, with a theatrical air, pulled out a broken Waterbury watch, which was attached to a gold chain, saying: "You see, boy, it's like grandfather's clock, 'stopped short, never to go again'; but it helps to keep the chain in its place, and no one knows that it's any better than a scooped-out turnip, or a Sam Slick clock. But, lad, I can tell you the time pretty nearly for all practical intents and purposes. You see that star there, on the verge of the horizon? Well, when that sets it's twelve o'clock; so now, as the poet says, 'This dead of midnight is the noon of thought.' Boy, I didn't think you were so interesting, for conversing with thee I forget all time."

With this compliment, he gave Harold a hearty slap on the back, saying: "How does that strike you, lad?"

"Rather hard," replied Harold, feeling more palpably the stroke on the back than the force of the flattery; "but it also strikes me that we should have been asleep long 'go. I thought it was later, though. The nights seem long."

"Ah, ungrateful boy!" exclaimed Oberon. "'Sleep then, and peace to your dreams,' as the poet said."

Chapter VI

" How far must I wander?   O God, how far?
I have lost my star! I have lost my star!"
                              —J. BRUNTON STEPHENS.

HAROLD was awake by daylight next morning, notwithstanding the late hour he went to sleep the previous night. He was accustomed to rising early, from his camping-out experiences on the journey up to the station, for Mr. Brownlow always believed in getting away from camp before sunrise.

Harold got up, dressed himself and washed, then took a walk outside, leaving Ponsonby Oberon sleeping soundly in the green-hide bunk. No one was awake at that hour on the station; even Mr. Brownlow, an early riser, was yet fast asleep. The cocks were crowing loudly in the kitchen yard, and a few quiet old horses were feeding placidly on the luxuriant couch grass, which was growing thickly all about the premises, and covering the ground with a green carpet so completely that not an inch of earth could be seen. He next went down to the creek, and there he saw several wild ducks in the weeds and lilies, which covered the shallower borders of the lagoon. At this sight Harold's sporting proclivities were aroused ; he thought of the old guns and firearms in his sleeping-room, and straightway he hastened to get one, and bring his very limited shooting experiences into practice. It was some time before Harold could loosen a gun from the old and shrunken leather straps which secured them to the wall-plate. At last a rusty old single-barrelled fowling-piece broke suddenly from its fixings, and came down with such a crash as to arouse Mr. Oberon at once into a sitting position. He rubbed his eyes, and called out excitedly to Harold:

" My gracious, boy ! what are you doing, fumbling round there, and making a row this hour of the night ? "

"It's daylight now," said Harold apologetically; "and I just came in for a gun to shoot some ducks I saw on the creek."

" Well then, my lad," replied the drover, "take one, and let me sleep. I have a big arrear of 'nap' to work out yet, for you kept me awake with your 'pitch' till all hours last night. At the same time, my sonny, let me tell you that some of those old guns have been loaded for the last quarter of a century; they have swan-drops, and bullets, and slugs, and I don't know what else may be stuffed down them. Beware then, thou innocent boy, for know you not what the poet said, 'The villainous saltpetre hath laid many a good, tall fellow low.'"

" Oh, I'll be ever so careful," replied Harold.

"Be it so then, my lad, and remember that discretion is the better part of valour, and distance

E

from danger is the safest guard. Let me tell you again to blow down the muzzle of your gun before you attempt to load it, and if you can get air at the nipple—well, it may be right enough, and the chances are about even that it won't burst. So now go, my lad, in peace, and my blessing with you, remembering what the poets say, ' That folly shoots at flies,' therefore aim at nothing that's not good food for powder. Bring back, if you can, half a dozen ducks, and you will thus earn my gratitude for the day, as I'm a lover of stewed fowls and soup, and the salt beef now is very dry and hard."

By the time Ponsonby Oberon had finished this speech, Harold had loaded his gun, and seemed quite prepared to risk all the dangers of it bursting. The drover laid over on his pillow, and very soon was sleeping happily as before.

Harold had very few of the instincts of the good old English sportsman, who would consider it murder to fire at a bird on the ground. Neither did he have any taste for fancy shooting, such as taking down the first bird and the last bird out of a flock flying past him. He patiently crept along the ground till within range of the birds on the water. He raised his head from the reeds and long grass, but, alas! before he could aim the timid wild fowl had flown, and Harold, for the moment, was left vexed and disappointed. But he was not discouraged. He followed the direction the birds had taken—again he crept through sedges and water-grass, and again

he was disappointed by the wary wild fowl. He was
now out of sight of the head station, but he knew the
direction to return to it; and, as it was still early
morn, he resolved to again try his luck before going
back to breakfast. He tramped about the bush for
nearly an hour, but ill-luck seemed to attend all his
diligence and patience.

"Well, I'll go back to the house," he said.
"I suppose Mr. Oberon will have something to
say about my shooting. He'll try to be funny
at my expense; but anyhow, I ain't wasted much
powder and shot." With these words Harold
changed his gun to the other shoulder, and, impelled
by a sturdy appetite, he stepped out bravely for his
breakfast. He walked on cheerfully and lightly for
about half an hour. He was perfectly happy, and
delighted with the wild scenery all around him—
everything looked so beautiful in the early morning.
Nature, in fact, seemed to have awoke refreshed after
the rest and silence of the night. Very beautiful, too,
those gorgeous wild-flowers of the Australian bush—
sweet scented and many coloured—seeming to be
half bashful of their fairy loveliness as they peeped,
dew-spangled, through the luxuriant grass. All
around, on every bush and tree, strange melodious
birds fluttered and warbled a strange medley of
song—a gladsome pæan to Nature in her wildest and
most delightful form.

Harold now looked about him. Surely he must
be getting near the house, but as yet no evidence

of the station could he see. He began to feel a
little uneasy as to the route he was travelling.
He looked about him again, and then somewhat
altered his course, for he was now beginning
to have grave doubts and fears as to the exact
locality of the station. Another hour passed, and
yet no sign of the station homestead—the boy
wandering in sad perplexity, not knowing what to
do or what course to take.

Hour after hour went by, Harold aimlessly
wandering through the tangled Lignum of the
water-courses, then out on to some flooded flat,
studded with strange gnarled Coolebah forest.
Next perhaps he would cross some wild Macka-
garoo, or swampy clay pan, abounding with wild
fowl and game of all sorts, but which now had
no interest nor attraction for Harold. Here and
there a large brown snake would rear his head for a
moment in a threatening attitude, and then, with a
hiss, disappear mysteriously into the long grass. Or
it might be a yellow iguana that next would rush
bustling through the dried leaves and dead fallen
branches, and then into its burrow in the earth, or
perhaps take temporary refuge in a hollow log.
Harold was no less startled by these reptiles than
they were by him. He walked in fear and dread
through the tangled grass, thinking every moment
to be bitten by a venomous snake, or else that he
would tread on some sleepy adder, and then the end
would be certain. Of the deaf, dead-looking, silent

adder he had the greatest dread. Closely resembling
in colour everything in its environment, the adder
might be easily mistaken for a dead stick or a harm-
less, decaying piece of loose bark. Thus Harold got
many an unnecessary scare—many a time he shied
at the mere shadow of a danger, when the reality
was perhaps far away.

In these hours of futile wandering Harold
became very weary, footsore, and hungry. He
realized now that he was lost; and in his desperation, caring less for himself than the dear mother
at home, he prayed that her sorrow for his death
might be light and be soon forgotten. He sat
down on a fallen tree, wiping the tears from his eyes,
and, in the intervals of a repentant sobbing, saying:
" How my poor, dear mother will grieve when she
hears of this. As for myself, I don't mind so much ;
but after I'm gone she'll be there in pain for me. Oh,
I am bad ! I know it, I feel it now ; but I never
thought of it before. I know I'm not worth much,
and I think I must ha' been always a bad case ; but
for all that she'll be mourning and grievin' after me
as if I was the best in the world. If I only died out
here in this wild bush, knowin' that she would never
hear of it, and that she would never care, I could
now be all right ; but for my own self I don't care—
no, not in the least."

He stood up and looked out across a plain
towards a Mulga hill in the distance ; then, with
a firmness and resolution, he said : " Anyhow,

I'm not goin' to stay here and die while I can move a step. I'll keep travellin' anyhow, though it may be for nothin'." With these words he stepped out bravely towards the Mulga hill. It was now nearly sundown, and the prospect for Harold seemed as gloomy as the night that was falling fast. On he went ; the sun went down, the stars shone out, the wind blew monotonously across the bleak plain, but still no beacon light nor camp-fire in the distance for that poor, aimless, wandering boy. Then, sudden and loud and plaintive, would come the cry of some mournful dingo across the silent plain—a weird, hopeless, despairing yell. After that perhaps the long, loud, piercing screech of the woeful curlew would break, like a bell of distress, on the silence of the night. The air seemed filled with the cries of the forlorn and desperate. It seemed as if all manner of crimes were being committed out here on these lonely wilds, and that the cry of the poor sufferers met with no response but the distant wail of some fellow creature in like sad measure of dis-tress.

Harold had now left the creek and water-courses, and his constant tramping had made him very thirsty ; but out there on that lonely plain Nature had no succour for the thirsty and the hungry. In weariness and utter exhaustion he sat down, and, looking up at the stars, he said : " They are just the same as they were last night, just as bright, and cheerful, and happy lookin' ; and they seem to look down on me just the same as I always knowed them. Anyhow, I suppose at this same moment they are lookin' down on plenty of others who also don't know what to do. I suppose, too, they are lookin' down on many others at this same moment who ain't got any cause to complain."

After this Harold for a long time sat in silence, appearing absorbed in some great thought which only came remotely and vaguely within the pale of his understanding. At last he said: "It is very wonderful to think of. God is here with me on this great plain, and in that little star so far away, He is there also; and if I could only look beyond that again, there He would be also. Beyond and beyond and ever so far—that's what I can't imagine; you can never reach the end." And thus the lost boy fell asleep in trying to form some conception of the infinity of space and God's omnipresence.

Chapter VII

"Where the dingo's trail was the only track."
—*New Country*—MARY HANNAY FOOTT.

DESPITE his situation, Harold slept soundly. He awoke about daybreak, refreshed, though hungry and somewhat weak from want of food. It did not take him long to realize his position, and so, according to his custom, he offered up his devotions, and then shouldering his gun, resumed his wanderings with a conflicting mixture of apprehension and of hope. The sun rose, and revealed a prospect of plain and scrubland, which gave no token of human habitation. Later on, as the day grew warmer, he again experienced that feeling of parching thirst, which had left him in the coolness of the night. As he walked on through the burning plain, his thirst became more and more intense.

At last, far out on the verge of a line of timber, Harold espied a white object, which appeared to be a tent or a white-washed hut. This cheerful sight gave the wanderer fresh hope. He thanked God most fervently for this timely relief in his hour of need. Soon Harold came on what appeared to be an old dray track, and as this led directly to the white object on the borders of the plain, he

followed it, though no better travelling than the track-
less plain. Very weary, very exhausted, he gradually
drew near. But now what could it be? Not a house,
certainly. Not a tent. Neither was it a cart or
vehicle of any sort! Drawing nearer still he saw—
God! it was a grave. Harold sank down hopeless
on the plain. That grim evidence of death had more
meaning and horrible significance for him now than
it could possibly have at any other time. There
seemed no room left for anything but despair.
Harold rose up, saying: " I wonder what poor fellow
died here." He tottered over to the grave, which was
enclosed by rough, sawn palings, painted white. At
its head was a large slab of iron bark, also painted
white, and bearing in quaint, irregular letters the
following sad inscription :

"George Clay, aged 28. Perished of thirst."

" Perished of thirst," repeated Harold ; " perished
of thirst. And I suppose, poor fellow, that you
had a mother who you thought of when you
laid down here. Well, I can't go any farther.
So I must stop here ; stop here, I suppose, till the
judgment day, and till then the same head board
can do us both. My God! how hot I feel; how
burnin' hot and terrible thirsty I am."

   * * * * *

Far out on the plain, four objects are groping
slowly, very slowly through the trees. They seem as
if in search of something—they are turning here and

twisting there, and now they come along more quickly
in a direct line.   Suddenly a wild shout breaks across
the plain, and one of the objects in the distance starts
out at a great pace, making directly for the grave.
The other three follow, but not at such speed. Nearer
they come ; nearer, and Harold, turning as the wild
shouts break upon his ear, recognises Ponsonby
Oberon racing across the plain at the utmost speed
of his horse. Before many seconds he arrived at where
Harold was standing. Jumping off his horse, he
caught the lost boy by the hand, gave him a hearty
hug and squeeze, saying excitedly at the same time :
" Thank God we've found you.   Thank God you're
not lost and gone before, like poor George there.
One more lost sheep returned safely to the fold."

" Water!" cried Harold, in a muffled, hollow voice
" Water ! "

" Yes, yes," said Oberon hurriedly, " Here's the
water-bag.   Drink, drink, and, as the poet says,
' Drink deeply, for shallow drafts intoxicate the
brain.' "

Just then Mr. Brownlow came cantering up, calling
out, " Ponsonby, you idiot ! take the water-bag from
the boy.   Take the water-bag from him, I say, you
fool."

Ponsonby Oberon replied indignantly : " Fool,
you say ! Mr. Brownlow.   Haven't you the sense to
see that the boy is as thirsty as a sponge on a dry
stage ? "

But Mr. Brownlow paid no attention to Oberon's

explanation. He jumped from his horse and jerked the water-bag from Harold's mouth, saying, "You young fool, you've given us enough trouble already without giving us the bother of burying you."

"Drink!" exclaimed Harold, trying desperately to regain the water-bag. "Give me a drink. I'm per-ishin'; I'm burnin' thirsty. Give me back the water."

"Yes," said Oberon warmly. "Give him back the bag. By gosh, Mr. Brownlow, as the poet says, 'You're cruel as death and merciless as the grave.' Give him back the bag, can't you."

"To the deuce with you and your confounded poet, Ponsonby," exclaimed Mr. Brownlow. "Will you ever have sense? Will you ever be anything but a fool? Be satisfied that I'm doing everything for the best. Get on your horse now, Ponsonby, and come away some distance."

Oberon obeyed, as he always did when his master became peremptory. But he muttered to himself as he mounted his horse, "This, I suppose, is what the poet would call 'Cruel to be kind.'"

"Now," said Mr. Brownlow, pouring out about a glass of water into a pannikin, "Ponsonby, you take this and leave it about a hundred yards out there on the plain, and when the boy drinks it, bring me on the pint again. We mustn't give him too much water at a time. We must quench his thirst gradually. Your idea of dealing with him would have pegged him out in one act."

Harold, thinking he was about to be deserted by

them, followed Brownlow and Oberon, calling out,
" For pity's sake give me a drink. Don't leave me
here to perish." He came along to where the drop
of water was left, drank it at one gulp, throwing
away the pannikin and following Mr. Brownlow,
calling out wildly for water, more water.

Oberon took up the pannikin as directed and followed Mr. Brownlow, who in the meantime had gone
another two or three hundred yards ahead, and left
down another small vessel of water. He took the pint
which Oberon brought him, and again going some
distance out on the plain, left down another drop of
water. Harold followed eagerly, calling out piteously
for water, and drinking such small quantities as were
left for him at intervals along the plain. Ponsonby
Oberon, whose duty it was to bring on the empty
pannikins, had much to say about the hardness,
cruelty, and madness of this peculiar scheme of saving
a creature from thirst. He quoted poets, and wildly
exhorted Mr. Brownlow to stop and give the boy a
drink. But the old squatter was firm. " Ponsonby,"
he said, " you're a natural born fool. You just stick
to your poets and bring me on the pannikins." After
Harold had been led on in this way for over a mile,
he exclaimed, "Leave me here to perish, then. I'll
not follow you another yard. You're both brutes.
You came out here for the fun of seein' me perish.
Only I threw away the old gun, I'd shoot you both,
and then I would have your water-bags, and could
have a good drink, anyhow, before I died."

With this volley of threat and invective, Harold sank down in the shade of a stunted Gydia tree, and called out to his persecutors to let him perish in peace.

" He's all right now," said Mr. Brownlow. " Let us go on about half a mile or so, and we'll make a pot of tea, and in the meantime a camp under the Gydia tree will do him no harm."

" Look here, Mr. Brownlow," said Oberon excitedly, " the torture of Tantalus by the gods pales into insignificance, when compared with this diabolic contrivance of yours for perishing this poor boy by slow degrees. To use the sublime words of Milton, 'Your scourge is inexorable in this torturing hour.' Can't you let him have a good drink out of the water-bag, and then he can have a drink of tea and a snack afterwards. But if you leave him there, your pot of tea won't be much use to him by the time you get it boiled."

" Well," said Mr. Brownlow, " I don't understand all you say, because I ain't got my pocket dictionary about with me ; but I understand this, and that is that you are a natural born fool." Oberon tried to give a sarcastic laugh, and said, " 'Where ignorance is bliss 'tis folly to be wise.' And now, Mr. Brownlow, you can make a personal application of that piece of wisdom of the poets. How does that strike your deck-house ? "

" Look 'ee here, Ponsonby," said Brownlow, " it's not exactly the time for me to be standing around here arguing the point about mad potes with a natural born fool like you."

With this triumphant retort, Brownlow stuck spurs to his horse, called out to the black boy with the pack horse, and cantered on to a clump of timber at no very great distance away. There he lit a fire, put on a quart of tea, and stretched himself contentedly in the shade awaiting results. In the meantime Oberon quoted all the worst curses of the poets, and hurled them with gigantic force after the retreating form of Brownlow. These thunderbolts of the muse, however, fell short of the mark. Ponsonby wiped his face with a red silk handkerchief, and said, "Certainly I'll not desert the lad in this evil hour of his adversity. I'll stand to him like a Casabianca. Though I haven't got a water-bag, yet 'a fellow-feeling makes us wondrous kind,' as the poet said."

With these words the faithful Ponsonby got off his horse, and coming over to Harold, said, "See here, my boy, though all is lost, Oberon is with you." He clapped his hand dramatically on his chest and continued, "here is a man who never turns his back on friend or foe. Harold, wake up, arise, as the poet said, or be for ever fallen."

Harold looked up, and said, "So you have come back. You didn't think it right to let me perish. Now give me a drink, will you?"

"My boy," exclaimed Oberon, "old Brownlow took my water-bag as well as his own, and I got nothing to offer you but my sympathy and good wishes. I have come, in the language of the poet, to lighten the burden of another's care."

"Well, then," said Harold, "you can leave me. You're no use to me without your bag of water."

"Ah, ungrateful boy," said Ponsonby Oberon; "and this is the way you treat me for my dog-like faithfulness in sticking to you to the last. What does the poets say? 'The blackest of all crimes is ingratitude.' But look there; old Brownlow has pulled up. He's making a fire, and, I suppose, will put on the pot of tea he talked about. Come on, Harold, let us be after him. Here, you take my horse and I'll walk."

Harold readily consented to this arrangement, and soon they reached the camp, where Mr. Brownlow had made the quart of tea. "Now," said he, "come and have a drink of this tea, you young rascal. I'm not sure, after all, but that you didn't deserve to perish for giving us all this trouble. A nice picnic it is for me—hunting up stray new chums out in these dry plains in weather like this. This is always the racket. As soon as I bring a jackeroo up to the place, the first thing he seems to think it his duty to do is to go and get lost."

"And now shouldn't we be glad that we found him?" exclaimed Oberon. "Does not the Scriptures say, that there is more rejoicing over one stray sheep returned to the fold than over a hundred that had never been lost?"

"That's all rot," broke in Mr. Brownlow; "one stray, useless jackeroo will give a man more worry and bother than a hundred good useful stockmen, who know their work and never get lost."

Chapter VIII

" To waste long nights in pensive discontent."
—*Mother Hubbard's Tale*—EDMUND SPENSER.

" I TELL you what it is, Mr. Oberon," said Harold, " I don't like Mr. Brownlow. I can't like him, and I'm going to go away."

Such was the remark our hero made one night about a month after the events recorded in the last chapter. During those four weeks he had rather a stirring experience of station life. Mr. Brownlow kept him at work of all sorts, giving him neither ease nor quarter. As soon as one task was finished Harold was set at another, and so on from early morning till late at night. Mr. Brownlow's Unionist notions were remarkable and characteristic. He worked on the eight-hour principle, but it was eight hours before dinner and eight hours after ; and his idea of giving a man a day's rest was to keep him carting firewood from early morning till dewy eve.

Ponsonby Oberon pushed his smoking cap back on the back of his head, and said, with a paternal earnestness, " Yes, Harold, my boy, you're right. Go back as soon as you can to your people. Complete your education, and don't waste your sweetness in the desert air like me."

64

"I wouldn't like to go back so soon," replied Harold. "Wouldn't they laugh at me at home. Wouldn't they tease me and poke fun at me the whole day."

"Ah, nonsense!" exclaimed Ponsonby Oberon, giving Harold a wild clap on the back; "nonsense, my lad. Know you not what the poet says, 'Laugh where we must, be candid where we can.' So you just laugh with them. Say that this little escapade of yours on the bush was one of the grandest affairs you ever had in all your time. Make the most of it, tell your experiences candidly; and, as Shakespeare says, 'Tell truth and shame the devil.' Tell that little affair that happened to you the other day where you fell off your horse without any cause, and how old Brownlow was going to give you a good whipping for it, because the horse ran away and lost the saddle. Boy, as the poet says, when you get back you will be able to tell such a plain, unvarnished tale as will make their hair stand on end."

"I don't want to go home yet," said Harold.

"My lad!" exclaimed the mercurial Ponsonby, "lucky you are that you have a home to go to. Look at me—man of talent as I am—I got no home. As the scriptural poet says, 'The foxes have holes, and the birds of the air have nests; but the Son of man hath nowhere to lay His head.' Here I am to-day, away to-morrow; sometimes in rain, sometimes in sunshine; sometimes with a few bob in my pocket, but more generally hard-up. We drovers

are like old King Cole, we're merry souls. We take
no thought for the morrow ; we spend faster than
we can make. We run the credit system for all it's
worth, and wherever we go you can track us by the
broad highway of debts we leave after us. ' We're,' as
the old song says, 'all for fun and noise.' We have
no Semitic grasp of cash, and we have no ambition,
excepting it might be to run a pub in our old age,
and that more for the sake of the drinks than the
profit. But look here, Harold, here is a riddle, as
the poet says, 'which I would fain unravel, and which
doth vex my soul.' If you don't want to stay here,
and you don't want to go home, what do you want
to do ? "

"Go somewhere else," answered Harold."

" Ha ! ha ! " roared Mr. Oberon, " soon you would
find yourself like Noah's dove, no rest for the sole of
your foot, and you'd come back, like the prodigal in
the Scriptures, ready to eat of the husks of the swine
yard. I see you have been reading that novel in
which life in the bush is described as a continual
picnic. Well, it may be so ; but I can tell you that
the perpetual damper and salt junk picnics have
not always charms to soothe the stomach of man,
to use the language of the poet. But here's another
thing, my little man : old Brownlow won't let you
slip away like that. You're in his charge, and he'll
see that you don't go wandering about the country
like a pariah and an outcast, 'seeking fresh woods and
pastures new,' as the poet says. If you don't want to

stop with him and complete your colonial education, then he'll safely pack you home to the bosom of your family; and so, as the song says, you'll get there just the same."

"And do you really think that's what he'd do?" asked Harold.

"Why, of course it is," quickly retorted the restless Ponsonby. "You're old Brownlow's *protégé*; and, in the language of the muse, beggars can't be choosers. It won't be his fault if you wander about the country like a stray dog that's lost its collar. Why, it was only last year that a young jackeroo—something of your own age—was sent up to old Brownlow, and after he was here for about three weeks, he took it into his noddle that—like the mouse described by the poet—he'd see the wonders of the world for himself. So he took his departure and left no card. But, be gosh! old Brownlow was on to his tracks like a shot out of a shovel. He overtook him before he got any distance, and from there to the station he whipped the offending Adam out of him, to use the language of the poet, and that with such a double action vengeance as would make your hair stand on end. What between old Brownlow's curses and the boy's wailing and gnashing of teeth, it seemed as if the two of them had a very exclusive monopoly of chaos and confusion all embroiled, and discord with a thousand various mouths, to conclude with a fitting quotation from Milton."

"And what happened after that?" inquired Harold.

"Why," replied Ponsonby, "old Brownlow packed the youngster off next day to his fond and loving parents, gave him the hearty blessing of a stockman, and predicted that, all going well, he'd be hanged some day. Now he's a rising clerk down in a Melbourne office, and often tells how old Brownlow acted a father to him."

After this Harold remained silent for a considerable time ; but Ponsonby Oberon rattled on in his usual erratic manner, misquoting poets and telling miscellaneous experiences in his own career. At last Harold broke in on him and said, "Mr. Oberon, I'll say good-night to you ; I'm going to bed."

With these words he rolled himself up in his blankets, and, despite Ponsonby Oberon's efforts, could not be again aroused.

The worthy drover gave Harold a pat on the head, saying,—

"'Sleep breathes at last from out thee,
My little patient boy.'

So said the worthy Leigh Hunt, and now I think I'll follow suit."

Chapter IX

". . . those than run away and fly."
—*Hudibras*—BUTLER.

THE hour might have been twelve, when a small bearded form, clothed in mole-skin trousers, and an old overcoat, stealthily made its way from the room in which Ponsonby Oberon was sleeping. This was no other than our hero, Harold. As he gained the high road, he muttered to himself, "Now I must make the most of my time from this till mornin'. I suppose Mr. Brownlow will be after me, like he followed the fellow last year, but this horse-hair beard and old slouch hat will help to pass me off."

With these words, he stepped out boldly on the road for Queensland, and by sunrise had left Mr. Brownlow's old station many a mile behind. But now he was beginning to get hungry. He brought no food of any sort with him, but the demands of nature are imperative, and soon the inward boy began to assert himself.

"I see a carrier's camp in front of me," said Harold; "but I don't know if it's safe to go near him. He might know me and tell Mr. Brownlow."

The carrier was having his breakfast, and as Harold passed at some distance away he called out to him,

"Hullo, mate; come and have a drink of tea? You're early on the wallaby this morning."

Harold paused for a moment, but soon the still small voice of his stomach spoke through his lips and answered, "Thank you, I will have a drink of tea."

When the bushman invites you to partake of his billy of tea, he always means you to take a share of the edibles as well. It is the conventional way of asking you to dine with him, or breakfast with him, as the case may be.

"There's a knife there in the tucker box," said the carrier, "so help yourself to the grub. The beef is not too good, but you'll manage to pick a feed out of it. I ain't got any extras to offer you—ran out of them a few days ago. I spect to get to old Brownlow's to-morrow, and get rid of my cargo. You know I'm loaded for him. He's a rusty old bloke, ain't he? Suppose you know him? Not a bad sort, though some people reckon he's a hot 'un."

Harold drew his old felt hat well over his eyes, and answered the carrier as briefly as possible with an occasional "yes" or "no" as the case required. He lost no time in eating his breakfast, and then, thanking the carrier for his hospitality, he once more started on his way. He travelled till about noon, and then, feeling very tired and exhausted, he went off the road to where there were some bushes, and stretching himself in the shade, he was soon fast asleep. He woke again a little before sundown, and resumed his march with new vigour. He did not go more than half a mile, when he espied a horseman coming cantering along the road to meet him. A second glance, and he saw to his horror it was Mr. Brownlow himself. Quick as lightning Harold made up his mind to act the part of a surly old shepherd, and be as curt and surly as possible. He drew the old felt hat well down over his face, and in a few moments more Mr. Brownlow reined up his horse in the roadway before him, saying: "Good-day, me man. Did you see anything of a boy back along the road?"

"No," replied Harold, with all the gruffness he could muster, and not lessening his pace for a second.

Mr. Brownlow looked after him for a moment or so, feeling very angry and pugnacious. Then he broke out, "Well, anyhow, you're an ignorant, surly wretch, that wouldn't pull up and bid a man the time of day and answer a civil question properly." After this he stuck spurs to his horse and started into a good smart canter—making his way for home. Harold shortly looked round and was glad to see the figure of his severe old master disappearing rapidly down the road.

"He must have passed when I was asleep," said Harold to himself. "Well, I reckon I'm in debt to the old slouch hat and horse-tail beard for passing me off like that." Soon the sun set and the stars began to appear. It was a dark and lonesome night, and the prospects for the wanderer seemed neither cheery nor hopeful. He passed over a low hill, and then suddenly he saw a bright camp fire in the distance. It seemed to him a beacon light and star of hope, and he stepped out in the direction as fast as his tired limbs could carry him. When he drew nearer, a man on horseback came out to meet him. " Hey ! " he said, " go round the other side and don't rush the blooming cattle to Kingdom Come off the camp." Harold obeyed, and gained the camp fire by another route. The drover's men were having their supper, and invited him to "come and have a feed." The wanderer required no great pressing. He cut off a piece of beef and damper for himself, and quickly retired from the betraying glare of the camp fire to eat unscrutinized and at leisure.

The drover and his men were a merry set. They laughed and jested over their past experiences, and talked hopefully of all the fun they'd have when they'd get to town. The drover himself was a hard-visaged, loud-voiced man, who talked with great eloquence on the different Melbourne Cups, and discussed with most critical acumen the various merits of all the likely horses engaged for the next great classic event to be run on the course at Flemington. He was, in fact, a walking turf guide—a breathing cyclopædia of horses' pedigrees, their times, places, and performances, and every now and then he was ready to lay a wager that such and such were the cases. His men however, in bush parlance, "stood off him," when it came to the point of making a bet. They felt that the boss had facts and figures too well at his fingers' ends to make many mistakes. At last he said to one of his men, "Dash it all, the cook has had a pretty stiff 'dog watch.' You better go out and square a circle round them 'hornies,' and let the dough banger come in." The fellow got up, called out to the cook to bring him the horse, and soon he was riding around the cattle, singing at the top of his voice a very popular bush song, called "Clancy of the Overflow."

Harold in the meanwhile had eaten his supper, and was now spreading out his miserable rag of a blanket—making his bed for the night. He folded up his tattered overcoat for a pillow, and silently laid himself down to rest. Just as he was dozing off to sleep, he suddenly bethought him that he had not said his prayers. Immediately he sat up on his blanket. He was about to go down on his knees and offer up his devotions, when he looked up and saw those wild, unholy bushmen jesting, laughing and cursing all around him. Ridicule is the severest test that religion can be tried by. Harold was a brave lad, and devotional practices had been more or less ingrained into him, but still the ordeal of going down on his knees and praying before these men was too much for him. But after a little while he compromised the matter with his conscience by reasoning that God would be better pleased with him if he did not bring religion into ridicule by practising it before these profane scoffers and unbelievers. "Yes," he said, "the Lord would be angry for having religion poked fun at ; and, besides, it would be makin' these men worse, and adding more sins to them if I was to be the cause of them laughin' at holy things."

This sophistry, perhaps, would not have stood test of severe logic, but Harold's conscience could not trace a *reductio ad absurdum*, and consequently was well pleased with the wisdom and result of the whole argument. "Now," he continued, "I will say my prayers quietly lying down, and God, who sees my thoughts, will know that I'm doing it for the best."

Thus conscience and religion by a little tact and science gained a decisive victory over "the Evil One." Harold rolled himself up in his ragged blanket and repeated the old prayer, which he had often said at his mother's knee—"Our Father, which art in Heaven." Then in blissful slumber his eyes closed, and the innocent, sinless boy slept the sleep of the just, and dreamt perchance of his school days and his once great victories in the cricket field. Once or twice in the night he was wakened by the whispered conversation between the man going out to do his watch and the one, who had just come in. The latter would say : "Look out for the polly cow, that we killed her calf yesterday. She's tryin' to make away there at the back of the camp. All the rest are settled down to it. Here's the watch. I think you call Bill next. Is there any cold tea in the billy ?" Then the man would have a drink of tea and a smoke, and rolling himself up, clothes and all, in his blankets, would be soon contributing his share of melody to the nasal chorus round the flickering camp fire.

Chapter X

" I've wandered east, I've wandered west,
Through many a weary way."
                    —WILLIAM MOTHERWELL.

FIVE weeks passed away since we chronicled the last event in Harold's career. He had now, by various means, found his way far up into Central Queensland. Much of the way he travelled on foot, but sometimes he'd get assistance from a drover returning with plant and horses after " doing a trip south" with fat bullocks. Once he went horse-hunting for a hawker, and on another occasion a good-hearted coachman, who had no passengers, gave him a lift for several miles. Bush life, he was certainly seeing in its various phases, and despite all its hardships and privations, it seemed to have a peculiar charm for him. He had long ago thrown away the false beard, and the hawker, in consideration of his services, supplied him with a blanket and a new suit of clothes. He still continued to say his prayers on his knees when he was by himself; but when he got in with a crowd of unsympathizing bushmen, he had resort to stratagem, and made his thanksgivings comfortably on the broad of his back.

One day he was plodding along a weary piece of

road, which stretched across a shelterless plain, when suddenly he heard the rattling of bells and hopple chains, and looking back he beheld to his great surprise no other than Ponsonby Oberon. The worthy drover quickly dismounted and, catching Harold by both hands, exclaimed with great effusion : "'It was even thou, my guide, my companion and mine old familiar friend,' as the poet said ; I'm glad to see you, by gracious I am. Where have you been all this time ? What have you been doing ? In the name of Cornelius à Lapide, as the poet said, how did you live ? Well, it knocks all my previous experience into 'pye' to think that I should meet you out here. Tell me all about it now."

"Did Mr. Brownlow send you to look for me ? " asked Harold.

" Perdition catch my soul, as the poet said ; but don't talk to me about old Brownlow. I have balanced my account with him, and for all the insults and injuries he's done me I have had the generosity to square them off to the profit and loss of all my grievances. Yes, Harold, I'm a large-hearted, broadminded man. I'm not what old Johnson would call a good hater. I bear charity and good-will to all mankind, and I forgive old Brownlow with as generous a magnanimity as old Socrates himself."

Ponsonby Oberon in this speech got worked up to a high pitch of excitement. At last he pulled the sealskin cap from his head and dashed it on the ground, exclaiming : " Harold, it is only the great man who can stand a great injustice. By heaven, only I have as strong and philosophic a mind as Plato's, the injustices done me would work like madness in my brain, as the poet said."

"Well, I feel sorry for you, Mr. Oberon," said Harold ; " Mr. Brownlow must have been very bad to you to make you go on like that."

"I tell you, boy," said Oberon warmly, "that I'm as cool as a cucumber. I am just telling you of my troubles in a cool, calm, stoical manner."

" But you haven't told me anything yet," protested Harold. " You didn't say what harm Mr. Brownlow done you."

" Ah, boy," said Oberon sadly, "the heart distrusting, asks for facts, as the poet said. I thought I had your sympathy. I thought a fellow-feeling would have made us wondrous kind to one another. But, lad, what are we doing here on the middle of a dry stage. Come, shove your swag there on my pack horse, and catch one of my loose nags. I got a spare saddle ; so let us get under way, and, as the poet said, push on—keep moving."

Harold readily availed himself of this means of getting over a very dry and uninviting piece of country.

"Now that we are horsed and once more on the march," said Ponsonby Oberon, " I can tell you that when it was found that your place on the station knew you no more, that there was some mounting in hot haste, as the poet said, and a general wild

hullabaloo to try and find you. Old Brownlow
caught his best horse, and brought a stock-whip with
him that he said he'd wear to the bitter end on you.
He said to me : 'Ponsonby, I reckon this is rough
on a man. It seems to take me all my time Jackeroo
hunting. One day they go and stray away and go
within an ace of perishing, and then soon after the
wretches will give a man leg bail and clear like red
shanks or a myall nigger with a black trooper after
him. When the sheep were on the station they
helped to cultivate many a grey hair in my head ;
but, by gosh, Ponsonby, this Jackeroo racket will
make me as bald as a coot. Lucky for you that
you're a natural born fool and the world never
troubles you.' With that he dug spurs into his
horse's flanks and raced away like a madman with
the devil barking at his heels. Well, anyhow, after
being out all day he came back late at night, and as
the poet said, was a sadder and a madder man.
After he had got a glass of whisky into himself and
had eaten his supper, he said to me : 'Ponsonby, dash
me buttons, if I'd care a curse, only I promised my
old friend Merton that I'd look after the lad. I was
to give him such a sick'ner of station life that he'd
never hanker after the bush again. And now here's
the go. Just when I was knocking all the romance
and nonsense out of him, the fellow takes to his
scrapers, and bust me if I know where he's gone to.
Deuce take me, if I have any idea of how I'll tell old
Merton about it. He'll reckon, I suppose, that I ill-

treated the boy, and you know, Ponsonby, that I
gave him good quarters, and the only thing I ever
did to him was to make him stand up to his graft.
There is no mistake I had bad luck. I never met
any one that I could make enquiries of, excepting Bill
the carrier, and a surly old wretch of a swagman,
who wouldn't stop to bid me good-day.'"

"That was me!" said Harold. Then he told the
whole story of how he escaped from the station, and
his wanderings up to date. Oberon listened with as
much patience as his restless nature would allow him,
and at the conclusion of the narrative clapped his
hands, quoted a poet, and exclaimed, "There is no
mistake you're as wonderful a little man as ever
'humped a bluey.' Now do you know what my own
dodge is at present? No. Well, I'm travelling on
the game. I explained that once before to your
clouded understanding, as the poet said. Now I
want you to come with me, and I'll make you as
sharp as a new razor. After six months there won't
be a move on the board that you won't be up to.
There is nothing like travelling on the game to brush
a youngster up. It makes him as wide awake and
keen-eyed as an Argus. Some will tell you, boy, that
there's blue ruin and damnation in this sport of
kings. Well, it may be so ; but I think my favourite
poet was not far out when he said :—

> 'Well, those were harmless pleasures enough,
>   For I hold him worse than an ass
> Who shakes his head at a neck in the post,
>   Or a quick thing over the grass.'"

Ponsonby Oberon rattled on in this pleasant mood till he saw a water-hole by the road side. Then he said to Harold, "Here, let us camp for dinner, for, as the poet said, eating maketh a full man, and drinking a merry man. Let us outspan and put on the billy."

When the horses were hoppled out, and while they were waiting for the tea-can to boil, Ponsonby Oberon unfolded his plan.

"Now see here, Harold," said he, "at the next township there's to be a grass-fed race meeting. It is for all horses that have never tasted corn for three months, and that will be clean into my hand. We must be there, lad, and there will be such a scooping of the pool as was never heard of."

"But," said Harold, "if it's for grass-fed horses only, how is it you feed those two of yours? Just now you gave each of them a nose-bag full of oats."

Ponsonby Oberon laughed loudly and heartily. "Ah, my lad," said he, "you're a long way yet from taking your degree in this sort of education. As the poet said, you're compounded of many simples. Well, know you not then that this is the per-centage that I take for the risks I run. The philosopher, said the wise man, leaves nothing to chance. If my horses get in light for the handicaps, I'm going to back them for all I'm worth. If the weights are dealt out to them too roughly,—why, then, I must only run them stiff and back against them through some one else. A man has to run a crank race now and then or these bush handicappers would never stop till they stacked a church on his horse. No ; in travelling on the game there's a time to lose and a time to win ; remember that's one of the first principles in our philosophy. As the poet said, you're only a babe and suckling yet. You have much to learn in the ways of men. You will find it's a case of the survival of the fittest, and the best rogue wins."

Chapter XI

" Preferred to 'spread-eagle' the ruck,
And make a long tail of the 'field.'"
                    —*Kingsborough*—H. C. KENDAL.

Συμμισγόντων δὲ τῇ ναυμαχίῃ Καδμείη τις νίκη τοῖσι Φωκαιεῦσι
ἐγένετο.—HEROD.

PONSONBY OBERON and Harold travelled on till they came to the bush township, where the grass-fed horse races were to be held. They camped at a small water-hole at no great distance from the course, and there Oberon, assisted by Harold, prepared his horses for the coming events. Every morning and evening they gave their horses steady exercise on the racing track, but contrived to escape the observation of the township touts. Every night, Oberon would leave his horses and camp in charge of Harold, whilst he himself went up to the township to gather what information he could about the other horses likely to be engaged in the forthcoming races. He would generally return in the small hours of the morning, singing like a sand-boy, and with a bottle of whisky in his pocket. This he would offer, liberally enough, to share with Harold, but the lad steadily refused—so the worthy drover, perhaps not unwillingly,—was obliged to drink it all

himself, saying : " Well, as you won't have a booze,
I suppose I must only drink a double health to thee,
as the poet said, but it wouldn't do you any harm to
return the compliment. It seems to me unnatural
and unsocial to let a man drink by himself."

One night, returning very late as usual, he said to
Harold : " I've been just after sounding the man who
has been appointed handicapper, but his fine sense of
honour, as the poet said, could not appreciate the
wager I wished to make him—ten to nothing that my
horse wouldn't win. Deuce take him ; but I think
the long and the short of it will be, that I'll have to
run my horse a stiff 'un and back against him."

" Well, I don't very well understand it all," replied
Harold, " but it does sometimes seem to me, Mr.
Oberon, that your plans are not honest."

Ponsonby Oberon laughed and said : " You see, my
lad, it's this way ; racing is like the heathen Chinee,
as the poet said, for ways that are dark and for tricks
that are vain, the turf is remarkably peculiar. It's
like sitting down to a game of cards with men who
play all they know. You understand and take it for
granted that the other side will shuffle the cards and
stack them to suit his own taste, and he is also aware
that you will do the best you can for yourself when
it comes to your turn, as the poet said, to have
patience and shuffle the cards. It's simply a contest
of wits. The man with the most cunning and who
has the most dodges will always come out on the
top."

"But that seems very bad on both sides," put in Harold.

"My lad," exclaimed Oberon, "your code of ethics is a very narrow one. In all gambling transactions there are always two negatives, and you, who have come from school lately, know that they must make a positive. You know that I am playing dishonestly. I am aware that you are doing the same. Therefore it's just the same for me as the other. As the poet said, 'fair is foul and foul is fair.'"

"I think it is all so false and dishonest," mused Harold.

Ponsonby Oberon got up and gave him a hearty slap on the back. "Just so, my lad," said he. "You have struck the nail remarkably square on the head. As the poet said, all is false and hollow. In travelling on the game, it's nothing but a case of diamond cut diamond. It is just exactly the same with everything else in the world—nothing but deception and lies. Man is a bundle of falsehoods—he not only deceives his fellow-man, but he deceives himself."

The night before the races Ponsonby Oberon went back to his camp rather more drunk than usual. "Harold!" he shouted, pulling the blankets off the lad. "What! fast asleep and snoring like a grampus, when I thought you'd be all anxiety to hear the result of the handicaps. It is wonderful to think of your stoic indifference at an exciting time like this. Well, the wretched old handicapper has dealt out my weights with an open hand, as the poet said. As

it is, I believe I could win in a canter, but I must
have an eye to the future, my boy, and this time
my plan of action is to run a slanter. I got a fellow
up in town to lay all he could get against my horse,
and to make matters easy for him, I told every one
that the big money is a dead bird for me. Of course
they reckon that I'm egregiously an ass, as the poet
said, for to send my horse up in the market like that,
but I'll teach these bush-whackers a lesson that will
make them remember me. Yes, Harold, John Armstrong must ride for me to-morrow—a losing race is
often the one that pays the best, though not so as a
rule for the general public."

"And who's this Armstrong?" asked Harold. "Is
he a good jockey that you know?"

"There is no mistake, your innocence surpasseth
all understanding, as the poet said," laughed Ponsonby Oberon. "Well, this Johnny Armstrong is a
ubiquitous sort of fellow, very subject to palm oil,
and as his name suggests, can take a very powerful
hold of a horse, and has generally the misfortune to
run in the ruck or perhaps last. He is not a popular
jockey, though there is hardly a racecourse that he
doesn't get a mount on."

"Mr. Oberon," said Harold, "sometimes I think
you're a clever fellow, other times I can't make out
if you're a fool or not, and generally I got a notion
that you're a dishonest, good-natured fellow. Very
often I don't know what to think of you, unless it's
that you're mad."

Ponsonby Oberon gave a wild, loud laugh and threw his cap at Harold, exclaiming : " My lad, you make me out to be a strange complex personality of the first water. But a man of genius is hard to understand ; he is always working the art that conceals art. You're so child-like and bland, as the poet said, that I know you say what you mean ; and when you put me down as a fool you paid me a compliment that I'm proud of. The rule is, always endeavour to persuade your opponents to take you at a low valuation—the world always accepts a man at his own price, and you know, as the poet said, it takes a wise man to act the fool."

" Well now, let us get to sleep," protested Harold. " I suppose you want to be fresh for the races to-morrow."

" Yes, by gosh," exclaimed Ponsonby Oberon, " I must do my sleeping in camp and not be caught napping on the course."

With these last words both the wanderer and the adventurer went to sleep.

Early next morning Harold aroused his companion, who was not by any means thankful for being cut short in his slumbers.

" Lad," said Oberon, " I never saw the like of you. You go to bed at sundown like a fowl, and like an old hen that has an egg to lay, you're up by starlight, and cackle all about the place, making chaos and confusion in the whole camp, as the poet said."

" Very well, Mr. Oberon," said Harold, " sleep on

till sundown if you like. "Them racing fellows up there most likely will put back the sports to suit your own time."

"Egad, my boy," exclaimed Oberon, starting up in his blankets, "you're learning to cultivate a fine sense of sarcastic humour. There's a Diogenes in embryo in you, my lad. Cultivate your talent, as the poet said, and you may rise to the dignity of a cynic's tub yet. Be gosh, though Harold, another sort of tub wouldn't hurt you just at present. Have a look at that bottle there and see if I left a drop in it at all. My coppers are as hot as a boiler fit to burst. What! not a drain left. Harold, you should have known that I'd want an eye-opener this morning. The least you could do was to leave me the makings of a pick-me-up."

Harold protested, "Mr. Oberon, you know I don't drink."

"Well, you'll learn it soon enough," was the reply. "As the poet said, it's a costly habit on thy purse. Now I must get away up to the pub, and find a hair of the dog that bit me. A small bottle of champagne is a great reviver after a night's boozing. You have old Masquerade up to the course by ten o'clock. I'm going to scratch Clodhopper."

With these words Ponsonby Oberon hastened away for his morning's refreshments, and Harold was left to get ready his own breakfast.

Punctually at ten o'clock Harold led old Masquerade to the track. There he saw Oberon, who was bustling about in the crowd, with a roll of notes in his hand, and shouting out excitedly at the top of his voice.

Two or three small races were run, and then the jockeys mounted for the principal event, in which Oberon's horse was engaged.

" Now, see here," said he to the rider, taking him quietly on one side ; " as soon as the flag drops send your mount clean away to the lead—go to the front hands down, as the poet said, and when you get round to the back of the course pull the old fellow off the track on to the heavy ground, and keep him jigging there as as long as it's safe. Run him as wide as you like round at the back as long as the stewards don't see you. Bring him back on to the course again when you're drawing towards home, and by that time the wind will be knocked out of him, and he'll no longer be fit to hold his own in the front rank, as the poet said."

Oberon, after these instructions turned round, and whispering to a small-eyed, cunning looking man, who stood close at hand, said : " He'll look a winner all over for the first part of the journey, so wager all you can against him. Make hay whilst the sun shines, as the poet said."

After this, the worthy drover hurried about through the crowd, making his roll of notes very conspicuous, and shouting out with the voice of a Stentor : " They'll never see his tail for dust. He'll lead them a merry jig from start to finish. He'll win, pulling double with his mouth wide open. As the poet said, it's all over bar the shouting."

At that moment the flag dropped, and Oberon's jockey, true to his instructions, sent his horse to the lead at once. Just then Harold came up and said: "Mr. Oberon, before the horses started I heard a fellow make a wager of twenty to nothing with your jockey."

"Oh, don't bother me, don't bother me," shouted Oberon, mad with excitement.

"And," persisted Harold, "your Johnny Armstrong said 'thank you sir.'"

"Peace be with you, as the poet said," exclaimed Oberon in a wild frenzy, and not hearing nor heeding the information that Harold proffered. Oberon went on in a loud monologue: "He's going grand, grand. That's it. Now it's safe to take him off. Run him off track you fool, there's no time to lose. Gosh! did ever any one see the like of it! He's sticking to the course like a barnacle to a ship's bottom. Pull him off the course, pull him off the course! By the Gemini, this is terrible—five lengths to the front hard held, as the poet said, and still in the inside of the track. By the sacred nine, this is enough to make me mad. There, most of the race is run. Too late, too late! You wretch, you have thrown me over. In he comes up the straight and nothing near him. I'm done, I'm ruined! There, past the winning post by half a dozen lengths, and it's all over."

With these words, Ponsonby Oberon ran over to his jockey, calling out: "You traitor, you have sold me like a fat bullock in a sale yard. I'll have you down from your high estate and send you weltering in your blood, as the poet said."

"Keep back from the horse till the jockey weighs in," shouted the clerk of the course.

But Oberon took no notice of this command. He came on determined to take summary vengeance, but was seized by Harold and held for a few seconds, When Oberon got away, the crowd had closed round the jockey, who was now weighing in.

"Weight," said the clerk of the scales; and at that moment Oberon broke through the circle of spectators and aimed a blow straight for the jockey's head. The fellow artfully ducked his head one side, and in return sent out a terrible right cross-counter which, catching the excited drover square on the jaw, sent him with a crash on to a gambling table, which was immediately at his back. The table was broken, and the result was that the man who owned it was so enraged that he lost no time in dealing out a hearty kick on Ponsonby Oberon's ribs. This caused the unfortunate drover to cry out : "Murder here—I'm mobbed by a host of jockeys and forties, and a fellow with a sweat table is staving in my ribs. Murder! or my blood be on your heads, as the poet said."

Harold, hearing these cries of distress, immediately

came to the assistance of his friend, but in the
general excitement he received a hit in the eye,
which caused him to retaliate, and in the general
crowd, he struck the wrong man. This led one or
two more into the scuffle, and matters were fast
assuming the appearance of a faction fight, when
the only policeman in the township made his appearance on the scene. The result was magical; the
rioters dispersed in a moment, and the worthy
constable, catching Harold by the collar of the shirt,
exclaimed triumphantly: "Come on now with me.
I'll chain ye up for disorderly conduct and disturbing Her Majesty's pace. Sure did ever any
one see the like of such a spalpeen to be after
causin' an insurractshun on the racecoorse?"

As Harold was led off by the faithful guardian
of the public peace, the cry went round, "a protest
—a protest is lodged against the winner."

Ponsonby Oberon hurried off as he heard this,
and in wild, excited exclamation, asked: "What's
this I hear? What's this at all? First I'm cheated
by a rascally jockey, and now I'm to be done out
of the miserable satisfaction of the prize and probably have my horse disqualified. Truly was ever
man beset by such a host of troubles, as the poet
said? They come not singly and alone, but in
battalions."

The cause of the protest was soon known. The
owner of the second horse lodged an objection
against the winner on the ground that he was corn

fed. The stewards quickly called a meeting, and the man who entered the protest produced some damaging evidence in support of his statement. First, one fellow was brought up, who said that he detected several grains of undigested oats in the horse's manure. Then another came forward and said that after several nights' careful watching he found the animal with a nosebag on. Finally, a third made affirmation that he saw several grains of horse-feed scattered about Oberon's camp. The committee were very incensed by these strong evidences of fraud. They called up Ponsonby Oberon, and in language more forcible than polite, informed him that the case against him was one that left little doubt in his favour, and then asked him if he had anything to say for himself. Oberon replied that he was so astounded by such barefaced, groundless accusations that he didn't know what to say. "I'm clean knocked of a heap," said he, "and the only thing I can tell you is the remark made by King David, that all men are liars, and of this you have three splendid examples in those fellows who just came forward, and who coolly built up from airy nothing, as the poet said, a story like the baseless fabric of a vision. Gentlemen, I can only say that these men have nothing of the still small voice of the inward monitor, and that they've got the most splendid imagination for facts that I've ever seen or heard of in all my time."

" Rot, rot, rubbish and bluff," broke in the chairman of the committee; "that sort of stump orator's gab won't do here. Have you got anything to say for yourself, or can you produce any one who'll try and clear you of these charges?"

"What's the use? What's the use?" exclaimed Oberon excitedly, as he dashed his cap on the ground and walked up and down talking loudly and wildly. "You have prejudged my case, and I could not now convince you to the contrary—even if I was such a logician as Belial, who could make the worse appear the better reason."

He paused for a moment, and then suddenly slapping his forehead with his hand, he exclaimed: "Yes, yes—of course. The young fellow who was with me from the time I commenced training, will be able to tell you that I acted strictly on the square."

"Well, call him up," said one of the stewards, "and we'll hear what he has to say."

"Gentlemen," put in the man who entered the protest, "I beg ter object. This young fellow belongs to the same push, and course he won't say nothing ter make things look blue for his mate."

The chairman quickly turned round to the man, and said with a snarl: "And, of course, *your* three fellows are of a different sort. Bring up this lad at once and let us have no more wasting time."

"He's taken away to the booby house, sir," shouted three or four at once.

"Well, I suppose that means that he's on the chain. Call Constable O'Brien here."

The constable soon made his appearance, and the chairman, who was a Justice of the Peace, said: "O'Brien, we want that young fellow for a few minutes, whom you took away a short time ago, I understand. We have an important matter here under consideration, and the chap's evidence may be of some importance. Will you kindly bring him round to us for a few moments?"

The result was that Harold was brought up before the committee. The lad looked very much confused and ashamed, and for a few minutes his words seem to stick in his throat. As soon as Oberon saw him, he bustled over quickly, and giving him a slap on the shoulder, said: "Now, my lad, tell the truth about me. They accuse me of feeding my horse. They got a villainous tissue of lies in support of their vile statement, and now, my boy, I want you to tell the facts of the case. Tell the solid truth, Harold—as the poet said, tell truth and shame the devil."

The chairman turned on Oberon and said, with no very gentle grace: "Will you be so kind as to leave the examining of this boy to us. There is no necessity for coaching him in his part. We understand very well what you mean by this off-hand candour you assume."

Ponsonby Oberon quickly put his hand to his head with the intention of dashing his cap on the ground. In this he was disappointed, for the much abused head cover was already in the dust, where it had been thrown a short time before. He contented himself with picking it up, and saying to Harold with forced calmness : "Tell the square, honest, plain, unvarnished truth."

The boy looked at Oberon in hopeless confusion, then he glanced at the committee, and from them his eyes again wandered appealingly back to Oberon. Harold was not used to this sort of an ordeal, and consequently his ideas were confused, and words somehow would not come to him. The chairman saw this, and said kindly : "My lad, take your time. Do not get yourself nervous and flurried. I know that I felt very mixed and uneasy myself the first time I went to talk to a crowd. Steady yourself now, my lad. Do not be bashful. We just want you to tell us what few facts you may know about this horse-feeding business."

Harold drew two or three long breaths and then said : "You want me to tell you all I know about Mr. Oberon's horse ? "

"Yes, yes"; exclaimed the stewards and Ponsonby Oberon almost together. The latter adding significantly : "You know, Harold, my whole case rests on you telling the truth."

Thus encouraged, Harold, in sentences somewhat broken at first, began his evidence. He did not go far when Ponsonby Oberon discovered, to his horror, that the boy was telling a plain unvarnished tale, as he said. Harold went on describing everything truthfully and in detail. The whole story and secret of the corn feeding came out. It was a complete exposure; and Ponsonby Oberon was so struck by the marvellous candour of the boy, that he didn't know what to say. At last his tongue found utterance, and he exclaimed with great agitation: "Harold! Harold! In the name of all that's sane, what are you talking about? You have added ruin upon ruin on me, as the poet said. You——"

"Stop, stop," said the chairman; "we don't want to have any of this sort of hypocritical frenzy."

Ponsonby Oberon bounced off—making his way through the crowd, and wildly vociferating that he was Ishmael, and that every man's hand was against him. The chairman turned to Harold, and said: "My lad, we have to thank you for your clear and straightforward statement." Then turning to the constable, he said, "O'Brien, what have you got this boy on the chain for?"

"Well, sur," said the policeman, "I caught him in the very act of being dhrunk, and disorderly, and fightin', yer anner."

"Oh, you did," said the chairman cynically. "Well, then he must have sobered up wonderfully quick."

"I never drink at all," pleaded Harold, "and I'm sorry that I was in the row."

"Oh, well; that's all right," said the chairman. "Now look here, O'Brien, I'll be responsible for the conduct of this boy. You can let him go."

"But, sur, shouldn't he——" The constable was

interrupted by the chairman with "Yes, yes, yes. Should be brought up before the Court in the morning, and go through the usual formality and all that, but in this case you needn't mind that."

Thus Harold was released, and the stewards then turned to consider Ponsonby Oberon's case. They were not long in coming to a conclusion. Oberon was called up, and the chairman, with firmness and severity, said: "Sir, the case against you is clearly proved. We are determined to put down this knavish, rascally and dishonourable conduct, and let every man understand that we will do so with an iron hand. We get up a little sport for the amusement of the people in the district. Our club is a small one, and we can only afford to give small prizes. Therefore it would not pay to corn feed, and we decided horses should be off the grass. But here you come with a horse corn up to the neck, and a dead certainty for any long distance races. We consider it as criminal an action as forging a cheque, robbing a till, or going through a man's pockets. Every true sportsman is a man of honour, but there is always here and there some rascally fellow with neither principle nor integrity, who goes about like a wolf in lamb's clothing, making endeavour to cheat and circumvent the true and honest sportsman. We intend to sternly put that down. We will protect the honourable man, and at every opportunity we will make an example of the rogue. In this I know we have the sympathy and good will of all straightforward men. It now remains for me to tell you the decision of the committee—Yourself and your horse are disqualified for the period of eighteen months. Let that be an example to you. Go."

Chapter XII

"Paid is all thy debt in time."
—CHARLES HARPUR.

PONSONBY OBERON returned to his camp.
There he saw Harold sitting quietly on a bag
of oats, and apparently enjoying a rather late lunch,
which consisted of johnny cake, dry salt beef, and
black tea. Oberon gave a wild excited laugh, and
throwing his cap at Harold, said : "Boy, there is no
mistake, you gave me away clean. Your facts were
stubborn things, as the poet said, and they had the
same result on my case as a sledge hammer on an
egg. And to think that I should have had you
called up myself to do me this good turn—ha, ha, ha.
You see, lad, that he who loses can laugh as well as
he who wins. A philosopher, you see, Harold, is a
large-hearted, large-minded man—blaming no one
—not even his friends. No mistake, you're the soul
of truth—you're a perfect Epaminondas. I thought
you'd have a little imagination for facts, and be
able to lie like the truth, as the poet said. But no,
you found no pleasure so great as standing on the
vantage ground of facts. Harold, my lad, we must
lose no time—the publican here has an account
rendered for refreshments against me that would

make your hair stand on end. We must sneak away, going forced marches, and this place must know us no more."

"When will we go?" asked Harold.

"When!" exclaimed Oberon; "I tell you there is no wasting time, my brother, in a case like this. As the poet said, we must be up and doing, with a heart for any fate. We must pay for the publican's refreshments at the rate of eight miles an hour, and if we keep up the pace for the best part of to-night, I think by to-morrow the account will be about balanced."

An hour later Ponsonby Oberon and Harold were making their way through a stretch of low Gydia scrub, and escaping as quietly as possible from the scene of so much disaster.

"Ah," exclaimed Oberon, "there is no mistake, we struck a red hot streak of ill luck in this con-founded place. Fortune played against us with false cards, and by the hokey we went down, and as the poet said, great was the fall thereof."

"You see, Mr. Oberon," said Harold, "that there are others just as good as yourself at travelling on the game."

Ponsonby Oberon, with a gesture of impatience, threw away the match he was striking, and taking the pipe out of his mouth, said: "Croaker of a boy, you speak the taunt before my face, as the poet said. You think because I went down with a thud that I'm not up to my label. Where I failed was in having such implicit confidence in human nature, for I thought that all men were like myself—true, honourable and trustworthy. If I had been guided by the poet, who said truly, men are deceivers ever, and if I had only said, Ponsonby Oberon, look out, it's not every man is as square as yourself, then you'd have seen different results. It was my noble-hearted faith in man that blued my arrangement. I have nothing of the Rochefoucauld about me—pity that I haven't, or I wouldn't trust those I reckoned my closest friends."

Oberon struck another match, lit his pipe, and said, with a laugh, " Now you needn't think, Harold, that my last remark was a cap made to fit you. But look here, my boy, we must move our pegs a bit quicker. We are only paying the publican at about the rate of four miles an hour as yet. Let us take a canter and square accounts a bit faster, for, as the Scriptures said, owe no man anything."

Thus this strangely assorted pair travelled that day. Sometimes going along steadily, other times suddenly breaking into a canter and going for several miles at a smart pace. They travelled like this till long after sundown. At last Oberon pulled up, saying, " My boy, I think now we've honestly done the best we could, so surely we are deserving of a rest, for, as the poet said, virtue has its own reward. Let us hopple out here for the night, and, in the language of the muse, rest from the labours of the day."

After they had let their horses go, and eaten supper, Oberon lit his pipe and prepared to talk. For some time he babbled on, and Harold answered with an occasional "yes" or "no." Oberon was satisfied as long as his companion was listening. But at last the drowsy monosyllabic answer gave place to a contented snore. Oberon looked over to where Harold was stretched. Then suddenly an idea struck him. He leaped to his feet, and giving the boy a hard clap on the chest, said, "I'll go bail now, my lad, that you haven't said your prayers. You haven't thanked the Lord for taking you out of the house of bondage, as the poet said. Have you now? Have you?"

Harold sat up, rubbing his eyes and, looking at Oberon with a dreamy stare, muttered, "What's that you say? Prayers? Ah, yes, to be sure, I didn't. Thank you, Mr. Oberon, for reminding me. I'll say my prayers now."

"That's right," exclaimed Oberon, rubbing his hands approvingly. "Know you not what the poet says :—

"'Who goes to bed and does not pray
Maketh two nights to every day.'"

Harold, with half-closed eyes, rapidly mumbled through his devotions ; then he tumbled over on his blanket and lost no time getting to sleep. Ponsonby Oberon looked at him in disgust for some time. Then he broke out: "Yes, there you lay in a horizontal position, your head without a night-cap and full of the foolishest dreams, as the poet said."

Oberon always gave the poet credit for all the sayings which he misquoted. It did not matter to him whether it was sage or romancer who said all these fine things, they were always put down to the glory and honour of the muse. Oberon puffed away impatiently at his pipe for some time, but the silence was too much for him. He went over to Harold, gave him a rap on the ribs, and shouted out, "Boy, don't you know that it's not good for man to be alone, and, I may also tell you, as the poet said, that few and short were the prayers you said. I really think, my lad, that you ought to add a bit of an appendix to that short orison you uttered. Why, bless my soul, it wasn't longer than half a dozen 'Amens.' To tell you the honest truth, you commenced your Paternoster just as I started to light my pipe, and, by the hokey, Harold, it's a fact you were rounding them off as I was throwing away the match. Don't you know what the poet said—or is it in the Koran I read it—Woe to him who is negligent in his prayers. But it's no use— no use. The fellow sleeps like a dead log, a sort of sleep, as the poet said, that knows no waking."

Ponsonby Oberon, finding it was useless trying to keep up a conversation with Harold, was at length forced to betake himself to his own blanket. There he settled himself down and in a loud monologue · went on : "There is no mistake, it's rough on a man having to be cut short in his grog like this. Not a drop in the camp, or within miles of it, and I feel just this night as if I could give my life for a refreshment. Well, well, it's a different caper to last night, when I was all for fun and noise, as the poet said, and our glasses clinked merry as a marriage bell."

Suddenly he leaped to his feet and called out with all his voice: "Well, why not take a hand then; give them a recitation—How we beat the favourite—let the curlews and plovers have a Roland for their Oliver, as the poet said."

Then he altered his tone to a sort of cracked shriek, and the stunted Gydia echoed to his voice. The crickets ceased their chirping and the curlews and the wildfowl flew away screeching, the while Oberon shrieked out with much gesticulation his favourite poem. He broke off suddenly, saying, "No use, that's a fact. Things are a bit too dull for one man's vocal efforts to make them cheerful."

He made another attempt to wake up Harold and get him interested in an erratic dialogue. But the lad felt that he was better engaged, and so Ponsonby Oberon gave up the effort in despair. He went over and stretched himself out on his blanket again, trying with an effort to compose himself to sleep. Just then a dingo gave a loud, piteous, mournful wail at no great distance away. Ponsonby Oberon jumped to his feet, exclaiming, "What's that? What's that? Ah, it's only a dingo after all. Be

gosh, I'm as shaky as an aspen leaf.   I haven't now
the firm nerves that never tremble, as the poet said.
I believe I'm on the verge of 'the blues'; a glass
of grog would do me all the good in the world."

However, after many futile attempts to wake up
Harold, the mercurial Oberon at last found rest.
Morning broke and the magpies commenced their
joyous carols all around the camp.   Harold soon
awoke, and after sitting on his blanket and rubbing
his eyes for some time, he got up and had a wash.
Then he raked the slumbering coals together, made
a fire and put on a billy of water for tea.   After
that he picked up his bridle and started after the
horses, which were camped on the farther end of
a great level plain.   He had some trouble in finding
the camp again on his return; in fact it was only
by the merest good fortune that he was not bushed
altogether.   When he came to the fire, he found the
billy had boiled over and there was not a drop
of water in it.   He picked it up, but alas! the
bottom fell completely out of it.   Harold gave a
start, and uttered, "What will Mr. Oberon say?   It
was my fault in putting on too big a fire."

But Ponsonby Oberon was quite oblivious to these
petty accidents.   Harold considered for a moment;
then he went over to Oberon, and giving him a
rough shaking, said, "The bottom is out of the tea-
billy, what will we do?"   But there was no response,
excepting a grunt and a yawn.   "Mr. Oberon," continued Harold, "won't you wake up.   The sun is

high now—very high—and the day is going to be hot. I have brought the horses up, so let us be getting away while the morning is cool. Ah, I can't wake him. He's a terrible man to sleep, especially in the morning. Mr. Oberon, do wake up. Just get your eyes open a bit and have a wash and then you'll be fresh and all right."

Harold shook Oberon again and again. But his efforts were all in vain—the only answer was a drowsy muttering of "let me sleep; go away out of that."

Harold, finding that it was all no use, went away and sat on a log. After contemplating for some time, he suddenly got up, saying to himself, "Well, there's the beef billy, I can scour and scrub that out and make it clean enough to boil the tea in." With that he again set to work and soon had another can of water boiling. He put on some tea, and after he let it cool, he again went over to Oberon, saying, "Now, wake up! I have made some tea, and if you'll just have a drop of it, you'll be freshened up wonderful—great thing a drop of tea to make one keep his eyes open."

Harold's persuasions and efforts were all without result, so he consoled himself by going over to the pack bags and having his own breakfast. After he had finished, Ponsonby Oberon gave a loud yawn, and stretching out his arms, muttered, "Time to get up, I suppose. What a fool I was to sleep on the sunny side of the bush—the bright orb of

day, as the poet said, always wakes a fellow up
in the morning. Good thing always, Harold, to
sleep on the western side of a bush, you always
get the benefit of the shade, you see. You don't
have the sun burning a hole in your blanket at
unearthly hours in the morning like this. Ah, I
see, you got the billy boiled—good lad. Always
spare your poor old mate as much as you can ;
as the poet said, respect grey hairs. Mine, though,
are not grey yet, but they will be some day. Anyhow, Harold, you see I got rheumatics and I can't
knock round a camp like I used to."

After that he got up, saying, "Harold, I don't
think I'll have any breakfast this morning ; lost
my appetite somehow ; but, be gosh, my boy, I see
you found it, judging by the hole you made in the
johnny cakes. Well, I'll have a drink of tea anyhow,
though a drink something stronger would be more
into my tomahawk. Harold," giving the boy a slap
on the back, "never apply hot and rebellious liquors
in your blood, as the poet said—the after clap is
too much. I had a good bit of fun one way or
another back there at the township, but now the
re-action equal and opposite has set in, and I kinder
wish I never had been born, as the poet said. But,
what's this—made the tea in the beef billy ! What
sort of a mixture is this, me lad—a sort of a new
dodge in cooking, eh ? Giving us the soup and
the tea in one act. Great saving of time in that.
I hope, Harold, you didn't boil the beef in the tea.

Your principle of cooking is very original, my lad. I see you got a notion that they didn't know everything down Judee, as the poet said. They weren't up in this sort of a caper anyhow, and I think just as well for their tummies, too, that their ignorance was bliss."

"I'm sorry for it, Mr. Oberon," said Harold regretfully, " but the water I put on boiled away while I was after the horses, and when I came back the bottom had melted out of the billy."

"Run to my arms, my son," exclaimed Oberon, "you're a perfect George Washington for facts. Another boy would have said a horse put his foot through it, but your want of imagination made you give the true bill. Well, let us pack up our bed and walk, as the poet said.

Chapter XIII

"Men are never so likely to settle a question rightly as when they discuss it freely."

—Lord Macaulay.

A FORTNIGHT passed away since the conversation reported in the last chapter. Since then our two adventurers had travelled many a mile. Ponsonby Oberon had fully recovered from any effects he might have felt from his late disasters and he was now eagerly looking forward to a race meeting, which was to take place at a township some hundred miles away.

"Five days' steady travelling, Harold me boy," said Oberon with enthusiasm, "five days and we'll be at the scene of action, and Richard will be himself again, as the poet said. No mistake, for excitement this sport of kings is a great game—nothing like it, too, for exhibiting a man's talent and showing the dodges and moves he can make."

"I thought your horse was disqualified," said Harold. "You can't run him for a long while yet!"

"Ha, ha, ha," laughed Oberon. "Well, I thought I was making you a bit cunning by this time, but I see you still think it's folly to be wise, as the poet said. You must know then, foolish boy, that as for the disqualification, I only regarded it as a mere matter of form. I can get round that as easy as falling off a log. By the time we get to where this next race meeting is to be held we will be nearly 400 miles away from the unlucky little township where old Masquerade was disqualified. Not very probable then that there will be many at this next meeting who will know him. That doesn't make any matter though—I don't care if they be all there. A wise man, Harold, you know leaves nothing to chance. I am not going to run the risk of people recognising him. I carry the whole plant with me for making useful alterations in a horse's appearance. Ah, bless him, Harold, who invented dye. But why do I ask you to bless him ? You young rascal, you know that you didn't say your prayers last night, and the blessings of the unrighteous availeth not, as the poet said. Well, well—it doesn't make any matter —you can do a double shift to-night and that will put you square. However, as I was saying, the man who invented dye must have had some experience in travelling on the game. Anyhow, to a man of talent it supplies a long-felt want, and, like charity, it covers a multitude of sins, as the poet said. You see the old fellow is a bright bay at present, but when I am done with him, he will be a beautiful coal black. I also mean to be neat and artistic—put a good finish on my work as it were. I'll have a nice blaze down his forehead, and I'll make his hind fetlock white. That

will look well when I'm handing in his description on
the night of general entry. I'll be very particular
about details, for that shows a methodical and exact
man, as the poet said. Now just keep your mouth
closed and don't interrupt me till I explain to you
what a genius I am. You see the old fellow has got
a stumpy tail. Well, there's a tale attached to that
tail, ha, ha, ha. What about that for a pun? The
poet says that the man who'd make a pun would pick
a pocket—the truth of which I'm not going to dispute just now. However, that stumpy tail was the
means of getting him two stone lighter in a handicap
one time. Now, you see, Harold, it's the fly season,
and it would be cruelty to animals to let that poor
old crock go about with that little brush only to protect himself. No, the good man is always good to
his beast, as the poet said, and I mean to make some
amendments and alterations in that stump. It is
quite piteous to see the way it goes through the form
of wagging, and yet the flies are only laughing at it.
That horse has only little there below, but I must
make that little long, as the poet said. Well, the
fact of it is that I got a tail in my pack bags that fits
him to a critical nicety. You see, my boy, a wise
man always looks well ahead of him, and I have
carried that spare tail in case of an emergency such
as will take place at the next meeting."

"But what about the horse's brands?" enquired
Harold.

"Pshaw, sweet innocence," said Oberon, with a

dramatic wave of his hand. "Do you think he was the only horse ever bred of that brand? But even there, my attention to details will show itself. I will act well my part, as the poet said, for there all the honour lies. Did you never hear of such a thing as 'faking a brand,' or 'plucking' or 'blistering a brand'? My true genius comes out in little fine touches of art like these. Do you see the P on his shoulder? That I'll change into an R or a B. The number I I can easily make into an E. All that is simply done by plucking out the hairs with a small tweezers and you make a brand that looks as natural as life. You can also make brands to taste by a little drop of carbolic acid, but then that doesn't always do because it makes a permanent affair. Another simple recipe for a temporary brand is this:—Make your iron red hot, then get a wet bag and place on the horse, where you wish to leave your sign manual—press the hot iron against it, and you thus blister an impression that looks as if it had been on him since he was a foal. It does splendidly for the time and after a month it wears off again and leaves the spot a *tabula rasa*, as the poet said, on which you can make any other brands you like in any future case of emergency. There is also what they call the 'frying-pan dodge,' but it is only a botch who goes in for that. My system is an art that truly conceals an art, and unless I have some good-natured friend to give me away, I am as safe as a church. Somehow though, from my last experience, I am inclined to think with the poet—save me from my friends, I'm not afraid of my enemies."

"Mr. Oberon." said Harold, "you're cunning right enough, but somehow it seems to me like cheatin'."

"You dunderhead of a boy," shouted Oberon, as he took off his cap and struck Harold with it, "do you want me to be going over the same old ground again and again to satisfy your conscience in a simple ethical matter like that. According to your moral notions and your fine sense of honour, everything that's clever and shrewd must be wrong. I suppose, on the other hand, you reckon that everything that's foolish must be right. Well, Harold my boy, you see this is how it is. It's only one man in a hundred who can do a clever, brainy trick, and because the other ninety-nine can't follow suit they straightway set the smart man down as a rogue and a rascal. Envy and jealousy, my boy, and remember they're grievous sins—so keep in the path of virtue and good works, as the poet said."

"But that's only what one man thinks—what you call the clever man," protested Harold.

"Right you are," exclaimed Oberon, with a clap of his hands. "Now these ninety-nine stupid men are always doing foolish things, and if they were to be shot for it they couldn't work a smart dodge. Then you see there's all that crowd against me. They hold the majority of opinion, that nothing but stupidity is right, and thus we got the standard of good and evil. Now that I have made it clear to

I

you — you can understand the difference, can't you ? "

Ponsonby Oberon's sophistries were very much mixed and confused, and Harold could make no intelligible deduction from them. He thought for a time and then answered with a reluctant, " Yes."

" Ah," said Oberon triumphantly, " I thought I could cause the dawn of reason to break on your clouded understanding, as the poet said. I'm glad of that, because you have been bothering me so much lately about little matters of so called right and wrong, that I was beginning to think that you had missed your vocation, and that your proper place would be a cloister, where you might go about with shaven crown and sandalled feet and visage grim with fasting, as the poet.said."

" And yet," said Harold musing, " when I come to think over it, all that you have said don't seem to have any more sense in it to me than a lot of words shaken up in a hat and taken out anyhow ! "

" Ah," returned Oberon with an effort to appear sad, " all my logic is wasted on you. Your conscience has got such a monopoly of your understanding that unless you choke that still small voice, as the poet calls it, or unless you put an iron gag on it, you'll soon be beyond the pale of hope and reason."

Chapter XIV

"Where there is mystery it is generally supposed that there must also be evil."   —LORD BYRON.

HAROLD and Oberon had now arrived at the little township, and lost no time in getting their horses ready for the races.

"Harold," said Oberon with a burst of enthusiasm, "you must ride for me this time. With the practice you've had in training you'll be well able to fill a place in the pig skin. I'm not going to trust those jockey blokes any more. Why, boy, they are so naturally crank that they'd throw a man over just out of pure force of habit, even though they had nothing to gain by it."

"I don't think I could ride good enough," modestly protested Harold. "Anyway, not good enough to get up against them sort of riders, as knows all about it."

"Me dear little boy," exclaimed Ponsonby Oberon, giving Harold two or three hard claps on the back, "your humility fits you as if it had been made to order. I'm a truthful man though—so I must tell you at the same time that as a jockey you got nothing to boast of—you're a perfect dooda in that

line.   However, it's a case of two evils, and the less
must be chosen, as the poet said."

"Mr. Oberon," said Harold, with a show of dignity,
"if you think I'm so bad, get Johnny Armstrong to
ride for you again.   I see you reckon I ain't any
good."

"Ah, well, it's all right," said Oberon, frankly; "just
keep your hair on, me boy, you'll be bald soon
enough.   Well, perhaps you won't be so bad after all.
Maybe now you won't be such a duffer as you look.
Yes, yes—oh, yes, be gosh—I'd rather trust you,
pan-cake maker though you are, than all the fly
jocksters about this township."

Harold was not too well pleased with these left-
handed compliments and mixed flattery.   The boy,
indeed, considering the practice he had, was not to
say a bad rider.   His mistake was that he thought
perhaps the professional jockey was not so much
superior to him in horsemanship after all.   Sitting
under a bush, he brooded over the matter for some
time.   Then suddenly a thought flashed across his
mind, and he got up and went back to where Oberon
was busily engaged in giving old Masquerade a new
coat of dye.

"There he is now!" exclaimed Ponsonby Oberon,
with evident pride in his own artistic efforts, "neat,
precise and dux, as the poet said.   Looks well, don't
he? painted to a hair, literally, and seeming as if he
was to the manner born, as the poet said.   Never
thought, be gosh, that I was such a neat hand with

the brush as what I am. Egad, there was a real
Landseer thrown away in me. He was a great
painter of dogs, you know, Harold ; but I don't
know that he could give me much of a start in the
line of painting a horse. And the tail, Harold !
Look at the tail ! Fits him and becomes him by the
hokey—now don't it ? "

"I wouldn't have hardly knowed him," said Harold.
"No mistake, he do look different. Now, Mr.
Oberon, what I come to ask was how yer goin' to
run him ? Because, you see, I don't somehow think
it honest if you don't run him to win. Anyway, I
wouldn't pull him, you know, 'cause the people might
be backin' him. And you see——"

"Oh," broke in Oberon, " it's to be real dinkum
this time—fair and square on the go. As the poet's
motto was, go for yourself and go to win. I'm
going to enter him as a maiden—that's a colt that
never ran before. He'll get in with a light weight
because he'll have neither pedigree nor performance
to make the handicappers think well of him. Then
I'll back him to win the double for all I'm worth,
and all the coin I can raise in any shape or form will
be stacked on him. He's got lashons of pace, as you
know, from that Cadmean victory at the last meeting,
and in this out of the way bush township he'll have
nothing to meet but crocks. As the poet said, it will
be a case of Eclipse first and the rest nowhere. Be
gosh, boy, there'll be a depression in the township after
we've done with it. There will be nothing but wail-

ing and gnashing of teeth, as the poet said. Our
visit will be a landmark in their memory for years
to come. Banks may bust, but to these little bush
places it makes no difference. Let a dark horse
come along though, and he makes a financial wreck
at once. The bush whackers go down like shot, and
most of them are working a dead horse for twelve
months to come."

"Now that it's to be a fair race," replied Harold.
"I can tell you, Mr. Oberon, that I'll do me best to
win. I thought you might be wantin' to pull 'em
again, and so I didn't want to ride a cheatin' race."

"Right you are, says Moses," broke in Oberon.
"He's to be on the job, and the public who back him
will get a fair jig for their money. Yes, Harold;
honesty is the best policy, as the poet said. Of
course, though, to protect myself I must give the old
horse a deuce of a bad name in the betting market,
I'll try to credit him with such a terrible reputation
that the public will have nothing to do with him in
the way of backing. You see, me boy, I want to
do all the wagering on him myself, so I can't afford
the general public to have much of a cut in. No
matter what weight he gets, I'll grumble and growl
and rage about it, so that the handicapper will kinder
wish he never had been born, as the poet said. I'll
talk about scratching him and I'll make such a row
about my weights that most people will think my
chance a very off one. Of course every one won't
think so, because that's an old dodge—kicking up a

racket about your weights. Now you take the old moke up to the course and give him his exercise while I go up to the town to hear the news."

With these instructions, Ponsonby Oberon hastened away to the township. After an absence of three hours, he came back in a high state of excitement. " Harold," he shouted, " what do you think ? Jerry Brown has just arrived in town with the celebrated race horse, Discount. He's got another old crock too, a horse that never did anything, but it's Discount that's causing all the excitement. You see, he's got a great record, and his reputation is all over the country. There's not one in the township has ever seen him before, and yet by repute he's familiar to them all. Jerry Brown, though, is egregiously an ass, as the poet said. Do you know what he's doing ? Why, instead of giving his horse a bad name, he seems to be quite proud of him. Instead of saying he's lost all his pace lately, and that he's a bit wampy on his legs and gone in the wind, he's telling every one that he's the greatest horse in the country. In fact, he's joyous over the big weights he carried to victory, and by the way the fellow is talking you'd think he's inviting the handicapper to stick a church on his horse. Yes, you'd think, by the way he's going on, that he didn't come to race, but to raffle the horse for all the money in the district."

" Yes ; but," said Harold, " perhaps the man is goin' to do the same as you done at the last races."

"Never a fear of that," interrupted Oberon. " Jerry

Brown's reputation is too well known for the public to take him at his own valuation. They won't back him at any price, so he won't have much to gain by running a slanter. No; *his* only line is to run him square and back him on his own account. The people may bet against him if he gets a very big weight, but they'll never wager on him no matter how he's let in."

A few nights after this Ponsonby Oberon returned to his camp after having been up at the township for most of the afternoon. He was in great good humour, and shouted to Harold before he came within fifty yards of the camp: "My lad, rejoice with me! I have been let in with bottom weights in the two handicaps. Discount was commissioned to carry three stone more than anything else in the race, and Jerry Brown cursed and swore, and scratched his horse as soon as the handicaps were posted up. He then went and got drunk, and now he's dead to the world. And now, as the poet said, there is no impediment in my fancy's course—old Masquerade—I mean Slow Tom—must win. I have taken him with two bookies already in doubles, and I'll get all I can on him to-morrow. We must look out, my boy, that none of the push get prowling about near enough to give him a bait. They'll try to stiffen him when the coin is stacked on him. I'm making arrangements to raise money on my horses; so, if by any chance I go down, I lose all and will have to carry my swag away from the township."

"Oh, I think you oughten ter ha' done that," protested Harold. "You see, your horse might fall, or he might break his leg, or something might happen to 'em."

"Bar these remote possibilities, Harold," said Oberon. "My horse is a moral for the double. There will be nothing to trouble him now that Discount is scratched. As the poet said, we're surer of prosperity than prosperity could have assured us."

"And has Jerry Brown got nothing in now for the races?" asked Harold.

"Oh, yes," replied Oberon, with a laugh and a wave of his hand; "he's got a forlorn hope—the crock I spoke about when Jerry first came to town. He hasn't got the ghost of a show though. Anything that he has ever done was to run unplaced at two or three little public-house meetings. No, as the poet said, defeat and fall for him is certain."

"But your horse, Mr. Oberon," asked Harold; "ain't there a chance that he ain't so quick as you reckon?"

"It's no question of chance at all," burst in Oberon, with a clap of his hands and throwing his cap on one side. "I tell you, boy, a wise man leaves nothing to chance. My horse, not such a great time ago, cut out his mile in 1.45 and carried a slick of weight at that. A nag that can do that is good iron anywhere. You can stake your life on him in a bush meeting, and now that he's on with a light weight, as the poet said, assurance is doubly sure."

Chapter XV

"We knew too much, but not quite enough,
And so we went to the wall."
—A VOICE FROM THE BUSH.

THE morning of the races Harold came up to the course leading old Masquerade. Ponsonby Oberon on seeing him immediately left the crowd, where he had been shouting and going on in a most excited manner. He came over to Harold, saying, "My boy, just keep him away for a bit, for, as the poet said, 'out of sight out of mind.' The Flying doesn't come off for half an hour, and in the meantime I'm laying everything I own, or ever will own, on him. I'm backing him to my bottom dollar. I'm going a real plunger. If any one comes about to have a look at him, be sure you don't let them put a hand on him. Some of these racing push wear rings with poisoned needles concealed in them, and if any of these blokes come round to give the old fellow a friendly, admiring clap on the neck, you'll know what they're up to, so knock them down with a stone. Remember, as the poet said, diseases desperate grown by desperate appliances are relieved, and again, to be forewarned is to be forearmed. So don't let any one put a hand on him ; don't let any one come near him. My whole fortune depends on it. I'll be a clean mucker if they stiffen him."

With these instructions Ponsonby Oberon again disappeared in the crowd. But although he could not be seen, his voice could be heard all over the course. After a while the bell rang for the Flying Handicap, and Ponsonby Oberon came rushing out to Harold, and exclaiming with great excitement, "Now go and get your colours on and weigh out. I'll take care of the nag. Be sure you don't leave the scales too neat. Your weight, as you know, is seven, seven, but ride two pounds over, so as to be on the safe side. Be gosh how the old fellow will fly with that weight, and he's as fit as a fiddle too ! "

Harold went away to weigh and to put on his colours. When he returned Oberon gave him a pat on the back, saying, "Now, lad, my whole fortune is wagered on you, so you must do or die, as the poet said. Here, give me your leg till I give you a lift up. Now that's the style. How are the stirrups ? Right ? Well, then, you can go and give your canter past while I go and draw for you. Just give him a steady preliminary, and when you are going past the post shout out, ' Slow Tom two pounds over weight.' We must act according to rule, for, as the poet said, ' Order is Heaven's first law.' "

Ponsonby Oberon went over to where a man was shaking a hat and calling out, "Now then, come on, you fellows, and draw for places. Think I'm going to stand bareheaded in the sun here all day, waiting for your leisure."

" Right you are," said Oberon ; " I draw for Slow Tom, so let us take a dip into that canteen of yours, as the Irish poet said.

He plunged his hand into the hat, pulled out a paper and looked at it for some moments in disgust. " Oh gosh ! " he exclaimed, " I've drawn the outside place of all. Dash it, old man, let us put it back and have another go. This luck is too bad for a stranger in a strange land, as the poet said. What, you won't ? Well then, suppose I must make the most of my usual ill luck."

He gave Harold his number, and would also have given him a long list of instructions how to ride had not the starter called out, " Now, you boys, I tell you I won't wait."

" Well then," said Oberon, " go ; and remember, as the poet said, that your place must be in the front rank all through."

" I'll do my best," answered Harold. " Mr. Oberon, they'll be no gammon ; I 'sure you I'll do my hones' best."

After the starter had the usual little trouble with one or two over eager jockeys, he managed to get the horses into line. Then down dropped the flag and away they went. From the moment of starting two horses shot conspicuously to the front. There was a dead silence in the crowd for a few moments, and then loud shouts went up of " Jerry Brown's horse and Slow Tom! By the living jingo the pace is terrible; they're clearing out from everything!" Ponsonby Oberon's excitement bordered on madness. He rushed out into the straight shouting out, " Ride for your life—ride for your life, or I'm done!" The clerk of the course just managed to get him back when the horses came thundering on with Jerry Brown's horse leading past the post by a short neck.

It would be impossible to describe Ponsonby Oberon's feelings when he realized that his horse was beaten. He raged and raved through the crowd in a perfect frenzy—throwing his cap in one place and his pipe in another, and crying out he was " ruined, ruined, ruined!" After a long while his excitement calmed down, and he began to take a more rational view of his case. He came to Harold saying, " Well, my boy, I suppose you did the best you could, but I have lost one leg in the double, and now it's a case with that lot. No mistake, as the poet said, the slings and arrows of outrageous fortune have let loose their dogs of war on me right enough. The first meeting, when I didn't want to win, the jockey throws me over and gives me a Cadmean victory. Now, at this gathering, when it was my whole hope that my horse should come in first, a dooda jockey messed away my chance. Gosh, did ever any one hear of such ill fortune ?— it might pass into a proverb—the luck of Ponsonby Oberon."

Harold interrupted with, " Mr. Oberon, I didn't do nothing to deserve you gettin' on to me like this.

I done all I could to win, but that horse of Jerry Brown's was the best. The people told me I rode well. Anyhow, I rode honest, and if you think differen', Mr. Oberon, I won't ride for you any more. Same time, I'm sorry you was beaten."

" Ah well, ah well," pleaded Oberon, wildly waving his hands ; "don't take too much notice of me, Harold, for luck has so fixed me with her threatening eye, as the poet said, that I deserve to be excused for whatever slips from me. I feel that all the world and his wife are against me, and that they're scoring a great innings to the bowling of my bad luck."

" Yes ; ah yes," said Harold, thoroughly pacified; "I know you must feel it, and I'm very sorry that things turned out so bad."

Ponsonby Oberon was now getting more reconciled, and he answered, with a dramatic gesture, " Well, after all, Harold, I'm a philosopher, and I laugh at it all—ha! ha! ha!—the fickle dame plays strange freaks with us all. 'The wise man takes with everything and smiles,' as the poet said, as if he mocked himself. Now I must tell you the big money is eighty pounds, and if I can win that I'll be able to redeem my horses. If I don't come in first in that, it will be a clean cooker with me. I'll have to leave the place carrying my swag. Think what it means to me, Harold, and you must ride as never did man before, as the poet said.

In due time, after lunch, the horses were once more drawn up in line before the starter. This time they were to run off the big handicap—by far the principal race of the meeting.

Ponsonby Oberon, mounted on a sorry old horse he borrowed from some one on the course, rode here and there shouting out loudly at the top of his voice. Suddenly the flag fell and the cry went up, " They're off!" In the first turn past the post three or four local horses in a bunch were leading the way—three or four lengths away came Harold on Masquerade, and, almost last, Jerry Brown's horse going steadily. After they had travelled about three quarters of a mile, some of the horses in the rear began to move up and join the leading bunch. Jerry Brown's jockey brought his mount up to Masquerade's quarters, and thus both horses travelled for about two hundred yards. Everything else in the race had now gone past them, and the light-weights in the front rank were cutting out the pace at a merry rate. Next for half a dozen strides, Jerry Brown's horse came on. Then he fell back again absolutely last—a cry from the grand-stand, "He's done! he's beaten!" The jockey took off his cap, held it over his head for a moment and again put it on.

Just then Harold, drawing near a post, gave his mount a sharp prod of the spurs. The old horse wagged his tail, but so close was he travelling to the post, that the splinters from it caught the artificial appendage, and once more—suddenly and unexpectedly—old Masquerade became a cob. Jerry Brown's jockey was astonished beyond all description.

Seeing the tail hanging on the post as he passed he was moved by a sudden impulse to pull up. He lost two or three lengths by this, but immediately recollected himself, and dashed both spurs into his horse's flanks.

In the meanwhile Harold, perfectly unconscious of what had taken place in the rear, was sending his horse along at a terrible pace. Old Masquerade seemed two stone a better horse for having thrown off so important a part of his disguise. He swept past several jockeys, who stared in wonder at his stumpy tail. Now they were all rattling past the bend which led into the straight, and at that moment Jerry Brown's colours came flashing through the beaten horses—leaving them as if they were standing—and stride after stride overtaking Harold, who, with something in hand, was three lengths to the front. On he went, on, stretching out to it, ears back and fully extended, gaining at every stride—steadily, surely. Out came the whips at last, and the two horses, now side by side, neck and neck, strode on locked together—the finish of a splendid race. Half a length from home Jerry Brown's horse, by a tremendous effort, just managed to forge his nose first past the judges' box.

Chapter XVI

"Madame, tout est perdu fors l'honneur."
—*Francis the First to his Mother.*

"Φθείρουσιν ἤδη χρῆσθ' ὁμιλίαι κακαί."
—MENANDER.

A TALL, bookmaker-looking man came up to Harold and said, with an air of easy self-confidence,—

"Now, my lad, I'll jest treble you for that nag, and bloomin' nice bargain I got in him too—disqualified, and bowled out, and all that. Great asset, ain't he for forty quid?"

"I'm not goin' to give you this horse," said Harold, staring all around in the hope of seeing Ponsonby Oberon.

"You needn't look about for your mate," put in the bookmaker-looking man. "The fact is, he's skedaddled." Then he added, with a knowing wink, "About the best thing he could do, too, for the game's up. It's a clean go, old man, I tell you ; and this meetin' has been a real boil over for him. Here, I got the receipt of his horses and turn-out— I couldn't stand him plunging in my books unless I had some sort o' security. He left the receipts in the publican's hands, and now he's up a stump."

Harold handed over the horse without saying a word, and then made his way straight for the camp. The first thing that caught his eye, as he stood looking around him, was a note written in pencil, and bearing the name of Ponsonby Oberon. It commenced :—

"Alas! dear Harold, we must now part. As the poet said, my luck has run me to earth, and I'm a clean mucker. Urgent private business calls me away, so I cannot stand upon the order of my going, as the poet said, but I must go. Did ever any one get such a body blow from luck as I did? Fortune is trying me to see how much I can stand ; and, be gosh, being a philosopher, after the last act I seem to be able to stand a great dose of adversity. If I had only wasted down a bit myself, and ridden in the races, there would be a different tale to tell. It was my confidence in dooda jockeys that put me away. It's enough to make a man mad, Harold, to think of how you chucked away my chances. However, as I have often told you, I'm a philosopher, and I can laugh even on paper—ha! ha! ha! Great thing to be a wise man, my boy ; always, as the poet said, let the dead past bury its dead. But it's enough to make a man go and shuffle off this mortal coil to think of what a pancake rider you are. Even as it is I'd be right enough, only I had such deep-rooted faith in human nature. I thought it was such a certainty I must win, that I reckoned it only a matter of form to hand over the receipts of my horses to the publican. Of course I did not mean him to stick to them; only just to hold, as the poet said, as a guarantee of good faith. If I had not trusted a dooda jockey, I would not have gone such a plunger. As it is, I have to clear out on one old crock, and not as much money in my pocket as would buy one nigger a chew of nail-rod. So now it is, as the poet said, farewell the neighing steed; for I suppose I'll see old Masquerade no more. One consolation, anyhow, he's disqualified for the fellow who got him; for that stumpy tail clean put him away. To you also, my young friend, I say with the poet, farewell, a word that must be and hath been. May we meet again, and in the meanwhile do not neglect to say your prayers, as you've been doing lately. Anyhow, you can't say that I didn't try to keep you in the path of virtue and good works. I'm going Kerara way; but if any one asks about my health, tell them I'm gone the opposite direction. It is necessary for the present that I should 'hide my talent under a bush,' as the poet said. My boy, accept my blessing.

"PONSONBY OBERON."

When Harold read this he stood for some moments in doubt and perplexity. He did not expect that Ponsonby Oberon would have taken his departure in such a sudden and unlooked-for manner. However, the fact remained, Ponsonby Oberon had gone, and he found himself once more alone. While he stood thus undecided what to do, he was suddenly aroused by a voice calling out, in a rough, loud tone,—

" Well, young fellow, you seem a bit mixed this evening. Your mate has taken to his scrapers, ain't he? I can tell you straight wire, old man, that he didn't make no mistake in giving them sheroka. There'd a been the devil of a racket over that stumpy tail moke. Why, darn your eyes, every one knows him now that he's got the paint washed off, and they seed the faking you push made of 'is brands."

" Now, say no more about it," retorted Harold impatiently. " I suppose you think you're tellin' me something great? Well, you ain't then."

" Darn your eyes," replied the other, " I'm not a blamin' you a bit. I'm only just reckonin' that your little game didn't pan out accordin' Hoyle. You fellows didn't get home, and your little apple-cart was upset; consequence was your whole caboodle went a mucker, and now, I suppose, you're stiff, an' your mate's stiff. Never mind, though, old man. Come up to the settlin' to-night; there'll be plenty o' cheap booze knockin' round, and you can deal an 'and drinkin' an 'ealth as well as the rest of us."

" I don't know, somehow, what I'll do," said Harold sadly. " One thing, I ain't got much to stop here for. Everything's gone 'cepting my little swag, and I ain't got any supper in it for to-night."

"That'll be all right," quickly replied the fellow, who called himself Bill Jones. "You just come up to the pub and get a square feed. Darn your eyes, there ain't no cause to starve! If a fellow gets rid of his bit of stuff, why he can soon make a peg or two to set 'im up again."

"I'll go up with you then," replied Harold; "but, somehow, I don't feel very jolly to-night."

Harold went with the man, and, after he had eaten a not altogether hearty supper, he was told that the "settling up" would shortly take place. Harold had some curiosity in the matter. When the time arrived a somewhat miscellaneous crowd of bushmen assembled in the long dining-hall of the hotel. There the prizes were handed round to the various winners, after which Jerry Brown, as the principal gainer, called for "a couple a dozen fiz."

The publican, with a far-reaching smile, responded with the bottles. The air was soon filled with the "popping" of champagne corks, the noise of glasses, and the babel of the eager crowd. Then the chairman stood up, and, in a humorous speech, proposed the health of the principal winner, Jerry Brown, coupled with the names of two or three other gentlemen of the turf, who scored in the minor events. At the conclusion of the toast the whole crowd of sunbrowned, bearded bushmen stood up, as best they could, and yelled out in what was meant to be an eulogistic song, "For they are jolly good fellows," repeating the line with heroic persistency, and adding finally, "And so say all of us." Then three stentorian "Hip! hip! hurrahs!" and each man drained his glass to the dregs.

By some strange impulse Harold found himself standing up and cheering with the crowd. Some one thrust a glass of champagne into his hand, and, in like manner, he made no exception in drinking it. It was his first experience of the sort, and, though he did not like the drink, he felt somehow carried with the tide. Soon he found himself in excellent spirits, laughing, singing, and cheering with the rest. More healths were proposed and drunk, the flow of champagne going on apace, and the broadening smile of the publican showing evident signs of becoming set and chronic.

Such a variety of toasts were proposed that night as might well satisfy the dreams of the most thirsty and ambitious drinkers. Nobly, too, they responded to the call of, "Charge your glasses, gentlemen; I have a 'ealth to propose." Healths became scarce in the end, and as the tide of champagne was still flowing, some excuse for drinking it had to be found. So one man of resource proposed the health of the bellringer, and another imaginative individual struck on the happy idea of toasting, "The man with the sweat table, who did so much in his own line of biz to make our little meetin' so pleasant." Most of the crowd were by this time laid low, but such as survived the persistent charging of glasses made a final heroic effort, and, in a brave, determined, but somewhat unsteady manner, responded to the health of the " gentleman " with the cards and dice.

Chapter XVII

"Gloriously drunk, obey the important call."
—*The Task*.—COWPER.

NEXT morning Harold awoke with a terrible pain in his head. He felt cold and uncomfortable, too, as well he might, for he had put in the night on the hard floor of the dining-room, and had neither blankets nor pillow to add solace to his irregular slumbers. Two or three others were also stretched about in various attitudes on the floor, and as many more found rest on the table—one having the luxury of a champagne bottle for a pillow.

"Ah, by scissors," said one unkempt, woe-begone looking fellow, "that fiz is terrible stuff to put a head on a man. Catch me drinkin' it again. Never felt half so bad in all my life. And how did you weather it, young 'un?" he added, addressing Harold.

He replied, "Oh, feel something awful. I wish I hadn't touched that stuff they gave me. It waren't nice, either, only I saw the others drinkin' it."

"Well, well," said the other, "it's no use in whippin' the cat now; the only way is, let us take something to pick us up and get us straightened out somewhat. Come now and have an 'eye opener' with me."

" No, no," said Harold, " I don't want any, and I don't want anything to eat either.   I don't feel hungry."

" When a fellow is off his feed," replied the other, " there is nothing better than three fingers of whisky fired into him, especially after he's been a-boozin' too much the night before."

But Harold steadily resisted.   He felt so sick and disgusted that he thought he could never look at a glass or bottle again.   Nevertheless, later on in the day, by dint of hard pressing, a good Samaritan induced the lad to take a glass of weak whisky.   He took it with loathing, though he was told that he would feel better after it, and that it would help him to eat something.   It had that effect sure enough. He felt better and more light-hearted, and he felt a sort of vague gratitude for the man who had done him this good service.

Chapter XVIII

"Video meliora proboque ;
Deteriora sequor."
—*Metamorphosis.*—OVID.

A YEAR has passed since last we heard of Harold. Those twelve months have done much to work a change in the character of the youth. After the eventful evening, when Ponsonby Oberon disappeared, and the "settling up" took place in the long dining-room of the hotel, Harold became employed by the publican. First, with an old cart-horse, he used to draw the wood and water for the hotel. From that he received promotion in looking after the horses of the place, taking them into water in the daytime, and hoppling them out on grass at night. In the evenings he learned to play billiards—a game in which he took a considerable degree of interest, and in which he quickly acquired a certain amount of proficiency. From that he got to be billiard marker, and there his social success commenced.

He became very popular with poor gamblers, and thoroughly liked by those that were better off. To the former he allowed many games on the credit system ; and to the latter he acted the general part of fetch and carry when the time came for drinks,

being moreover good-natured, obliging, and civil—
three qualities which, when regularly carried, never
fail in having a good effect. He found it looked
like being disagreeable, unsocial, and odd to constantly refuse treats. So at first he said he would
have lime juice or lemonade ; but one night, these
drinks running short, he took wine as a substitute.
He liked the wine so well that he never after went
back to the lemonade. Some time later, however,
when a crowd of shearers were in town, the billiard
table became in great demand, and the calls for
drinks in consequence were more than common.
Harold was always asked to join, and though he
made one or two efforts at refusal, no denial would
be accepted. His wine glass was therefore filled
very often that night, and towards morning he de-
clared that he saw four lights on the table, although
he was only aware of two, and the man who was
playing at the time seemed to be holding a double
cue. After that he remembered nothing till some one
aroused him some time after sunrise. He found then
that he had gone to sleep on the floor of the billiard-
room, and although he had had an unusually successful night with the table, yet the only tangible
result he could show for it was a threepenny bit with
a hole in, and a black and dirty copper very much
battered, owing to having gone through a long career
of " headen 'em." But he had withal, as a memento
of the night, a racking headache and a terrible
sensation, such as he never experienced since the

night of the settling, long before. Now, as on that occasion, the good Samaritan came to him and strongly suggested whisky ; told him never to get boozed on wine, as it played terrible havoc with a man's headpiece, and left him out of sorts for the day. This seemed sound advice.

At any rate, Harold remembered that the whisky did him good on the first occasion when he had taken too freely of the champagne ; and he did not see why it should not act as an antidote when he had over-indulged in a commoner wine. He tried the experiment, and, finding it a success, he resolved in the future to show his gratitude to the whisky by not neglecting it for wine. He argued with himself that soft drinks did not agree with him, and that his stomach on occasions seemed to require the support of strong stimulants. The result of all this was, that, as time went on, Harold, glass for glass, could hold his own with the most accomplished drinker coming to the little township.

He had learned to smoke, too, and though he had forgotten many things, he used, as a rule, to say his prayers. They were certainly more a mumbled matter of form than anything else, for generally he would be thinking of some other matter. At the conclusion of his devotions he would say, " God bless me and make a good child of me." It was the little prayer he had learned at his mother's knee when he was indeed a child, but now repeated with such careless formality that he did not pause to consider how out of keeping it was with his present age. Cursing and swearing are consequences of environment and association, and living in such an atmosphere Harold could hardly avoid expressing himself forcibly at times. In short, though he was not as profane as the average bushman, his language was far stronger than would be expected from a youth of his age.

Thus time went on, Harold gradually changing and becoming more and more in conformity with his surroundings. " Why, bless my soul! " some bushman from time to time would say, " but you're getting to be a real man of the world, Roldy. When you fust came to these Clearings, you would neither smoke, drink, gamble, swear, nor kiss the girls. Now you do all these things better than the most seasoned hand among us. You show us we're gettin' behind the time. Well, well, I suppose the younker must come on and fill our places in the ranks of sport ; but, darn me, but they needn't make the pace so hot in the beginning."

Harold used not to take such remarks as compliments, but would thereupon straighten himself up, and for a short time after, he would be observed not to drink so much, and a certain air of melancholy would mark his demeanour. After a time, however, he would recover himself, and his voice would be loudest, and his glass the oftenest filled of any in the room. But there was one remark had a great effect on him. A stranger came to the township, and his

business keeping him a couple of days at the hotel,
he had ample time to observe Harold. He remarked,
"There's a young fellow who is certain to land in
either the prison or an asylum before long." The
young billiard-marker overheard the observation, and
such a sensation came over him as made him feel
quite sick and weak. It seemed to him as a pro-
phecy, and it came with all the force of such. He
felt indeed at the time how changed he had become,
and yet how stealthily and unperceived this change
had arrived. For two days after that people thought
he was ill, as in truth he felt—ill at heart and conscience. He did not taste any liquor during that
time, and the billiard-marking he left to some one
else. Some one recommended him to take a glass
of whisky every now and then, and the well-meaning
man who gave this advice received such a sharp
rejoinder from Harold as to make him think the
young fellow was already drunk. "By the blooming
Jupiter!" exclaimed the man, "but you'd snap a
cove's head off for a darn little." Harold looked at
him with blood-shot eyes, and said bitterly, almost
savagely, "Well, then, don't you mind tellin' me what
to do. Leave me alone, I say, leave me alone. It's
fellows like you that's made me what I am. Curses
take you all!"

The man looked at him in astonishment, mingled
with anger. He seemed as if he were about to say
or do something, but suddenly altering his mind, he
passed on muttering to himself, "Poor devil! He's

sufferin' a bad recovery all right. Well, can't be helped, I suppose, A fellow must pay the piper when he's 'ad 'is fun."

But in a few days this also was forgotten, and Harold returned to the old habits.

Chapter XIX

" My punishment is greater than I can bear."
—*Genesis*—THE BIBLE.

WE have, so far, given a brief and rapid sketch of Harold's career since he was deserted by Ponsonby Oberon. From time to time he would look back upon it, and a certain remorse would come over him, making him periodically reserved and bitter. But to it all there came at last a crisis. A party of merry drovers and their men came to the little township, and there for two or three days they stayed, enjoying themselves after their manner, and, to use their own words, "painting the town red." But one evening they went perhaps a bit too far. At any rate a sort of faction fight took place in the billiard room, which was full of drunken and excited men. Harold was insensibly brought into the disturbance, or rather he was drawn into it in spite of himself.

A conceited, cowardly little fellow struck him a blow with the billiard cue on the head, and then, to avoid the possible consequences, took to his heels, and kept running around the billiard table, with Harold after him in full cry. He kept his distance from his pursuer, every now and then shouting back taunts and insults, as he hurried round the table. This was too much for Harold, who picked up a billiard ball, saying, with a gnash of his teeth, "You little brute, if I can't catch you myself, I'll send something after you that'll take a short cut, and smash in your bloomin' crust." He threw the ball, which struck the man on the top of the head, and bounding from there passed through a glass window, striking a constable who was hastening to the scene of the disturbance. At this result, Harold stood for a few moments wonderstruck, and before he could recover from his surprise, the worthy constable had given him the "hammer-lock," and clapped a pair of handcuffs on his wrists. In the meantime the man who received the billiard ball on the head made his escape with all possible haste through a back door, and, thanks to the thickness of his skull, was very little the worse of his adventure.

The constable having secured Harold, looked about him to see what other captures he might make. But the disturbance was now settled, and not a single rioter could be seen or heard anywhere about the premises. The good guardian of the peace having secured order, marched his prisoner off to the lock-up. This building was a miserable little hovel, not much larger than a bath-room, and built roughly of galvanised iron. Harold was ushered in without much ceremony, a chain passed round his leg for better security, and then the door of the little prison brought to with a snap, the key turned in the lock, and all was still. All this took place in such a short time, that the prisoner could hardly realize it. When he did, there came to him a great heaving and bitterness of heart, and tears of shame, regret and anger welled into his eyes and trickled down his cheeks.

Next morning Harold was brought before the Court. It happened that it was the maiden case of a newly-appointed Justice of the Peace, and the worthy man conscientiously endeavoured to make the most of it. He heard the evidence of the constable, and one or two others, who were summoned to tell all they knew about the matter. Then he stood up, made a long speech, examined every part of the evidence in detail, said it was all *prima facie*. He made some remark about *habeas corpus* and *nisi prius*, concluding by giving a fatherly lecture to the prisoner and sentencing him to a week in the lock-up. At that Harold burst into tears, and looked as sad and dejected as if he had received the extreme penalty of the law.

That week in the lock-up was a terrible time for Harold. Not that he went through any physical hardships, or that he was badly or roughly treated, or in fact compelled to do any sort of work ; but it was the anguish of heart and mind at the thoughts of his position, and what he had come to in so short a time, that troubled and harrowed his soul. Solitude begets reflection, and one result of Harold's confinement was to make him very thoughtful and mindful of his past. Many a time indeed he shed tears after thinking of his mother and the days of his childhood. After that he would say his prayers with great earnestness, and,

feeling better and easier in his mind, would then lie
down to sleep. It was not till during this week in
prison that he gave any thought to what he uttered
when he offered up his devotions ; but from that time
the old familiar prayer was altered, for with great
earnestness he would say, " God bless me and make
a good *man* of me."

When the time of his release arrived, the constable
unlocked the door saying, " Come out now, and I
hope ye'll be better for the future. Sure it's not
throwin' balls at people's heads that'll make a man of
ye—unless, faith, it be a bad man."

This seemed to Harold like adding insult to injury.
His heart was a good deal bruised by his confinement,
but his spirit was not altogether crushed, and so he
looked indignantly at the man, and passed out of the
prison without uttering a word.

" Will yez wait a moment ? " said the constable ; " I
think I got a letter here for Harold Efferme, that by
the same token was given me this mornin', and begorra,
by the ould postmarks I would say the contints is
well sasoned by this."

" Well, that's me," said Harold ; " and it's so few
letters I get that I wonder who it can be from."

" Be Jabers," replied the policeman, " and sure
that's more than I can tell yez, from just lookin' at
the name in front and the postmarks behind. But
if yez will step over to the barracks here for a
moment, sure I can hand ye the letter and ye can
see for yourself."

"That's true," replied Harold, "and I'll go with you at once." At the barracks he was handed the letter, which was in a large square envelope with black borders. Seeing this he turned deadly pale, he felt his heart almost stop beating, and his hand shook as if palsied when he took the letter."

"My God!" he exclaimed, with a bitter anguish, staring wildly at the envelope he held in his hand; "this tells of death before I even open it. Oh, I can't, I can't," he said piteously, as he laid the letter down, a flood of tears streamed from his eyes, and he leaned helplessly against a broken bench.

The constable, who stood near, bent down, and patting him on the back, said, "Sure, me poor man now, you may be troublin' yerself for nothin', and in the name of God, just open your letter and let yere mind be at aise."

But Harold's dread of evil news so overcame him that he said: "Ah no! but you open it, will you—open it for me."

The constable opened the letter as instructed, glanced at it for a few moments, and then his countenance fell. Then, with a look of deepest pity, he bent over Harold, and said, with a touch of feeling in his voice, "Ah, me poor man, and faith it is bad news. God comfort you in grief, but your poor mother is dead."

"Ah, I thought so," exclaimed Harold, and then looking up with streaming eyes and a face racked with pain, he burst out between sobs fit to break his heart,

"I felt it; I knew it. Oh my poor, dear, dear mother, and I will never, O God! never see your good, kind face again."

The constable tried to utter some words of consolation and sympathy. In truth the worthy man, at the sight of the boy's grief, was not a little touched. But all he could say had no effect on Harold, for the boy seemed overwhelmed with sorrow, and deaf to all words of pity. After a while the constable walked gently away and left Harold crouching by the barracks gate, his face in his hands, his shoulders heaving with the great sobbing, and the tears trickling down between his fingers. Every now and then he would look up with a face already terribly careworn, and a look of anguish on it which showed only too plainly how much the poor boy suffered. Then he would make two or three furtive efforts to wipe his eyes with the sleeve of his coat, and again he would burst out sobbing, covering his face in his hands. Fully an hour after, when the constable came back, he found Harold in the same position as when he first left him, and crying as bitterly and pitifully as a little child. " Poor bhoy," he said ; "faith, ye have an affectionate heart, and God comfort ye in yere trouble. Come now, stand up, will ye, and we'll go and have something to ate."

Harold lifted up his face, with tear-stained eyes, and said, " Eat! Oh, I feel that I can never eat again." The constable muttered a few more words and then went away to his own dinner. When he came back after the meal, he found that Harold had gone. He was nowhere about, and no one in town had seen anything of him. The constable searched and enquired everywhere, but the poor bereaved lad, so lately released from prison, was nowhere to be found.

Chapter XX

"Free again! free again! Eastward and westward, before me,
    behind me,
  Wide lies Australia! and free are my feet, as my soul is to
    roam!"

—*Convict Once*—J. BRUNTON STEPHENS.

HAROLD had been gone some time when the policeman missed him from the barracks gate. He had resolved never to go back to the old occupation, and never again to be seen about the little township, which had been to him the scene of so much sorrow, disappointment and misery. He waited not to get rations, or swag, or quart, but just as he was—with no possessions in the world save his clothes—he stepped out into the roadway, and in less than half an hour was out of sight of the township and travelling he knew not whither.

He walked on till sunset that day, seeing no one, having nothing to eat, but feeling withal a load of misery at his heart. Sometimes he would halt, exhausted with the rate he had been walking; then, if there were a hole of water near, he would take a drink, wash and cool his head, and sitting down on a log or stone, would cry bitterly. After a while he would get up again, feeling very dazed and sorrowful, and with a

151

resolution that was almost pathetic in its earnestness, would again trudge along the dusty and uneven road. However, when darkness overtook him, he was obliged to halt. He felt neither hunger nor fatigue, but his head seemed swimming, and his heart sorrow laden ; feeling, too, that all hope and joy had gone out of his life for ever.

Next morning the hot sun rose through a cloud of smoke, and awoke Harold from a sort of delirious slumber, into which he had fallen for the first time only a little before dawn. He got up and staggered to his feet, feeling very lonely, very sorrowful, listless and weary. Then the thoughts of his bereavement came to him, and the tears once more started in his eyes, and grief renewed her burden in his heart. He picked up his hat, which had blown away some distance during the night, shook the dust from it, and placing it on his head, once more resumed his aimless journey along the forlorn road. After having walked most of the previous day, having eaten nothing since his prison breakfast, and put in a sleepless night without blankets, fire, or food, it is little to be wondered at that the boy was exhausted and miserable, and his mind partly wandering. Very slowly he tramped along the road for several miles. His pace was gradually getting slower and slower, and his steps less direct and certain.

One time he wandered a bit off the road, not seeming to heed or care where he was going. He fell into a deep rut, and for several minutes there he lay, looking up with a vague wonderment, and seeming like one who had awoke in a strange place from a long and deep sleep. After a time, he got up again, but now seemed more weary, sad, and pitiable-looking than ever, for his face was covered with red dust, and in one place his cheek was bleeding, and the blood was flowing down along his neck on to the collar of his coat. But he seemed to heed it not —in fact, he appeared to be unconscious of everything about him. Sometimes he would mutter some broken sentences to himself as in a dream, but they were vague, incoherent, and meaningless.

It is probable that he would not have been able to have gone much farther before he would have been overtaken by complete exhaustion. But just then, at a bend in the road by the river-side, he suddenly came up to a hawker, with a tilted cart, who was camped for the day. The meeting, though so unexpected, gave no surprise to Harold. In truth, he seemed to hardly notice the hawker or his cart at all. When he got that far, however, he sat down on a large rock, very weak, tired, and weary. The hawker came over, bade him good-day, but receiving such a vague and stupid answer, he went away immediately, not at all pleased with Harold's courtesy. After a long time the man came back again ; and staring at the lad with a mixture of wonder and curiosity, he said, " In the name of goodness, mate, what sort of a game is this you're up to at all—travelling in this wild part of the country with

neither swag, nor tucker, nor anything else? It's bad
enough to be without a horse, but without the other
things, why it's madness, and nothing else." Again
Harold's answer was wandering and almost meaningless. But this time the hawker saw the state the lad
was in. He took him by the hand, saying, "Come
over to my camp, you poor beggar. Darn me, but
I'll have to see to you, or you'll peg out your claim
somewhere about here, all right." Harold, not in
the least resisting, was led like a little child over to
the camp. There the man examined him and came
to his own conclusions as to his case.

Most bushmen are obliged by circumstances to
have some sort of a smattering knowledge of
medicine. Hawkers, especially—dealing as they do
so much in drugs and chemicals — get in time to
have a useful knowledge of the healing art. It
happened to be the case with the good man who
took charge of Harold. He indeed made a sort
of hobby of medicines; it was his weak point, and
he used to boast that he cured many a man, who,
only for his assistance, "would now be toes up
with cures." So he started to work on Harold,
and, as luck would have it, the first thing he did
was to give his patient a sleeping draught. This
relieved the overstrain, and gave rest. He lifted
Harold into the tilted cart, and with womanly tenderness placed a pillow under his head, and then
left him to a long-needed sleep.

Next the good man picked up an old gun and

wandered patiently up and down the creek in search
of game or wild fowl. "Well, he do seem used
up," said he, speaking to himself, and thinking of
Harold; "and a bit of duck or a pigeon, made into
soup, would be just the thing for him when he
wakes up." But he tramped in vain to every lagoon
and water-hole for a distance of two miles around,
and not a sign of a wild fowl could he see. Then
at last, when he was reluctantly obliged to betake
himself to camp, he kept repeating to himself, "No
mistake, it is hard lines that the very day I did
want a water-hen, or a duck of some sort, not a speck
of a darn one can I sight, and it the best thing I
could give him too—made into soup."

When he arrived at his camp, after being away
for two or three hours, he found Harold wide awake,
a far-away look in his eye, and every evidence of
pain and sorrow in his countenance. The hawker
looked in at him and said, "I have been all the way
everywhere about, to try and get a duck or something to make into soup for you, but I could sight
nothing—not even a cockatoo or a plover."

"Oh, thank yer, all the same," muttered Harold
wearily, "but I don't feel like eatin' anything."

"Ah, but you must," said the hawker, with emphasis; "when a man's stomach goes out on strike,
it's a case with the other parts of his carcase. Now
tell me when you had your last feed?"

Harold looked at his benefactor in a puzzled sort
of way and said, "I think it was yester mornin',

and now I'm not sure it weren't the mornin' before."

"Darn me!" exclaimed the hawker, "but you're
bad all right ; kind o touch of brain fever. So you
don't know when you had your last feed ?"

"Ah, yes," said Harold, as if to himself, "it was
the mornin' I was let out of jail. I remember
now."

"Eh? What's that? What's that?" interrupted
the hawker, "let out of jail! Holy Sailor, were you
in the chokey ?"

Harold seemed not to heed him, but went on,
"Yes, that was the mornin' that I got the letter, with
the—the—the——" A choking sensation came over
him, a flood of tears welled into his eyes and
streamed down his cheeks. The hawker, in a strange
mixture of wonder, compassion, and apprehension,
stared at the helpless boy and exclaimed, "By the
holy Moses, who'd 'a' thought he just come out of a
chokey! Well, by scissors, if he was right, he's not
the sort of a fellow I'd like to have about my camp,
—but now that he's down on all fours, I'm not the
one to turn him off, if he was the greatest robber
that ever stuck up an escort. Anyhow, it do make
a fellow feel curus how he come to be like this, and
what the tarnation brought him into chokey, and
where is his swag and turn out ? "

With these words the worthy man resolved to get
something delicate and nourishing for Harold to eat.
He scratched his head and mumbled to himself

" Dooce take it, but I got nothink very good and
light. I could make a bit o' stoo, and the salt junk
has got about as much flavour and substance as a
piece of wood. Well, well, I don't know what I can
do exactly." Then after a pause, he suddenly gave
an exultant shout, clapped his leg with his hand, and
said, " I have it now ! There are the two roosters I
was bringing home to the missis. Well, I must make
soup of one of them, though what the old woman will
say goodness only knows. And dear enough soup it
will be too, for the fowls sure enough cost me three
guineas apiece. And it's one of these I'm going to
kill for a chap I never seen before in all me life,
who's just come out of jail from all accounts, and
who, like enough, will try to rob my cart as soon as
he gets strong enough." He laughed at the idea of
his own folly, and after a while added, " The old
woman always reckoned I was a fool, and by George
I'll keep up my reputation in that line for this once
anyhow. So here goes for that rooster."

The worthy man killed his fowl, made it into soup,
and then, with a long-handled spoon, he fed Harold
as tenderly and carefully as if he had been his own
son.

Next day the hawker continued his journey, but
as Harold was very little better, the worthy dealer
made what he called " a doss down " in his cart for
his patient. As soon as he got into camp that night,
he took his gun and made another search for ducks
or pigeons. He met with the same fortune as he did

the day before, and returned to the camp very dis-
consolate, saying, "Very strange altogether; this
part of the country used to be full of game, and now
there's not a bloomin' one to be seen.   Well, I
suppose I must only kill that other rooster for my
young jail-bird patient in the cart.   It seems to be
the only thing he'll eat, and, darn him, but he's got
an expensive taste—six guineas for two feeds!—and
may be, after all, I'm only savin' his life till he's
hanged.   Ah, be George, a fool and a rogue has met
right enough.   No, tarnation take me, if I'll kill that
other rooster after all.   Time for an old codger like
me to be gettin' sense now.   No, the idea of the thing
is enough to make a cat laugh—killin' three guinea
roosters for a chap I don't know from Adam."

But when he arrived at his cart and looked in at
Harold, he cast resolution to the wind and killed the
other fowl also.   From that, day after day, he continued his journey, carrying Harold in his cart, and
every time he came into camp shooting ducks and
wild fowl to make broth for his patient.   Gradually
Harold got stronger, and at last became fit to take
care of himself.   The hawker came to a cross road,
and Harold, ashamed of having trespassed on the
good man's kindness so much, was glad of this
opportunity to get away, after much protestation of
gratitude for the kindness which had been shown
him.

Chapter XXI

" Sorrow, sad hearts, alas !
   And grieve, for loss we left behind must know ;
  Yet think that those who through Death's portals pass
   Have gain, not loss, to show."
—F. C. URQUHART.

AND now Harold once more went out alone. He had no particular course mapped out to travel, but like the drifting spar that is carried anywhere by the tides, he went whither the impulse of the moment led him. He took a road at right angles to the one the hawker was travelling, and soon in the stunted forest he lost sight of his kind benefactor and friend in the hour of need. He felt in his heart a limitless debt of gratitude to the unknown stranger, and at that moment he prayed that a boundless prosperity might be his reward. The good man, moreover, had given Harold a blanket, a supply of rations and a quart, and every time he was thanked he would pull his old felt hat over his eyes, and turning away, say, " Oh, it's nothin' ; it's nothin'."

Harold wandered along the road he had chosen for the whole of that day. Once at noon day he stopped by a little water-hole for a short time, boiled his quart, but finding he was not hungry, hurriedly drank his tea and continued his travels. The fact is,

his heart was very heavy, he felt terribly lonely, and
his mind was in such a state it would not let his
body rest.   Towards evening, as he was plodding
his way through a low stretch of Gydia scrub, he
thought he heard the whine of a native dog.   He
went along a bit farther when he heard the same
sound again, but now more resembling the call of
some one in difficulties or distress.   Then he stopped
and listened very intently.   Yes, he now heard it again.
It was some one crying, and sounded like the voice
of a boy, or perhaps it might be a woman's.   Harold
instantly got up from his listening attitude, and
saying excitedly aloud, " It must be some one in
distress an' wantin' help," hurried off at as fast a pace
as his legs would carry him.   When he got a bit
farther he could see a wagon, and as he drew nearer
at a breathless pace, he saw a girl kneeling on the
ground, her face buried in her hands, and sobbing as
if her heart would break.   The sun had now set, and
the darkness of a clouded evening made it difficult to
see far.   Harold could discern in the distance that
the girl was kneeling over something stretched on
the ground, but it was not till he drew quite alongside that he saw it was a man, and that he was dead.
The sudden shock of this gave Harold such a surprise
that he stopped at once and with a look of horror and
wonder stared at the stiff, outstretched form of the
dead man, and then with a questioning look at the
weeping girl, who could only brokenly articulate,
" Poor father !   Poor, dear father."   Then Harold's

tongue found utterance, and crouching down beside the girl, he took off his hat, and with a quivering voice burst forth, " Ah, poor little orphand, and this dead man here is your father ? Oh, I do pity you, I do so much pity you." Harold, with these broken words of sympathy, gave a most mournful sob. He was thinking of his own bereavement, which had so lately taken place, and the feeling of what he then suffered made him now have the fullest and heartiest compassion for the poor girl, whose parent lay there on the cold earth sleeping in eternal rest. He looked at the weeping girl, tears streaming down his own eyes, and he sobbed out, " I'd like ter be able to say somethin' to console yer, but I can't, and I do feel for yer more than I can say, because my mother is now dead and I am an orphand too. But, poor girl, God is good, and now let us here say one little prayer." He went upon his knees, but the bereaved girl was too overcome to follow all he said. It was perhaps one of the saddest and most touching pictures that man could witness or imagine, to see these two lonely orphans kneeling beside the prostrate figure of the dead man in the wild unbroken solitude of the bush, and there with sobs and tears mingling their prayers for the repose of his soul. It was a pathetic, an almost awe-inspiring sight to look through the shrouded gum trees at that moment, as the flickering camp fire threw a weird, ghostly flame across the waxen features of the dead man, then shone for a moment on the earnest, suppliant faces

M

of the mourners,—seemed to dance phantom-like through the ghostly forms of the giant gums and next was lost in the dark and terrible background which shrouded all.

After a time, the girl in broken sentences told Harold her story. She had been going to school at her aunt's place in Brisbane, and was returning with her father to the station where her mother lived, when her father was overpowered by sudden sickness, and died in less than an hour. He had been long subject to severe heart disease, and was frequently told by the doctors to avoid all worry and excitement. But, poor man, it was impossible for him to always keep cool and calm. A carrier's life may not be a very exciting one, yet there is frequently an amount of worry and annoyance about it, which tells severely on a man, especially if his heart be at all weak. Well, so it was that day, he had some trouble with his horses and his team, and the effects, as already stated, resulted in his death.

Harold was very much overcome with the girl's brief story. He could think of no words of consolation to offer, and so he sat there by the camp fire, not less sad and troubled perhaps than she, and feeling at times a cold shudder pass over him as he looked on the cold, calm features of the dead. The wind blew through the leaves and branches of the tall trees, and had a sort of melancholy, mournful sound like the wail of lost spirits. The sad, weird cry of the curlew would from time to time echo through the ghastly woods, and then as its plaintive notes died away, there would suddenly break forth the distressful, lingering yell of the dingo, like the cry of one in terrible pain and endless sorrow. The girl, in her loneliness and grief, felt all this most terribly. Once when the wind blew stronger, making louder the sobbing of the trees, there suddenly started a hideous chorus of dingoes and curlews, which caused the bereaved girl to start up at once, catch Harold by the arm, and exclaim : "Oh, I do feel so frightened. If it would only come morning. Oh, how I do long for daylight! Do you think it is near? It seems so long and long ago since the sun set."

But at that time it was quite early in the night. There were many hours to pass away before the god-like face of the sun would arise and dispel these phantoms of the night. It was a sad and terrible night for these two young people, situated as they were in the wild solitude of the bush, no house or homestead within perhaps fifty miles of them, and there, beside the camp fire, the dead man stretched in awful calmness —silent for ever. But at length, after many weary hours of watching and waiting, the birds began to twitter, and the faint streaks of dawn to appear. Then Harold said to the girl, "Ah, you poor thing, we must now do something. Yer father is dead, God rest him, and we must bury him."

But at this the girl only cried the more bitterly and wrung her hands in sorrow and despair. Harold then took everything upon himself. He went to the wagon, took a pick and shovel, and going over to a great gum tree, started a grave. For a long time he worked at it ; but at last, after hours of weary labour, he got it sank to a sufficient depth. Then he went over to the solitary mourner, and said : "God knows it's be a hard thing, but you must now say 'good-bye ' to your poor father, for we must bury him."

To this the girl in broken sobs replied : "I can't bear to part with him. Oh, to put him down in the ground and to never see him again—never—never." With these words she broke into a flood of tears and could not say any more. Through it all, Harold was very much overcome himself, but he felt it his duty to be acting. And so in his inexperienced way, he went on with great resolution to do all he could to the utmost of his power. He got a blanket, and wrapping it around the dead man, tied it at both ends ; and then, with a weary sigh, he said : "Well, we must now put him in the ground." But that was an undertaking which was completely beyond his power. The dead man was not by any means heavy, but it was more than Harold could do to carry the corpse to the grave. After many fruitless efforts he at length gave it up in despair. He shrunk from asking the girl to assist him, and thus he was in great despondency as to what to do.

Just at this crisis a horseman appeared upon the road, and Harold saw to his great joy and astonishment that it was Ponsonby Oberon.

Chapter XXII

"'They built his mound of the rough red ground,
 By the dip of a desert dell."
        —*Henry Kendall's*—II. EUROMA.

"MY 'joy is great to see thy face again,' as the poet said," exclaimed the enthusiastic drover, as he leaped from his horse and clasped Harold to his bosom, as if he had been a long-lost child. "But Harold, boy, I'm glad to see you after these weary months of waiting, as the poet said. But now, tell me all; you look as sad as the knight of the rueful countenance in Don Quixote."

Harold pointed to the grave, and then to the dead man rolled in his blanket, and said, "Mr. Oberon, we can't be cheerful at times like these; and look at the poor girl, crying fit to break her heart, poor thing. May God help her, for her father is dead."

Oberon looked, and then with great effusion said, "It's poor little Athnie." Then going over to her, he said, "Athnie, child, those tears are from the depths of a divine despair, as the poet said; and, who knows, but nature has done better for the good old man— your father? Weep not in vain then, as the poet said."

Over this part, then, we may indeed be brief. Ponsonby Oberon and Harold put the dead man in his grave, and Harold, to the best of his poor ability, offered up a sort of burial prayer for the rest of the departed soul. After that ceremony Ponsonby Oberon at great length, and with many quotations, told Harold the history of his wanderings since last they parted. He had some very interesting adventures, but they would be out of place to relate just here. In short, as he said, he was driven from post to pillar, till at last, without a shilling in his pocket, he was forced to carry his swag. "That sort of a life, Harold," he continued, "did not suit a man of talent like myself—so I began to think of old Brownlow, and the husks in his swine-yard, as the poet says. Somehow, in my wanderings I found myself, by some strange course of circumstance, drifting nearer to old Brownlow's residence. It may be that I found no rest for the sole of my foot, as the poet said. At any rate, the long and the short of it was that I found myself at old Brownlow's one bright afternoon. But I'll stop there," he suddenly concluded, with a spasmodic burst. Then after an attempt to smile cunningly, he added, "Harold, I have a surprise for you. But let us be getting under weigh, as the poet said, and be assured I have a surprise for you."

Harold, despite everything, could not shake off his sadness, and Athnie Brown, for that was the girl's name, was naturally very much overcome with grief. Ponsonby Oberon was sad for the few minutes of the

burial, but a mourning appearance did not come
naturally to him, and so he was soon back in the old
erratic mood.   He got together a rough and ready
breakfast, insisted on Athnic and Harold having
some, and then, with unusual energy, brought up the
horses belonging to the team, and with Harold's
assistance had them harnessed and in the wagon
in a remarkably short space of time.   When that
was done, he said, " Come here, Athnic, till I
lift you up into the wagon, poor child.   Alas, and
alas, but you're like sorrow on a monument weeping at grief, as the poet says."   Then turning to
Harold he added, " You take my horse, and I'll
drive the team, because I'm a man of many parts,
as the poet says, and I can do all these things,
Harold, me boy."

Harold, without a word, mounted on Oberon's
horse, and the worthy drover, picking up his whip,
with many flourishes started off the team, calling
out almost constantly " Gee whup," " Woe back,"
" Gee off," " Wee, woe ; come here, stumpy."

Every now and then he would look at Harold, and
say with great pride, " What do you think of that
now ?   Didn't I gee them off that tree well ?   Ah,
me boy, as the poet says, he who drives fat oxen
should himself be fat, but he who drives poor horses
like these are, must be a genius, Harold, and a lean,
thinking man like myself."

Thus they went along till lunch time, Ponsonby
Oberon rattling away on all subjects, perfectly un-

mindful that Harold and Athnie were—no matter
how interested they might be—unable to hear half
he said on account of the constant creaking of the
wagon.   When they halted at noon-day to boil the
billy for a hurried snack, Ponsonby Oberon lifted
Athnie from the waggon, and making a comfortable
seat for her under a tree, betook himself to a prepar-
ation of lunch.

During the meal Oberon said, "Athnie, child, how
swift the fleeting hours have passed since last I saw
you, as the poet said.   Why, then you were only a
little child, that I used to take on my knee.   Now,
though you are not like Elsie, mentioned by the poet,
who was a woman grown and wed the next time
he saw her, still you are a fine, big girl, bless you!
Child, tell me now, as the poet said, how many
summers have passed o'er thy fair head?"

"I was sixteen last birthday," answered Athnie,
whose grief was now more subdued, and who was
able to answer the drover in a simple and intelligent
manner.

"'Ah, happy age, ah, happy time,' as the poet
said," exclaimed Oberon.

"It has not been a happy time for me, Mr.
Oberon," said the girl sadly.   "If I live to be a
hundred years the terrible memory of last night will
be always with me."

"I hope not, I hope not," hastily put in Oberon;
"for, as the poet said, a sorrow's crown of sorrow is
remembering sorrowful things.'"

"Mr. Oberon," said Athnie, with a painful effort at a smile, "I have never heard of that version of the famous quotation before. Perhaps you are thinking of the lines in Tennyson's 'Locksley Hall,' where he says :—

> 'This is a truth the poet sings
> That a sorrow's crown of sorrow is remembering
> happier things.'

The poet he speaks of is Dante, who, in his 'Inferno,' says :—

> 'Nessum maggior dolore
> Che ricordarsi del tempo felice
> Nella miseria.'

Your own favourite poet, Lindsay Gordon, did not seem to be aware where it came from, or he would not have said :—

> 'Some poet or other sings,
> That a sorrow's crown of sorrow is remembering
> happier things.'

Longfellow, as nearly as I can recollect, has given us much the same sentiments, and ——"

"Gracious, Athnie!" exclaimed Oberon, unable to keep silent any longer, "you say, 'and.' Were you actually going to trace the thing farther? Were you going to cite still older authorities to cast upon my head? Why, as the poet said, you have added ruin upon ruin, and rout upon rout upon me."

"Mr. Oberon," said the girl, now quite animated and forgetful of everything, "I could have gone on to tell you of a passage in Chaucer, who has been incor-

rectly called the father English of poetry. He has
a few lines, which contain the substance of what
Dante says with regard to sorrow. And then I could
have quoted to you those lines in Boethius, where he
says, 'In omni adversitate fortunæ, infelicissimum
genus est infortunii fuisse felicem.' Then I think I
could have quoted a few Greek lines ——·"

"Oh stop, stop, Athnie," burst out Oberon. "By
Heaven, you astonish me! Greek, eh? You have
already given me Latin and Italian. After the
Greek you will speak in a matter-of-fact way of
Sanscrit, I suppose. By the hokey, as the poet
says, the wonder is, and still the wonder grew, that
how the deuce your little head can carry all it
knew. But perhaps, after all," added Oberon,
throwing up his hands, "Athnie, you're like Mr.
Jenkinson in 'The Vicar of Wakefield,' whose 'The
world, sir, is in its dotage,' was the only piece of
learning that he had."

At this the girl blushed, but quickly recovering,
said, very pointedly, "Mr. Oberon, it is only fair
to myself to say that I do not wish to be classed
with those who

> "'For renown, on scraps of learning dote,
>   And think they grow immortal as they quote.'

or rather, Mr. Oberon, misquote—that's the word
—'just enough of learning to misquote.' You
might probably consider that I have been pedantic
if I did not stop to tell you that those very lines

from Tennyson, were once given to us as a subject for an essay at a Christmas break-up. I happened to be reading Dante and Boethius at the time, and made a note of the parallel passages in those two authors, and that is how I came to know so much about it."

Ponsonby Oberon jumped from his seat, threw his cap on the ground, and rushed over to where Athnie was sitting. "Child," he exclaimed, "I yield to thee the palm, as the poet said—the palm of my hand. There it is, so now shake hands and be satisfied that you have been too much for the famous Ponsonby Oberon for once. Of course I have had a few reserves, but a man of talent, Athnie," he added proudly, slapping his chest, "is always too gallant to call out all his guns on a lady." Then, turning to Harold, he added : "You see that, my boy. Take me for an example, and always let the ladies *appear* to conquer."

But Harold stood in mute astonishment. He felt thoroughly ashamed of himself. Here was a girl so much his junior, but standing as much over him in knowledge as does the Alps over a mole hill. He felt that he must look a despicable and contemptible thing in her eyes, and at that moment he would have given the most of his life to have been more industrious at school. So poor Harold said nothing, but remained perfectly silent, looking bashfully down his nose. But Ponsonby Oberon was nothing disconcerted; he went on, "And now tell

me, Athnie, how you have been getting on at
school?"

"Oh, well," she replied, with a certain pride in
her look, "I think I may say very well, Mr. Oberon.
This year I passed the University senior examinations in all the subjects I went up on ; I took four
medals, and would have passed my matriculation,
as soon as I went up for it, but——" She stopped
at once, and, covering her face in her hands, sobbed
bitterly. "What am I thinking of?   What am I
talking of?" she said feelingly.   "Poor father only
so lately dead, and here I have been talking as
if nothing had happened.   Oh, when I talk of books
and these things, I forget everything else.   Poor
father ; may God help me to remember you with
deepest gratitude to my dying day."   The tears
streamed out between the girl's fingers as she
covered her face with her hands, and sobbed so
loudly and pitifully that Ponsonby Oberon turned
his head on one side, and with his sleeve gave a
furtive wipe to his eye.   The girl went on in broken
sentences, "And, poor papa, how proud he was of
me ; and oh, how the dear good man worked to
find this money for my education, and I was to
do him credit some day, when I passed to be a
doctor."

Ponsonby Oberon tried to offer all the consolation
in his power, but Athnie seemed to pay no attention to what he said.   Then he lifted her into the
wagon, lit his pipe, and said to Harold, "Now,

me sonny, we are like the lated traveller, as the poet says, who must spur along apace to gain our journey's end."

Oberon started on the team, and the party travelled steadily till some time after sunset. Ponsonby Oberon smoked and talked and quoted poets, but now he turned round to Harold, and said, "I told you I had a surprise for you, and you'll see now, in an hour's time, if what I say is not more than a random-spoken word, as the poet says."

Harold, of course, asked what the surprise was, and Ponsonby Oberon answered, "Ah, me boy, it's a surprise in store for you, as the poet says."

In an hour's time they heard the barking of dogs, and shortly after they drew up alongside several rough buildings. Oberon lifted Athnie from the wagon, saying, "Go to your mother, me child." Then turning to Harold, he said, "Come here, me boy; as I told you I got a surprise for you." He led the way three or four steps, pushed in a door, and Harold was instantly astonished by a sight of Mr. Brownlow! Ponsonby Oberon gave a loud laugh, and exclaimed, "Mr. Brownlow, it's a case of the return of the prodigal, as the poet says." And then turning to Harold, he gave him a hearty smack on the back, and pushing him into the room, said, " My lad, didn't I tell you I had a surprise for you. There you are, and now you've 'crossed the bar,' as the poet says, 'and meet your master face to face.'"

Chapter XXIII

"A scholar, and a ripe and good one;
Exceeding wise."
—*Henry VIII.*—SHAKESPEARE.

THE story of this strange and apparently unlooked-for meeting is easily told. Mr. Brownlow, shortly after Harold's flight from the station, sold out his interest in the "run," and went to retire to town—as he said, to "rest on his oars" for the remainder of his days. But the spirit and instinct of the old bushman were strong within him. Life in the town was fast killing him. He longed again for the bush, and regretted having ever left it. Esau loved not his heritage of desert sand better than Mr. Brownlow loved the wild solitude of the bush, the cattle, the horses and the sheep; even the emu, the kangaroo, and all the wild birds and animals of the wilderness, were regretted by him. He longed ardently to see them again, and he determined at last to go back once more to the old life.

About this time the Crown land of Queensland became in great demand. All the old squatters of Victoria and New South Wales were rushing off to the northern colony and taking up large leasehold properties there. Mr. Brownlow, seeing all his old friends so enthusiastic in the matter, was also fired with the same desires and ambition. He was like an old soldier who hears the call of the trumpet and the drum, and who is immediately fired with the glories and the victories of his youth. He thought of his old pioneering days—all the troubles, the hardships and the privations he went through in those times were forgotten. He only looked back on it all with a feeling of happiness, and a pleasant remembrance of his success. So he started off and worked his way out into the back part of Queensland. But he was too late—all the good country was already taken up, and was fast being stocked. On his way back he called in at a station which had some time back been stocked by a young Englishman. The poor fellow knew nothing about cattle and station life, and things were not going too well with him. Moreover, he was a city man—a banker's son—and he felt that the terrible desolation of the bush was fast driving him mad. He was anxious to sell his station; Mr. Brownlow was eager to buy.

When two people are of such dispositions, a bargain is soon effected. Mr. Brownlow purchased the run—a splendid piece of well-watered Mitchell grass country—stocked with three thousand cattle and fifty well-bred horses. He was a happy man once more. Then he went back and brought his old servants to live with him. Athnie Brown's father was his cousin, and lived pretty well with Mr.

Brownlow from the time he first came to Australia.
They had many a quarrel together, but somehow
it never led to a parting. Athnie's father was a
good-hearted, but very sensitive man, easily offended,
but always ready to forgive or apologise, as the case
happened to be, whether he was in the fault or otherwise. Athnie's father worked for Mr. Brownlow till
he managed to get enough of money to purchase
a team for himself. Then he got married to the
daughter of a local storekeeper, and thus, with a wife
and a team, he was one of the happiest carriers on the
road. In time his wife gave birth to a daughter—his
only child. The good man himself did not trouble
much about finding a name for the infant. He was
always content to call her lovingly his little baby.
But that was a title she could not be always known
by, and sooner or later some form of a christening or
a naming would have to be gone through.

One of Mr. Brownlow's jackeroos had literary tastes
and subscribed to *The Athenæum*. This suggested to
the worthy carrier the name Athnie, and so, when the
parson came around, as he did about once a year, a
christening took place, and the child ever afterwards
was called Athnie Brown. Well, the years passed
over very quickly, and Athnie had grown into a
remarkably smart, intelligent little girl. She was
sent to the local school, and there she seemed to
swallow learning, to the great delight of her father.

The local schoolmaster, poor man, did not possess
any very brilliant parts. He had sufficient learning

to teach the three R's to the bush children, and now
and then he would be referred to as an authority by
two bushmen, who would have some dispute and
the inevitable wager over some simple problem in
arithmetic. These mathematical controversies were
generally about a snail creeping up a pole so much
one day and then slipping down so much the next.
What time would it take him to get to the top ?   Or
not infrequently, it would be about the difference
between a mile square and a square mile ; generally,
the good old time-honoured questions that we see so
frequently answered in the columns of the weekly
paper.   The good schoolmaster would work these
little problems out on a cracked slate, and then,
handing them over to the disputants, say, with an
omniscient air, " That's how it's done."

But after a while Athnie got to know as much as her
schoolmaster, and, to tell the truth, perhaps a little
more. Anyhow, the kindly old master was very proud
of her, and when some simple bushmen would come in
trouble about the contents of a tank or dam he had
made, the master would say, " Why, bless my soul,
that's the easiest thing in the world !   Here, Athnie,
just tot up these measurements for this man, and let
me see how quickly you can do it."   When it was
done, he would take the slate, glance at it through his
spectacles, and say, " Correct, Athnie," and then, turning to the dam maker, tell him it was only a child's
sum—so many cubic yards to the inch. The dam
maker would scratch his head, as he gave a puzzled

N

glance at the slate, mutter his thanks, and then go away to tell every one that the "hole schoolmaster up there were gettin' the younkers on great. Surprisin' the scholards he's makin' of them."

Then came a time, at last, when there could be no doubt but that Athnie knew far more than her master. He did not care to put it exactly in that way, but he represented to her father that she was so much in advance of the other scholars that it was necessary to put her in a class by herself, and as he had all the others to teach, he could not spare the time to do justice to one. Just about this time Athnie's father was going down to Brisbane to bring up a load of station supplies. He had a married sister there, and the idea struck him that he would bring Athnie down and send her to one of the better day schools. The girl was delighted with this. She had a perfect thirst for learning, and her father was so pleased with her that he determined to spare no expense in giving her every opportunity to improve her education.

At the school in Brisbane Athnie became fired with emulation. She passed through from class to class with wonderful ˺rapidity. At the "break-up" of the school she took away an armful of prizes, and passed the junior University examination first-class in every subject. In her second year at the school she had a brilliant career, and in the University examination had the same success in the senior examination as she had in the junior the year before. Then the father came down from the station with his wagon for goods, and was bringing Athnie home to stay with her mother during the holidays, when his untimely death cast the poor girl into such grief and sorrow, and cut short all her hopes of a University career and a medical degree.

Chapter XXIV

"Pursuit of knowledge under difficulties."
                    —Lord Brougham.

SINCE we related the last event in Harold's history six months have passed. He remained on with Mr. Brownlow; but although he found that gentleman no milder or more lenient in his manner than formerly, still, for some reason or other—perhaps owing to the adversity he had experienced—he became reconciled to his lot. It was no uncommon thing to hear the master of the station yelling out to Harold,—

"Haven't you got them cows milked yet? By the thunder, but you're too slow to catch mussels. You like work so well, you could lay down alongside of it. But you'll run away like a black fellow at night for all that—take to your scrapers without note or warning."

Not unfrequently on such occasions Ponsonby Oberon would happen to appear, dressed, as was his custom, in the best of style—a showy smoking cap on his head, and a pair of beaded carpet slippers on his feet. On hearing the old squatter upbraiding Harold, the erratic Ponsonby would exclaim,—

"Mr. Brownlow, how's it you're always nagging at that poor fellow? By heaven, as the poet says, you seem to have a rage and talent for abuse."

At this Mr. Brownlow would turn round in a fiery humour, and exclaim,—

"Ah, that's you, you gaudy jackdaw, is it? Dressed in carpet slippers, and a smoking cap of as many colours as Joseph's coat. You think now that going about in that rig makes you a gentleman. No, sir, it does not, any more than it made the jackdaw a peacock. It does not even make you look like one, but it makes you look exactly what you are—a buffoon, or a circus clown, or the natural born fool that I have always known you to be. See me, sir; I got more money in my trousers' pocket than a thousand such as you could muster in a life-time, and yet I'm content to go about in plain moleskins and a cotton shirt, and I wear bluchers instead of slippers. There's an example for you!"

Ponsonby Oberon was thoroughly irritated at this speech, and his ready tongue would find answer,—

"By heaven, Mr. Brownlow, you're an example of doing without soap. As the poet said, you wash with invisible soap in imperceptible water. Moleskin trousers and cotton shirt, be gosh! Well, we can only take your word for it."

At this point Harold would probably have finished the milking of the cows, and would walk away, leaving master and man exchanging the most sarcastic compliments with one another. Then

perhaps Ponsonby would hasten away, and, overtaking Harold, exclaim with great excitement,—

"See here, me shaver, all I'm suffering for you.
Taking your part, old Brownlow has turned on me
with a tongue that would clean out a chimney, and
in language more forcible than polite, as the poet
said. He has said things to me that, on my honour
as a gentleman, I am bound to leave the place at
once. Just as well, too ; a man of talent like myself
is only wasting his sweetness in the desert air, as the
poet said."

Such scenes as that were very common, but they
would generally end up by Ponsonby Oberon
expressing his remorse of conscience, and Mr.
Brownlow telling him, by way of acceptance of such
apology,—

"You're a natural born fool, of course, Ponsonby,
and, as a matter of fact, you must talk through the
back of your neck or bust."

Shortly after, perhaps, the strange pair would
be seen on the most amicable terms, arranging the
day's work.

It was Harold's duty to milk the cows every
morning, and if they were not done in good time,
Mr. Brownlow, in no very mild language, would not
be slow to tell him so. But Harold was very patient;
he took all the abuse that came to him in this way,
and felt that he deserved it. After he had had his
breakfast, his certain fixed duties were to catch a
horse, and ride across the bush in a particular direc-

tion, turning back all cattle that might be making away in that part. This generally kept him out all day, and on some occasions, after showers, he would not return till late at night : the cattle had given him trouble, and he had to follow their tracks for perhaps many a mile. At first he used to take no lunch with him, and, as a consequence, would come back very hungry as well as very weary. Athnie observed this, and so she used to wrap a sandwich and a piece of cake in an old newspaper, and always remind Harold to take it with him when he would be starting out.

"You don't know, Harold, when you may be back, you see," she would say ; "and it must injure the constitution to be riding about all day without food."

Harold, in an awkward, bashful sort of way, would take the lunch, and would offer many expressions of thanks for the girl's forethought in making it up. When he came back in the evening, he would report matters to Mr. Brownlow, and, after he had eaten his supper, would go round to where Athnie and her mother would be sewing or mending, and, getting the loan of a book from Athnie, would study it very intently till bed-time. Sometimes, with a piece of slate, he would painfully, and after many errors, work out some simple sum in arithmetic. Athnie would, from time to time, look over his shoulder, and say,—

"Really, Harold, you are making wonderful progress. Look, mother, don't you think his writing is better to-night than it was last night, and he seems to me to be getting better every time ? "

Poor Mrs. Brown, good, simple woman, would look and say,—

"To be sure now, Athnie, I do declare, it do look better. He seems to dot all his i's and cross all his t's, and he ain't got any blotches on his copybook neither."

And the good soul, with a benevolent smile, would go on with her ironing, or washing up, or whatever she might have in hand.

Somehow of late Harold had a great desire to remedy his defects of education. When he compared his knowledge with Athnie's, he felt himself the most ignorant and stupid of beings ; and it was perhaps this shame at his own mental deficiencies that made him now so eager to learn. Athnie had brought home all her school books, and was always glad to place them at Harold's disposal, and also to give him all the assistance in her power. The youth readily availed himself of these advantages, and would study very earnestly every night, till good Mrs. Brown, having everything washed and cleaned up, would say,—

" Now, Harold, my good fellow, sure it's time for you to close your book, because it's getting late ; and I was thinking of covering up the fire and winding up the clock."

The winding of the clock was the last thing she

did before retiring for 'the night, and it was also the
gentle notice for Harold likewise to go to rest. But
it was not uncommon that Athnie would be so interested in instructing her pupil that she would feel
loath to leave off.

"Oh, mother dear!" she would exclaim, "do just
stop for a few moments, will you? I am giving
Harold such an important lesson in grammar. He
just said now of himself, 'I don't know nothing';
and I told him he was getting a good opinion of
himself to say that. Then he thought that I mis-
understood him, and he replied: 'Just as I said,
Athnie, I know nothing.' I told him that he would
say anything after that, for he said one thing one
minute and contradicted himself the next. Of
course he looked surprised; and now I'm explaining to him that in the English language two negatives destroy one another, and are equivalent to an
affirmative, or, in other words, mother dear, two
'noes' mean 'yes.'"

"Laws! Athnie," Mrs. Brown would say, wiping
her hands in her apron, "to think that now, and
when I said to the little nigger just this minute, 'No,
no, you're not to take pannikin,' I was telling him
all the time to take it, and I didn't know it, and he
didn't know neither, because he went away without
it."

"Oh, you good, simple mother!" Athnie would
say with a laugh. "Now, that's different, of course;
that way of repeating 'no' only makes your refusal

more emphatic. But Harold seems to have got his notion of negatives from the French.

At this point perhaps Ponsonby Oberon would come in, and say, by way of doubtful but well meant compliment, to Mrs. Brown,—

"Ah, you cannot understand the niceties of the English language, my dear madam. But know you not what the poet said, ' Where ignorance is bliss 'tis folly to be wise.'"

At this Athnie, quick and sensitive like her poor father used to be, would fire up and say,—

"Oh, what a happy man you must be, Mr. Oberon!"

Thereupon Ponsonby Oberon would get very excited, and make some retort on Athnie, which the girl generally returned with double force. Oberon would then get more excited, and, slapping his chest, as was his custom, talk with great vehemence, and exclaiming,—

" I came round here to say a few polite words to you two ladies, and to give Harold all the influence of my encouragement in his studies, and this is how I'm treated. In the skirmish of wit, as the poet said, you know I'm bound to let you have it all your own way ; and now I go"—slapping his chest again—"and the light of my countenance, as the poet said, will never darken this room again."

With this he would bounce out of the room, and Athnie, going to the door, would call out,—

"Ah, Mr. Oberon, to use your own sweet manner

of misquoting, the most inconsistent of all strange men thou art."

Ponsonby would go off in great haste, and join Mr. Brownlow, who would be reading a newspaper in the dining-room, and would exclaim,—

" By heaven, Mr. Brownlow, as the poet said, order is heaven's first law, and I have come to tell you that you keep no order in this establishment of yours. All is chaos, as the poet said—a babel of stunning sounds and voices all confused."

"What in the name of all stupidity is the matter with you? Confound you for a mad fool!" Mr. Brownlow would exclaim, laying down his paper, and glaring at the excited drover.

"What is the matter with me! Ah, by the hokey, Mr. Brownlow, you might well ask, as the poet said. I went out to the pantry now to get a drink of tea, and those two women turned on me with a double-action vengeance, and by sheer force of abuse hunted me from the place ; and as a gentleman, of course, I was obliged to leave without saying a word. And the worst of it all, there was Harold with a mug of tea and a piece of toast in front of him, and grinning idiocy from ear to ear, as the poet said."

To do Oberon justice, in his excited state he thought things were exactly as he described them. But Mr. Brownlow had small sympathy for him,—

" Get away out of me sight, you natural born fool of a man! Coming complaining about women, eh?

Well, you're getting more and more of an imbecile every day. As for Harold, he can have as much coffee and toast as he likes ; it won't break the place what a fellow can eat."

Ponsonby Oberon would not wait to hear any more, but, hastening out of the door, would call back over his shoulder,—

" Mr. Brownlow, I give a week's notice ; and when I'm gone you'll know my loss. As the poet said, we never know the value of a thing until we've thrown it away."

Chapter XXV

"Improve each moment as it flies."
Winter—An Ode—SAMUEL JOHNSON.

DURING the six months we spoke of Athnie
made several attempts to induce her cousin, Mr.
Brownlow, to provide the funds to enable her to
complete her education. But the rough and ready
old squatter would exclaim,—

"My gracious girl, what in the name of common
sense do you want more education for? You got
more now than the whole of this district put together
has. No. That's where your poor father made his
greatest mistake. He would have kept sending you
to school till you got bald-headed as a coot, and went
about in a chronic state of spectacles on nose like
those bleary-eyed dames, who get lecturing all sorts
of nonsense to the other fools of women. No, Athnie,
if I could only do it, I would discount 50 per cent. of
the learning you now have : I would have you forget
half of it, girl, and then you would know more than is
good for you—certainly more than can be ever of any
use to you, and more than all our family and people
all put together ever knew. Too much learning
makes your stump-orator woman, your women's-

rights woman, your equality-of-the-sex woman, and
your goodness-knows-what woman.   My own mother
only just had enough of learning to spell through her
Bible—and during her long life she was as happy as
a sandboy.   She never felt any wish to mount a pair
of spectacles, collar a woman's-rights pamphlet and
address a temperance lecture meeting.   Women ought
to be well content to be what their mothers have
been."

To this Athnie would reply, "Why do you say
that, and how can you, when you really must know
better?   If women were content to be as their mothers
had been, we would be no better off than Eve when
she was turned out of the garden : there would be no
advancement, no general improvement of our race
from generation to generation."

"Ho! ho!" Mr. Brownlow would interrupt.   "You
take a bad example when you speak of Eve, my girl.
Only for her, poor old Adam would not have been
turned out of the garden at all.   And as for the
improvement in the general happiness of the race, it's
the men who have done all that.   We men run the
whole show and govern everything."

"No, no," Athnie would hastily break in, "'The
hand that rocks the cradle rules the world.'   Study
biography, and you'll find that there never yet was an
able man, who had not a clever woman for a mother.
We owe all that's best and greatest and noblest in
our nation either directly or indirectly to woman.
Cultivate the intellects of women and you advance

the standard of men's thoughts. Deprive women of
the rights and opportunities to learn, to know, and to
think, and in the next generation the mental de-
generation of men will make itself manifest. Continue
the process, and the nation sinks into pristine bar-
barism, and eventual annihilation by some superior
race, as is the case of the fast vanishing Australian
aboriginal."

This would be generally too much for poor Mr.
Brownlow. He would lose his temper at the idea of
how this chit of a girl could so easily vanquish him
in argument. With the loss of his temper he would
say all sorts of foolish things, and as Athnie answered
him coolly he found that what he said one minute he
contradicted the next, and the knowledge of this
would make him more angry than ever. He would
close the argument with a stamp of his foot saying,
"I'll give in that women can always talk more than
men—men are doers and thinkers, and women are
the gabblers." Then he would turn and walk away—
leaving Athnie in a state of bitterest disappointment
and regret. Several times she tried him, but all to
no purpose. She represented that she was qualified
to matriculate now, that she would most likely gain a
scholarship or a bursary, that her expenses would not
be a serious item, and that she would be able to repay
it all twofold after a time. In vain, and after several
futile efforts Athnie was at last forced to give up her
long-cherished hope. It cost her much, and she
shed more than one tear, as she said, "All is dis-

appointment and misery. Nothing comes that we yearn for and desire."

Nevertheless as time went on she gradually forgot this failure of her hopes, and became more reconciled to the dull, humdrum life of the station. Mr. Brownlow made her a present of a little horse, and she used to find much pleasure in taking long canters through the station horse-paddock—always careful, however, never to go outside the gate, for from there the wild bush extended without fence or limit. As for Harold, his mode of life was altering : his constant application to study had made a remarkable improvement in his mind. Over all the rough places in the path of learning Athnie was with him, assisting him here, instructing him there. " Men," she used to say to him, " have many opportunities, and it is but their own fault if they do not rise ; women have but few chances, and if they fail they are not to be blamed." Many a time coming home late, after a long day on the cattle tracks, he would take his books—or rather Athnie's—and study and read and cypher—till good Mrs. Brown would give the usual signal for retiring. Then he would look up and say, " I did not think it was so late. Well, I suppose I must be going. Athnie, will you kindly let me have the use of this book ? I will be ever so careful of it and bring it back in the morning, and, Mrs. Brown, may I take this slush lamp ? "

These requests were always readily granted, and as Harold would be leaving the room, Athnie would come to him and say, "If you have time to-night, I would like you to read this, Harold ; it is such an instructive book, and I am sure you'll like it and profit by it."

Harold would offer many thanks, say a gracious "good-night" to the two women, and then taking the slush lamp and the books, walk away to his little slab room. This, certainly, was a rough little room, when he first took possession of it. But one night after returning from his usual duties round the cattle tracks, he went to his little slab apartment to have a wash— when, lo ! he found it perfectly transformed. All the crevices were filled up, the walls were lined and papered with coloured pictures from *The Graphic*, *Illustrated London News* and other pictorial papers. Harold stood at the door for some minutes, not daring to enter. Then he said half aloud to himself, " Ah, some visitor going to take up his quarters here, and the place is done up most nicely for him too. I never thought such a change could be worked in so short a time. Well, well, he will have a nice place here now ; so I will take my swag and things, and try and find some little nook or corner about the stables."

As he finished this little soliloquy a light hand was placed on his shoulder, and a musical little laugh rang in his ear. He looked about and there he saw Athnie smiling. "So, Harold," she said, "you think you are going to be dislodged. Now this little room is to be all your own, and mother and I did it up for you to-day whilst you were out.   Don't you think it is so much nicer ?   Look at the little bookshelf we fixed up, and so I put several of my books in it that I know you will read and study."

Harold let the stockwhip fall from his hands, turned his head on one side and wiped his eyes two or three times with the sleeve of his shirt.   Taking Athnic by the hand, he said, with his eyes swimming, " Let me thank you again and again for the many kindnesses you have shown me.   My life has been so lonely, and I have been a wanderer and a pariah, and know what it is to want a friend, and you have ever been that to me, God bless you ! God bless you! and may I be able to some day show my gratitude for all that you have done for me.   Believe me, this kindness sinks deeply into my heart.   To you I owe everything : the reformation in my life—for I was fast on the downward path in my time ; I owe to you my education, my knowledge, my principles of life and all that's best and truest in me.   None, so well as the friendless orphan, can better understand all that— and none can feel in their hearts a fuller thanks."

He looked up, but Athnic had disengaged her hand and turned to go.   Harold sat down on the door-sill, and burying his face in his hands sobbed till the tears ran through his fingers.   The poor fellow's heart was full, for it was touched by kindness—such kindness as made him feel happier, nobler, and gave him a more ambitious desire to act and live above all things base.   He looked up once more and caught a glimpse of her white dress as she entered her mother's room. Then he perforce exclaimed, " Ah, God bless her ! May her life be ever happy, and may she never, never know sorrow and bitterness ! "

Many a night, though feeling very tired and weary, Harold, after leaving Athnie and her mother would sit up in this little room and study and read till the small hours of the morning. On one occasion Mr. Brownlow woke up after several hours' sleep and, seeing a light at Harold's window, jumped up out of bed, exclaiming, " What the deuce is that fellow doing with a light at this time ! Got some of the stockmen in there with him, I suppose, and they're playing euchre for bottles of rum. I'll put a few fleas in their lugs, by heaven ! " Dressed in a long white nightgown he walked over to the little window of Harold's room, and looking through the opening, saw, to his astonishment, that there was only one occupant in the room, and that he was busy working out certain problems in trigonometry on scraps of paper. Mr. Brownlow stood for some minutes watching the mathematician, and then without saying a word turned to go. But just at that moment there was a wild shriek behind, and Mr. Brownlow, not caring to be seen in his night-gear at such a place, made all haste to his room.

Chapter XXVI

"Stubborn unlaid ghost
That breaks his magic chains."
—Comus—MILTON.

MR. BROWNLOW tumbled into bed, but he had hardly done so when Harold came and said, "Will you come over, Mr. Brownlow? I don't know what is the matter with Mr. Oberon."

Mr. Brownlow exclaimed, "Oh, curse the chucklehead! there is always something the matter with him!"

With that he lost no time in getting on his clothes, and in his bare feet hobbled over to Harold's room, and there he saw the miserable Ponsonby standing with his hair on end, and a wild and frightened look in his eyes. Mr. Brownlow greeted him with "In the name of all that's mad, what is the matter with you, you stark, staring lunatic, as you look?"

"Ah, by heaven! my master," exclaimed Ponsonby, wildly waving his hands, "that's a question you well might ask. What is the matter with me? or doth mine eyes deceive me? as the poet said. As sure as you stand there, as sure as I am here, I saw an apparition—an apparition, as the poet said, seen and gone!"

Mr. Brownlow stared at him in utter astonishment for a moment; then he burst out, "An apparition, you natural born fool of a man! What's that? or have you lost the fragment of sense you had, or are you walking in your sleep with a terrible nightmare rattling in that white-ant eaten brain you're supposed to have?"

"An apparition!" exclaimed Oberon, with offended dignity, "you don't know what that is! I never gave you credit for knowing much, but, be gosh! as the poet said, your ignorance surpasseth all understanding; an apparition, sir, is a ghost."

Mr. Brownlow, on this, instinctively looked around the room for bottles. "Where did you get this grog from?" he asked with great indignation. "I told you more than once that there was to be no liquor brought on to this place, or anywhere that I am. I won't have people drunk and going about in the horrors here."

"You think I'm drunk!" exclaimed Ponsonby, putting his hand to his head to throw his cap on the ground, but no cap being there he gave a fierce drag to his hair, and shouted out, "Mr. Brownlow, I'm as sober as you are. But no, I'll not do myself that injustice, as the poet said. I am as sober as Harold here, and I tell you I saw a ghost standing there at that window."

Mr. Brownlow thought for a moment. He did not like to confess that he had been going about in his nightdress at that hour of night, but in order

to clear Oberon's disordered imagination he decided
to make known the fact.

"Why, you natural born fool of a man," he said,
"that was me. I saw a light in this fellow's window"
—pointing to Harold—and I thought he was playing
cards for grog, and came to see, when you must
come fooling round and shout out ghosts."

"Ah, a fine explanation," broke in Oberon, with
a wild, derisive gesture. "You the ghost, eh? Why
the face was very like yours, certainly, but it stood
fully fifteen feet high, was all ablaze in front, and
had a black devil at its back fully thirty feet long.
And, oh, the face of the ghost that was staring in
at the window was like the head of the Gorgon, as
the poet said. It was something hideous and re-
pulsive to look upon."

"Well, Ponsonby," said Mr. Brownlow hastily,
"your confounded run-to-seed imagination has gone
riot properly. You would make out a cat an elephant
if you thought it was a ghost. I tell you this dashed
poetry is enough to make a weak-minded fellow like
you madder every day. Now, I'll explain your
apparition, as you call it, in two words. I was dressed
in my nightgown, and a man somehow looks taller
in that rig: white is supposed to be the proper
colour for ghosts, and that was white. When I stood
at the window the light from the slush lamp inside,
as a matter of course, shone out on me, making the
all-ablaze appearance in front you describe; and
as for the black devil, thirty feet long, at the back,

it was my shadow; but a natural born fool like you would never look at things in that light, of course. Now I'm not going to be standing here all the night explaining the tricks of that wild brain of yours, so I'm off to bed, and don't you get shrieking out any more ghosts, waking people up out of their sleep."

With these words Mr. Brownlow bounced out of the room, and shortly afterwards could be heard slamming the door of his own apartment and cursing all the natural-born fools in the world.

When he had gone, Harold, who had been sitting quietly on the side of his bed during the explanations about the ghost, said, " Well, Mr. Oberon, you may not have noticed, and certainly Mr. Brownlow could not have, or he would not have perhaps taken things so quietly; but you were, no doubt, not complimentary to his good looks about that apparition."

"How so?" asked Oberon, who had now partly got over his fright on realizing that his vision was of a substantial thing of this earth.

"You see," explained Harold, "you first admitted that the face of the ghost resembled Mr. Brownlow's, and some time afterwards you informed him that it was so perfectly hideous as to give one the horrors."

" Ha! ha! ha!" roared Ponsonby Oberon, clapping Harold with both hands on the back, " be gosh! my young friend, you're sharp all right. I meant that knock for him all along, and I got this little scene up purposely to give it to him. Ghosts, of course,

I regard as but visions of our waking thoughts, as the poet said. Didn't I act my part well, Harold, eh? That's where all the honour lies, as the poet said. Ha! ha! ha!" clapping Harold again on the head and shoulders, "I believe I was cut out for the stage, my friend, like Shakespeare. It may be that all great intellects run in the same groove, as the poet said; certainly mine runs in the realistic acting line."

Harold smiled at Oberon's feeble attempt to explain away his fright, and was thereupon clapped on the back by the erratic drover, who said, "Ah, my young friend, that smile of yours does one good, it is so childlike and bland, as the poet said. What do you say now," he added with sudden enthusiasm, "if we give old Brownlow another fright? Let us both sing out 'Ghosts!' together, and tell him that the apparition has come again."

"I think we had better not, Mr. Oberon," said Harold, smiling again. "Mr. Brownlow keeps a shot gun in his room, and he'd just as soon shoot at a ghost as anything else that came prowling about at night. I think, in fact, he's got a notion that the average ghost is vulnerable, or, at any rate, will not stand fire."

"Yes, be gosh! you're right," put in Oberon, giving Harold a pat on the head. "You're, as the poet said, rich in saving common sense. Well, we have given him one good fright to-night, and the fun of telling him, in a geometrical way, so to speak, of what sort of a looking fellow he is. Ha ! ha ! Harold, you got a logical mind and can trace a *sequitur*, as the poet says."

"Mr. Oberon," said Harold, "I think we had all better get to bed. You have acted your part of Hamlet so well to-night," he added with a meaning smile, "that I'm sure your talent is deserving of a rest."

"I don't like that smile of yours," exclaimed Oberon, flaring up. "You smile and smile, as the poet said, as if you mocked me, but actually you're trying to grin a stupid intelligence from ear to ear as the poet puts it. Harold, my friend," he continued, after taking a breath, "I think I'll sleep on the floor of your little room here to-night, if you'll just throw me a rug."

"I haven't got a spare one," said Harold, "but why not go round to your own room and get the one you had."

"Ah, Harold," interjected Oberon dolefully, "I'm not well. Will you go and get it, and blessings light upon your head, as the poet said."

Harold, without a word, hastened off, and when he returned he found Oberon in his bed and calling out from beneath the blankets, "Harold, is that you? I thought you would never come back. I think now that you have got the rug that you had better sleep in it, my good young friend, for exchange is no robbery, as the poet said. I got the best of the exchange perhaps in this nice pillow of yours, stuffed with feathers too, and figures and flowers worked on it. You're a bit of a dooda to have such a thing."

"Here, give me that!" broke in Harold hastily, as he snatched the pillow from Oberon and smoothed it down with a sort of loving care.

'You're a bit rough on rats," called out Oberon. "As the poet said, every cow has a right to its own calf, and I reckon it follows that every bed has a right to its own pillow."

"Yes," said Harold with a curt "good-night," as he blew out the lamp, "and every man has a right to his own bed."

Chapter XXVII

"For whither thou goest, I will go."
—*Ruth*—THE BIBLE.

WELL, so the weeks and months went on: Harold, with an insatiable desire for learning and a wonderful capacity for acquiring and retaining it. And yet he never for a moment neglected his fixed duties round the cattle tracks. He got to be a marvellous tracker, too, with such practice, and could canter along a trail in unfavourable country that would have puzzled many a keen-eyed black tracker to have followed. He had also half a dozen cows or so to milk every morning before his breakfast, but he always had them done in sufficient time to allow him half an hour's reading and study before the meal was ready. Yet they were pleasant old humdrum days the same routine of duties to be constantly performed, so that one day seemed almost exactly like another Athnie frequently went for her ride through the small horse paddock, but she had gone over the same ground so often that it seemed every stone was familiar to her. At some distance outside the station paddock a broad belt of dark green timber extended. Athnie frequently looked on this refreshing sight of tall, shady trees, and many a time longed to go out and take a ride there. At last one day she was tempted to open the gate and canter out "just for a few moments," as she said. When she got into the beautiful green forest, she felt as one taking a larger liberty, and laughed in pure ecstasy as she cantered and galloped through the bush. Her little pony soon got winded with this quick exercise. Then looking down at him she exclaimed, "Oh, poor little Dodsie, you're fairly out of breath, and now I must let you go back a little more at your ease." With these words she turned her horse's head homewards, as she thought, but half an hour's ride in that direction, and still the country was all new and strange to her. Then she became a little eager, and started her pony cantering for several minutes. But, alas! the country became still more puzzling, and no sign of the horse paddock could be seen. Then the poor girl became thoroughly alarmed. In her fright and excitement she raced the little pony in all directions in the vain hope of striking some part of the paddock fence. Her long hair became loose and tumbled in a wild golden fleece all about her, reaching down and mingling with the chestnut locks of the pony's mane. Her pony was a fat little fellow, and, with this smart exercise, was blowing very hard, and the sweat was running down in streams along his sides. Athnie pulled up to give him a rest, and covering her face with her small white hands, she sobbed bitterly, poor girl, and from time to time would, in great anguish, exclaim, "Oh, my dear mother, what will she think of this? poor dear mother! God help me! but her heart will break."

Harold had been out till very late that day round the cattle tracks. In truth he did not return till about nine o'clock at night, for the cattle on his boundary had been giving him a lot of trouble, several large mobs having wandered away for miles. Thus it was, when he returned, he found all hands on the station in the greatest excitement and alarm as to what had happened to Athnie. Mr. Brownlow and Ponsonby Oberon had gone out to search for her, and poor Mrs. Brown could hardly say a word for crying. When Harold learned the state of affairs, he waited not to rest or eat, but filling a large water-bag and wrapping two or three sandwiches in a paper, he caught a fresh horse and started off at once.

Mrs. Brown had told him that the last she saw of Athnie was going out through the far gate of the horse paddock, and then riding close under a certain low leaning tree, which Harold well knew. He was glad to have this starting-point to go on, and made straight for the spot. A dim crescent moon crept from time to time through a fleecy mass of clouds and threw an uncertain light across the open plain.

When Harold came to the tree, he saw the pony's tracks there sure enough, but Mr. Brownlow and Oberon had evidently also been there, for the tracks of two other horses were clearly visible. Harold here, trembling and anxious, got off his horse, and placing

his hat on the ground, knelt down and prayed long
and fervently to God to assist him and guide him in
the trying and difficult task he was about to under-
take. "God," he exclaimed, "God,"—passionately
and earnestly,—"make my eyes doubly watchful this
night, and take from me all weariness that I may
follow unerringly the tracks of this poor innocent
girl, this angel girl, too good for this world ; but we
cannot spare her, O God, we cannot spare her ! Lord,
above all things, I now thank Thee for having made
me Mr. Brownlow's tracker ; for now I may be of
some use,—I may save the life of this good girl."

With these words he got up feeling strong and
firm. Just then the moon shone out from a wavy
streak of clouds and cast a light that showed to
Harold the three horse tracks very plainly. He
followed them for some distance anxiously ; then he
saw one of the tracks branching off from the other
two. "Ah," he said, "Mr. Brownlow and Ponsonby
have lost the tracks already, for that must be the
hoof prints of Athnie's horse making in a separate
direction." Harold looked intently. "Yes," he
continued, "those are the pony's tracks, sure enough.
Well, it will give me all the better chance, the other
two horse tracks might help to mislead me." Patiently
and earnestly he followed the trail till the moon set.

Fortunately at that time the tracks cut across a soft
plain, and even in the darkness Harold's keen eyes
could trace them. But it was so dark that he had to
get off his horse and follow them on foot. For hours,

slowly across this plain, he traced the pony's hoof
prints, till at last they led across a stony ridge, and
there in the darkness he could for the time do no
more. He thanked God for having assisted him to
do so much. He was feeling very weary, but he
would not rest, afraid he would oversleep himself; he
was hungry and thirsty, too, but he would not touch a
drop of the water, nor eat one of the sandwiches.
"God knows," he said, "Athnie will want them
badly enough when I find her, poor girl. But I must
keep all the strength I can in my horse, and, thank
goodness, he is one of the best in the district." With
that he took off the saddle, and hoppled the horse
with a stirrup leather. Then he patiently waited for
day, which was not far off, but it seemed to him hours.

Once, indeed, for a few minutes, he went off into a
sort of doze, and he dreamed that he had found
Athnie, and that she was out on a great plain dying
of thirst. And he thought then, as he went eagerly to
his water-bag, that he had lost it, and there was the
girl fast perishing of thirst, and not a drop of water
within thirty miles. But his horror was still greater
when, on looking around, he found also he had lost
his horse. He thought then he took her up, oh, so
gently, in his arms, and felt resolved to carry her himself across the silent, dreary plain back to the station.
Then he thought he could see the end fast coming,
and that the girl was dying in terrible agony and
calling out for water. With that he felt he started to
run, and the faster he ran the wider the plain seemed

to get. Then looking at her, he saw that she was
dead, and the shock and horror of it caused him to
yell out, when he awoke so suddenly that he could
hear the echo of his own cry. Then he found that it
was a dream, and he thanked God that it was so. It
was now clear daylight, so Harold lost no time in
catching his horse, and getting him started once more
upon the tracks. Long before the sun rose Harold
had picked up the trail and followed it through the
stony and rugged, hard ridges with the watchfulness
of an Indian pathfinder.

Chapter XXVIII

" And the wayfarer faints 'neath his lightened load—
    Yet the river of God is full."
      —*In Time of Drought.*—MARY HANNAY FOOTT.

IT was perfectly wonderful how Harold followed those tracks. For hours he rode along the barren, granite country, and at a good pace too, having no other evidence to go on than here and there a little dead twig snapped in two, a pebble turned out of its place, or perhaps a mark no larger than a pencil stroke on a rock. Several miles he went like this, and in all that distance he never once saw a clear hoof-print—only such minute evidences as a trampled leaf, and those described. Yet he was following those tracks without a single mistake, as surely, it seemed, as if they had been imprinted on sand. The sun had risen high in the heavens when the tracks of Athnie's pony left the ridges, and made out across a wide and desolate-looking plain. Harold surveyed the scene with terror and alarm, for it seemed to him as the plain of his dream, and at that moment he had a terrible dread that his dream would be realized. He broke into a canter, as the tracks got into better ground, but he had not gone more than a hundred yards at this pace, when the

water-bag fell from his horse's neck. No water was
spilled for the bag was well corked; but the fact of
dropping it suggested another part of his dream, and
he felt a nervous tremor pass over him and the flesh
at the top of his head creep and crawl with a strange
feeling. "Good God!" he exclaimed, as he picked
up the bag, "I know perfectly well that dreams are
but the images of the brain half asleep, and nothing
more, and yet I cannot overcome this feeling of
apprehension." The fact of it was that he was
nervous from the over-anxiety and watchfulness, and
the great strain he had concentrated on his mental
faculties in following the tracks through such terrible
country.

On and on he went now at a fast pace—for the
tracks were all through soft country—and at the
same time he kept an anxious look-out on the plain
ahead of him. It seemed to him that he might have
travelled across this great plain for a matter of an
hour and a half when he suddenly caught sight of
an object which appeared to be moving near the
timber at the far side. Still keeping on the tracks
he put his horse into a fast canter, and when he had
gone about half a mile he all at once lost sight of the
thing he had seen. This caused him to press on
more eagerly; but when he got to where he first
observed the thing moving, he could see nothing of
it. "Ah," he said, "it may after all be only an
emu." This thought had just passed through his
mind, when, on looking around, he all at once caught

sight of a horse in a little hollow close alongside of
him. A second glance, and he saw to his horror it
was Athnie's pony without his lost rider. The words
rose at once to Harold's lips, "Good God of heaven!
what can have become of her!" He felt his heart
sink within him with fear and dread as to what might
have happened; but when he recovered himself and
looked again, he saw that the pony was without
saddle and bridle. With this sight Harold breathed
again, saying to himself, "She must have let the pony
go for a rest, and taken the bridle and saddle off, and
he has made away." He then went over to the pony,
and found the poor little fellow really knocked up,
his flanks and sides almost stuck together for want
of water, and his eyes were sunk back in his head.
It was a painful sight, and Harold's heart bled to
look at it.

Suddenly he took the hat from his head, poured
about a pint of water into it, and held it to the pony's
mouth. The poor little fellow drank it up eagerly,
and had such a look of gratitude in his eye that
Harold could not bear the sight, but quickly mounted
his horse and rode away some distance. When he
looked back he saw the little pony following him;
"God of heaven!" exclaimed Harold, "if this water
were only for myself, the poor little brute should
have every drop of it, thirsty and hot and perishing
as I feel, but I cannot bear that look of agony, so I
will let him have the only drop of water I might have
taken from this bag myself." He took off his hat

again, poured another pint of water into it, and after he had given it to the perishing pony he mounted his own horse, saying, "I must follow his tracks back." With that he went almost at full speed along the pony's tracks : he was so anxious that he could not bear to go slowly now. All at once near a bush he came upon the side saddle and bridle, and his heart gave a great bound within him as he looked fearfully around for Athnie ; but there was nothing of her to be seen. He knew that she must have wandered away on foot, and said, "God help her ! for to follow her light little footsteps on this hard ground will be slow work." In truth, it was terrible work. Harold's tongue was parched in his head, and he was weak for want of food ; but now he braced all the faculties of his mind, and concentrated all the energies of his being to patiently and laboriously following out those tracks.

If the following of the pony's tracks on the hard ridges had been difficult, they were as a broad highway compared with the trouble now, but with noble and magnificent heroism Harold struggled : he heard nothing, saw nothing but the faint track that Athnie made as she wandered about in her light cloth boots. It was a great strain, and the stones were beginning to dance before his wearied eyes, and the plain to turn and whirl round, when all at once he saw a little shoe before him. All seemed blurred and hazy at that moment; and as he picked up the tiny shoe, the dread of what had happened to its wearer came over him in an overwhelming manner, and he seemed to lose his senses as he cried in bitter anguish over this little memento of the lost girl. Then suddenly he felt a pair of soft arms about his neck, and a wild mass of hair on his face, and a voice calling, "Oh, Harold, Harold! I knew you would come. God bless you! you have come at last!" It was Athnie.

All wearied and exhausted for want of both food and drink, she had laid down beside a little thorny bush, she had thrown off the shoes from her little swollen feet, and there she waited in great pain, knowing she could go no farther, and buoyed up with a sort of instinctive hope that Harold somehow would find her—that Harold the great tracker would come after her and find her somehow. Then she thought of the rough hard country she had gone over, and a sudden despair would seize her, and she would cry out, "Oh, I know for miles along there the pony never left so much as the sign of a track." Thus it was, whilst in this maze of conflicting hope and despair, Harold found her little shoe; and though she was only a few yards off he did not see her, but she heard his sobbing, and with great joy and fulness of heart, and in gratitude and welcome, caressed him as she would a brother. Harold, in the bewilderment of his senses, looked at her tenderly, and taking her by the hand said hoarsely, "So, Athnie, you knew I would follow you. God knows I would; and that I have found you alive, there never was a happier moment for me than now."

The girl's next words were: "Harold, I feel hot and perishing. I am very thirsty, and have been for hours." Then Harold gave her water, a very little at a time, and after awhile he made her eat a sandwich. But he would not eat nor drink anything himself, for he knew they were fully forty miles from the nearest water, and there were only two sandwiches and about a quart and a half of water to do it on. Harold then mounted his horse, and took Athnie up before him on the saddle; and when he told her about the little pony, she cried and said, "Poor dear little fellow, I took the bridle and saddle off him and let him go, to give him a chance to save his life, and I do hope he will get into water."

Towards sundown the horse they were riding got very tired. He was also badly in want of water, and Harold saw that unless he was given a rest he would not get into water, which was still many miles away. So with a stirrup leather he hoppled the good beast out, and Athnie saying she felt very tired, Harold plucked great bundles of leaves, and made a soft bed for her to lie on. All this time the tongue was swelling in his head for want of water, and he was almost staggering from weakness and exhaustion. He laid the remainder of the water and the sandwich before Athnie, but she pressed him over and over again to eat and drink it himself, but he refused with great firmness, for he knew that she would want it all. Fortunately he carried a little tomahawk in his saddle pouch, and with this he got about a quart of bitter water from the bulge of a bloodwood tree. On his way back from the tree he killed a fat iguana, and cooked him in a fire made by rubbing a Gydia stick against a sandalwood log. The bitter water and the iguana almost made him sick, but he made every effort to make Athnie believe that he really liked such food and drink, in order that he might leave her the sandwich and the water, without appearing to have made any great sacrifice on his own account in doing so.

Athnie rolled in the great bundle of leaves slept rather soundly, but the terrible strain and exertion had so worked on Harold that he was feeling very unwell, and fearing that something might happen to him before he got home with the lost girl, he caught the horse again long before daylight, and started on once more with Athnie before him in the saddle. But after he had gone some miles he found the horse giving in, so Harold dismounted and staggered along, leading the animal as best he could. He felt losing his senses—there was a buzzing in his ears, and he could not bear Athnie calling out to him to get up and ride and let her walk. All seemed blurred and hazy to him also, but still he kept on wonderfully in a direct course. Athnie had long finished the last of the water, and was feeling terribly exhausted and thirsty, when turning a point of timber she all at once caught sight of the station. She gave a shout of joy, but Harold heard her not, and soon after the poor brave fellow tumbled over, muttering incoherently, and too ill and exhausted to rise.

Chapter XXIX

"Gone a-droving down the Cooper, where the western drovers go."—THE BAJO.

"Virtutem primam esse puto compescere linguam."—CATO.

"BY all the nine gods, as the poet said, this is the most fumbling attempt at a muster I have ever seen in all my time. By the hokey! Mr. Brownlow, but half a dozen new chum Chinamen, blindfolded, and on a dark night, armed with bamboo sticks would make a better try. Mr. Brownlow, you're not trying to get me the best bullocks—you're mustering me all the scrags and scallywags, and you're keeping the good ones so that some other messer of a drover will make a reputation at my expense."

After a month on a bed of sickness these were the first words which appealed to Harold's reason. The long excited sentence was given vent to by Ponsonby Oberon in an adjoining room. Harold could just hear Mr. Brownlow's terribly sarcastic reply, and caught the words, "You do well to say some *other messer* of a drover," when he turned his head and saw that Athnie and her mother were sitting in the room. But his poor wandering brain during his month of unconsciousness had conceived so many strange visions that he thought this also was another. So he stared vacant-eyed at Athnie, who was stirring something in a bowl, and at Mrs. Brown who was knitting one of his socks. In fact, both mother and daughter, during his month of illness, watched over him with the most tender care, and that both day and night. Many a time good Mrs. Brown would find poor Athnie crying silently by the bedside, and would try to console her by saying Harold would surely be well again. And to this the girl would reply incoherently that it was through her he suffered all this.

' The events from the ending of the last chapter can be easily told in a few words. When Harold fell in sight of the station, it happened that a black boy came that way just then, and, at once, in great excitement, he hastened off to report the discovery to Mr. Brownlow. That gentleman immediately harnessed a horse to a spring-cart, and telling the black boy that he would always have plenty of shirts, and tobacco and pipes for this good news, he drove off as fast as whip could send the horse. Nevertheless, although in his secret heart he was greatly overjoyed at seeing Athnie and Harold again, he could not refrain from scolding them in the most liberal manner. But he might have said all the worst things in the world, as far as poor Harold was concerned, for the brave fellow knew nothing of what was going on around him, but occasionally he

might be heard to mutter something indistinct about
the plain growing wider, and the water being all done,
and such like. But as for Athnie she only wept,
and that not for Mr. Brownlow's harsh words, but
on account of the sad and painful state poor Harold
was in. Well, he was got home as quickly and
carefully as possible, but something like a brain fever
set in, and for a month he tossed about on his bed,
watched sympathetically and in constant anxiety,
day and night, by Athnie and her mother. In the
meanwhile the time had come to send away a mob
of fat bullocks from the station, and Ponsonby
Oberon was to take charge of them. The excitable
Ponsonby was so anxious to get a good mob that
nearly every hour of the day he would have a dispute with his employer, which to an onlooker would
seem as if it must end in a serious rupture. It was
in the midst of one of these altercations that Harold
regained his senses. As soon as Oberon heard of
the fact he hastened round to the invalid's room,
and taking the thin hand of our prostrate hero he
exclaimed,—

"Ah! Richard is himself again, as the poet said.
My lad, I'm glad to see you on the way to the
sano mens in sano corpore, as the Latin poet said,
for ever since you have been laid on all fours I
have had to bear alone and unpitied the whole heat
and burden of old Brownlow's abuse."

As he made this last remark he looked carefully
around to see that his employer was not within ear-

shot. Then, seeing that all was safe, he threw his cap on the ground, and his eyes blazed up with a wild gleam as he clapped Harold on the breast and said, " By heaven, my lad, there has never been such a man as myself since Socrates of old was scolded by his old rasper of a wife. I'm real patience on a monument, as the poet said, for nothing that old Brownlow can say will put me out, for wisdom can, of course, always afford to smile at folly. But it does make me mad "—here Oberon jumped on his cap—"to think that old Brownlow will not make a decent muster, and give me a chance to get a few good bullocks. If I could only get 1 per cent. of good cattle I'd whack every drover in the district when we got to market. By the hokey! Harold, the poets may talk about the injustices to Ireland, but the green isle never suffered half as much as I do. And a ministering angel thou, when man is in his hour of need, as the poet said."

Here he turned to Athnie, who was about to give something to Harold out of a bowl. But Oberon, in the act of giving Harold another pat, accidentally struck Athnie's hand, and all at once the hot gruel poured out of the basin on to the invalid's chest. On the impulse of the moment Athnie lifted the big spoon which had been in the bowl, and straightway she struck Ponsonby Oberon a hard smack across the ear with it, which, as the spoon was hot and full of hot gruel, caused him to yell out far louder than Harold did. But it did not end at that, for Mrs.

Brown laying down her sewing came up and gave him another vigorous smack with her thimble hand across the other ear. At this Ponsonby rushed from the room with his hands to his ears, calling out to "season temper with mercy, as the poet said." But in the back verandah Mr. Brownlow's voice could be heard cursing all the natural born fools in the world, and so for the time the poor drover had a painful turn of it.

Now we need not linger any more at this point of our story, excepting to say that after awhile Harold got strong enough to walk about, and Ponsonby Oberon after expressing much dissatisfaction had the mob of fat bullocks mustered for him. It was wonderful to witness his excitement at this time. The morning he got charge of the cattle, he was so fidgety that he hardly touched any breakfast. He tasted a mouthful of stew, and then jumping up, with his eyes dilated, he went to his horse and cantered off eager to see how his charge was getting on. He would then ride round them two or three times, and ask his men what they thought of the mob. They would generally answer, " Ah, a little lot of beauties ! Should be good doers on the road, and after a week will be as quiet as dogs. Reckon with this mob, Mr. Oberon, you'll upset the apple-cart of those other drovers. They are just a bit tetchy at present. Woe, boys ! Woe there ! Steady, now ! "

This last would be addressed to the bullocks, as they would give a slight rush, startled perhaps by the screeching of a bird or the breaking of a dead branch. Ponsonby Oberon would answer the man with, " Ah, the old fellow never gave me the best of the bullocks, and I'd have had all the worst of them only the way I used to keep him up to it. I moved the springs of action, as the poet said, but then of course I could not be everywhere. But then I'll get top price for them—I'll make the worse appear the better mob, as the poet said."

With that he slapped his chest and cantered back to the station. When the cattle were counted, and his " delivery note " made out, Harold—who was now fairly well—was deputed to go with him, and see him off the run for a few days.

Harold went with the cattle for about a week, and it so happened, that on the eve of the day he was to return to the station, Ponsonby Oberon with his charge camped at no great distance from a shanty or bush store, where liquor is sold without a license. His ration bags were now getting very low, and so he thought he would buy some stores at this wayside place before he ran altogether short. It was here that he had a remarkable and humiliating adventure, for no sooner had he arrived at the bar of the shanty than he called for a glass of spirits, and this being supplied him, he got so merry that he gave a long recitation with much dramatic gesture. Then he called for some more spirits, and Harold who had come up with him to help bring down the rations was pressed to drink also. This, however, he refused, and

told Ponsonby that unless he got his supplies quickly
he would leave him and go back to the camp.   Upon
this Oberon filled his bags at a little back room,
where he was served by a man who seemed to be in
a chronic state of drink.   Then he told Harold to
look after things, for, as he said, " I must go away for
a moment to refresh the inner man, as the poet said."
But being away some time, Harold went in search of
him, and was told at the bar by a dirty woman with
a torn dress that Mr. Oberon had just gone round to
the kitchen.   Thither Harold followed him, and there
he saw the happy drover with a large slice of cold
pudding to which he appeared to be doing great
justice.   When he had got through with this Harold
called him away ; then Oberon in great spirits went
up to a stout middle-aged woman, who was in the
kitchen, took hold of one of the loose locks of her
long straggling hair and said, " Now for all the gifts
the goddesses give us, as the poet said, I thank them
through you their representative for that bit of cold
pudding."   The woman was not by any means a
complacent sort of dame, and greatly resented her
hair being touched.   But Ponsonby Oberon was too
pleased with himself and everything to depart in
peace, and he cried out, " For one curl of these fairy
locks, as the poet said, I'd give the best part of a long,
useful life.   Give me a scissors that I may steal one
little velvet ringlet of this gold to keep remembrance
yet of thee, as the poet said."   With these words he
pretended to reach out for a knife, but the woman in

great anger, picked up a very dirty old frying-pan, which was nearly full of slush and bad· dripping, and was the grave of many thousands of flies. With this she struck the unfortunate Ponsonby fairly down on the top of the head. Now, it so happened that it was an old disused pan with a cracked bottom, being kept only to hold scraps for fowls and bits of kitchen refuse for the little pigs. Well, the force of the blow caused this broken bottom to fly completely out, and it seemed almost as sudden as a "Jack in the box," that poor Oberon's head popped up through the rim of the broken pan. It may well be imagined that he was in a dreadful state, poor fellow, for the sickly, foul-smelling slush all covered his head and streamed down his face, and ran down his clothes even into his leggings. His rage was indeed great. "By the sacred nine, as the poet said," he wildly exclaimed, " but I'll have your scalp for this, Mother Munroe, you villainous old woman, with a face that would frighten a Gorgon, as the poet said; but I'll kill you, I'll murder you, I'll slay you for this!" Alas! poor man, he might have gone raging and raving to this day, and yet be without power to do hurt. For, as I have explained, his head stuck up through the bottom of the pan, and its broken jags stuck so about his neck that he could not get it off. Moreover, stout Mrs. Munroe held the handle, and with a " rolly-polly " stick battered the poor prisoner on the head till, finding he could not escape, he changed his cry from threat to entreaty, saying, " Oh,

Mrs. Munroe! don't murder me! Don't kill me! I'm only a poor man with rheumatics : I'm only a poor man with rheumatics—with pain and age and faltering gait, as the poet said."

But to all this, the strong woman only responded with additional raps, calling out, " You got rheumatiz, has you ? I'll give you rheumatiz in the numskull, you impedant varmint you! Take that, and that, and that !" A staggering man, with a nose that loomed like a signal of danger, now came on the scene, and after abusing the unfortunate Ponsonby to the best of his power, he released him from the frying-pan, and told him to go to the land of eternal fire and brimstone ; but he so contrived as to put his hand into the pocket of the much-abused drover and from there he extracted a pouch, which he quickly slipped inside his own shirt. Now Harold had stood by all this time fairly dumbfounded, for the whole thing was acted so quickly that he had not much time for thought or action. Moreover, he felt a sort of restraint at the idea of taking a man's part against a woman, and so between conflicting feelings he was kept in doubt as to what he would do till the red-nosed man took Ponsonby Oberon's purse. Then he jumped forward and said, " Here, sir, hand back that purse at once. I saw you take it."

The man turned on him and said, " You jest hold that swallow-all-of-a-mug of yours, or I'll knock the hog's teeth down your throat."

Ponsonby Oberon now missed his pocket-book,

and he came up all covered in slush and dirt, saying
with great excitement and a burst of alliteration,
"You rascally, robbing, red-nose rogue, hand me
back my purse, or I'll make a wreck of you! as the
poet said." How the matter might have ended it
would perhaps be hard to say, had not the pocket-
book fallen from the fellow's shirt and thus plainly
bowled him out. Harold picked it up at once and
handing it over to Ponsonby Oberon, said, "There
you are now, and come away down to your camp at
once." With these words, Harold picked up the
rations and walked off. When he arrived at the
camp, he found that Oberon had not followed him,
so one of the men said he'd go up and get him down.
But he also being long delayed, another man said
he'd go up and see "what they were a-doing it on."
The end of it was that every man in the camp went
up to the shanty to see what had become of those
who had gone some time before. Towards sunset,
Harold—excepting a little black boy—was now the
only one to look after the cattle. He could not
leave them, so he rounded them up on camp, and
without a bite of supper watched them all night by
himself. Next morning Ponsonby Oberon and
his men came straggling back to the camp,
looking very woe-begone, and each blaming the one
bad nip of grog they took for making them, as they
said, sick as dogs.

When Harold got back to the station again after
seeing Ponsonby Oberon safely away, he did not tell

Mr. Brownlow any of the things above recorded, but it all leaked out through the little black boy, and the master of the station was very angry. He rated Harold up hill and down dale, as the saying is, and never a word was he answered back, for Harold felt that Mr. Brownlow had just cause to be angry.

Nevertheless he went up many degrees in Mr. Brownlow's estimation from that day.

Chapter XXX

Indocti discant et ament meminisse periti.
                                    —HORACE.

WELL, a year, and perhaps a month or two as well, may have passed away since Ponsonby Oberon started off with the mob of fats we have told about. Of course they were all sold long ago, and strange as it may seem for those who may have formed a bad opinion of Mr. Oberon's droving, he was only three short in his delivery, and the mob averaged within three pence of "topping" the Sydney market. Mr. Brownlow was delighted, and said there was nothing like a natural born fool for a drover after all, and though he had first intended to curse him from stem to stern for getting drunk at starting, he would now tell the agents to make him a present of £50.

In due time, the worthy Ponsonby returned to the station. He was all smiles as he clapped his chest and told every one, over and over again, how he went within a fraction of topping the market with a lot of scrags and scallywags. He repeated this so often that Mr. Brownlow got in a terrible rage at last, and cursed poor Oberon beyond hope of all redemption, calling him, as well, the most

natural born of all fools. Then the indignant drover
flared up into a great state of excitement. He
pulled off his cap and jumped on it, and the pipe
he had just taken from his mouth he threw off wildly,
not knowing what he did. The chances are, it would
have struck Harold right on the eye if he had not
seen it coming, with a great tail of fire, and caught it
in his hands. Then Ponsonby Oberon exclaimed,
" I will go at once, Mr. Brownlow. The blackest of
all crimes is ingratitude, as the poet said, and though
I worked and laboured and watched your cattle with
the greatest care, you think no more about it. Yes,
sir, I kept them fresh as daisies ! "

With a wild clap of his hands he bounced out of
the room, and Mr. Brownlow bellowed after him,
" Kept them fresh, did you ? By gosh ! you refreshed
yourself to dead drunkness at the first shanty you
came to ! "

But Ponsonby Oberon perhaps did not hear it.
At any rate, he hurried right on for the stockyard,
and there he caught two horses, and put a pack on
one and his riding saddle on another, and in a
remarkably short time he was mounted and before
the door, calling out, " Mr. Brownlow, I leave you
rather in pity than in anger, as the poet said. I take
my talent elsewhere ; I take myself and my great
droving abilities where they will be properly appreci-
ated. Sir, I go ; and when I am gone you will say,
as the poet said, we never know the value of a thing
until we have thrown it away."

With these words he clapped his chest with great force two or three times, and then he turned his horses, and galloped away. Mr. Brownlow stared after him for some time; then he burst forth, "Well, of all the natural born fools and stark, staring lunatics in the world, that idiot Ponsonby Oberon takes the palm! But he can go to pot for all I care. It's his loss, not mine."

Now, it was time for Mr. Brownlow to send another mob of fats away, and he had great faith in Oberon as a drover, and perhaps he had a certain liking for him as well, for old acquaintance' sake. At any rate, after cursing and bustling about for awhile, he caught a horse and cantered down the road Ponsonby Oberon had taken. When he had gone maybe a mile or so, he met the erratic Ponsonby travelling back in the direction of the station he had just left. Mr. Brownlow at this chuckled to himself, muttering, "Ah! he wasn't such a natural born fool as not to know on what side his bread was buttered. He's coming back now with the gas out of him, I'll warrant me."

At the same time, Ponsonby Oberon was clapping his chest and saying gleefully to himself, "Ha! ha! the old fellow didn't take long to find out he couldn't do without me. In his better senses he knows full well, as the poet said, that I am the mainstay and backbone of his whole business." A few minutes after this they passed one another on the road, and Mr. Brownlow looking

back said, " I have to tell you that you left most
of your traps behind, in your wild, mad hurry in
clearing out from the place."

And that's just what I was going back for,"
said Oberon with a dramatic gesture.   In truth,
he did not know that he had forgotten anything,
and, if we must be candid, he did not know what
he had taken away with him in his excitement of
packing up.   But a peep into his swag would
have discovered there one greasy legging belonging
to Harold; a kitchen apron belonging to Mrs.
Brown; and one dirty old cotton sock, the
property of Mr. Brownlow.   He had also an old
flour bag, all full of holes, the possession of no
one in particular, and certainly of no use or
benefit whatsoever, excepting, perhaps, to beat out
a bush fire with.   However, the ice was broken,
and shortly after both men might be seen riding
back to the station—Ponsonby laughing wildly,
quoting poets, and slapping his chest; whilst Mr.
Brownlow told that he must have a muster for
fats at once, and Ponsonby Oberon must take
charge of them and get away without delay.

Well, in short, it is some time ago since Ponsonby Oberon went away with this second mob of
cattle for market, and, as we have said, it is some
fourteen months since he took the first.

It would be wonderful to relate all that Harold
acquired in the way of knowledge of all sorts in the
meanwhile.   As a classical and mathematical scholar

he could easily teach many a schoolmaster; as a
thorough bookkeeper in all systems, he was fit for the
Society of Accountants, quite capable, at any rate,
of auditing the books of any business firm; as a
business correspondent, he could write fifteen good,
lengthy letters within the hour, all, too, clear,
thorough and to the point.

About this time travellers were beginning to get
numerous along these back country roads, for
several large sheep stations were stocking and
improving, and consequently giving employment
to a great number of men. So perhaps a dozen
times every day as many travellers would call
in at Mr. Brownlow's, and say they wanted to
buy something out of the store. Then he
would tell them that he kept no-store and didn't
sell rations. With this they would complain that
their ration bags were completely empty, and
couldn't they be sold a bit to carry them on. Mr.
Brownlow would generally curse them for not seeing to that before, as all the country should know
that he kept no store. Then he would tell them
that he would sell them a bit for this time, and
that would be the last. However, the end of it
was, he found that he had to keep a store, though
he grumbled very much at all the travellers it
brought about his place. When he got his goods
in, he put Ponsonby Oberon in charge of them,
finding him a full set of books, and telling him he
would have to keep all the accounts of the station:

but this arrangement somehow did not work. Sometimes a man would leave the employ, and at the settling up he would find that half the things he got out of the store were not charged to him. At other times the wrong man would be charged, and then, of course, there would be trouble—in fact, there would be nearly always trouble in the store during the short time Ponsonby Oberon was over it. Poor Ponsonby would get very excited, and throw his cap in one corner, and his pipe in another, and would be generally unable to find them again ; as for the pipes, the matter was not so much, for he would generally go to the box and take out a new one as occasion required.

At last he came to Mr. Brownlow and said, " Be gosh ! I can't stand this game any longer. It's too far below my talent, and I have to stoop my mind down very low to get level with it. Though I can be great in small things, as the poet said, still these small store-keeping things grate on me. Ha ! ha ! ha ! what do you think of that now for a pun ? Don't be afraid that I'll pick your pocket after it. In short, I have come to tell you to put Harold in the store—it will just come nicely within the range of his understanding ; as for myself, you don't require a Nasmyth hammer to break an egg."

The end of it all was, however, that Harold was put in the store ; but what a task he had ! Everything was out of place ; the wrong prices were labelled on nearly all the articles—in fact, the invoice book had not been worked out at all, and consequently values were set down anyhow. Sometimes the carriage would be left out, sometimes the duty; at other times, perhaps the wharfage, freight and harbour dues at port, or the commission, or insurance, or something else would be omitted in working out the landed cost of the goods; the result was that most articles were sold at a loss.

This was not the worst, for the journal and cash books were in such a terrible state, with cross entries, and single entries, and double entries, and, in fact, all sorts of entries, that no man in the world could post them up, or indeed know what they were about at all. There were also bundles of letters scattered about here and there, and all left unanswered and neglected.

Ponsonby Oberon had gone with the fats at the time Mr. Brownlow went with Harold through the store, and witnessed this state of affairs; but he cursed the good drover for a careless, useless, natural born fool of a fellow, with not enough of brain to bait a fish-hook, and enough of conceit to fill a cask. After he had eased his mind in this way, he told Harold to do the best he could, for he felt, as he said, that he'd get the horrors if he stayed to see any more of it. Harold did do his best.

In about a fortnight he had all the books adjusted, the goods properly priced, dusted, and put away on shelves, the store cleaned out, and everything as it should be. In the processs of cleaning out, he picked up fully two dozen pipes which had been thrown away by Ponsonby Oberon in his periods of short madness. These pipes were for the most part broken and damaged by the hard usage ; but Harold put them away carefully in an old case, for, as he said, they did just as well for the station blacks as new ones. In fact, he was the just steward, taking the greatest care of his employer's goods, and rendering account of everything. Gradually, too, Mr. Brownlow found out his uses as a clerk, and eventually made the most of him in that way. First, he used to give him all the unimportant letters to reply to. This was all done so well and promptly, that gradually Mr. Brownlow gave him more important letters to answer ; and finally—for Mr. Brownlow, like most bushmen, hated writing—Harold was given all the correspondence of the place, private, confidential, and otherwise : but nevertheless he liked the work, for now he could make use of every spare moment in reading, studying and improving himself.

Chapter XXXI

" I have heard of reasons manifold
Why love must needs be blind."

—COLERIDGE.

THESE were pleasant days indeed for Harold. Often there would be only himself and Mrs. Brown and Athnie on the station, for Mr. Brownlow would frequently be away camped out for several days, and Athnie would be often in the store with Harold for an hour or so perhaps at a time, and when he had closed up for the day they would go out walking together—sometimes, perhaps, shooting along the banks of the lagoon, or down to see the Chinaman working in the garden. Good Mrs. Brown never made an objection to any of these things; in truth, she saw something in Harold's countenance so noble, trust-inspiring, and honourable, that she felt any young girl might go with him anywhere; and so it was.

In all these walks, and on all these times the young couple were together, there was not one mention of love—nothing said that had any reference that way, and yet they were supremely happy. They talked of prose and verse, of the latest books as well as the oldest, and displayed a masterly, critical analysis in their opinion of all. Thus it went, and one and each knew not the other's heart—knew not, in fact, their own hearts—nor stopped to ask.

Now at this time an old gentleman bought a small sheep run which was adjoining Mr. Brownlow's place. He was a married man and brought his wife up with him to live on the station, and also a son about twenty-two years of age, and a daughter some half a dozen years younger; he had other children, but they were away at school. Well, the man who first owned the sheep station was a bachelor, and he lived in a miserable little hut, which could afford no accommodation to a man with a family. Thus it was that Mr. Brownlow invited Mr. Linden—for that was the gentleman's name—to stay with him for awhile until he could erect suitable buildings for his family.

This invitation was gladly accepted by Mr. Linden for the sake of his wife and daughter; as for himself he would be away nine-tenths of his time, seeing to the building of his new house, and other matters connected with the stock and management of the place. His son would be generally at Mr. Brownlow's place, for he was a young man fresh from college—having no idea of the bush, and caring less for it. He was a good-looking young man of taking manners, well up in the current small talk, and one who could make the fair sex pleased with him, for the reason perhaps that he had the talent of making them pleased with themselves. He soon got on friendly terms with Athnie, and as he had just taken his B.A. degree, he was, on the whole, able to discuss the classics and general literature with her, but Athnie with her private reading possessed a far wider scope of knowledge, and many things she spoke of were beyond young Mr. Linden's range. Such studies as were prescribed for him for his Bachelor of Arts course, he was on the whole well up in, and acquired more than a "cramming" knowledge of, but many of the classical authors were little more than a name to him. He could discuss Greek and Latin Comparative Philology, had Æschylus, Sophocles, Andocides, Plautus, and Gellius well in his mind, but, we are afraid, had no great appreciation of them, for his anthologies therefrom were not the most creditable. Well, he passed a good part of his time with Athnie discussing these matters, and it must be confessed that she was not round to the store so often as formerly. Harold felt this, and now, it must be told, he for the first time felt the state of his own heart: it was jealousy brought him all at once to this fact. It may be that jealousy is but abnormal love, but there are few things that make a man more realize the state of his own feelings —that make him understand all at once how deeply he is in love, and how strange it was he never knew this before.

One day Harold sat at his desk, feeling very heavy at heart, and wishing that young Linden had never come to the station, and hoping the time would soon arrive for him to go away. As he sat thus with his

hand to his forehead, he heard the joyous ripple
of a girl's laughter out in the dining-room of the big
house.   Strange as it may seem, it gave Harold a
pang, and he thought to himself, "how pleased she
must be with him !"   This silvery laughter breaking
out from time to time made Harold feel less and less
at his ease.   At last, we know not why—perhaps it
was to witness how happy Athnie was with young
Linden—but after fidgeting about, he got up and
went out to where the laughter was going on.   Then
he found that it was young Linden's sister who gave
forth these gleeful ripples of mirth, for she was
playing a sort of game of Blindman's Buff with her
brother, and being a glad-hearted girl would burst
forth in merry peals of laughter from time to time,
according to the fun of the game.   In a corner of the
room, writing at a little desk, sat Athnie, totally un-
mindful of all that was going on around her.

Simple as the little incident may appear, a great
load was lifted from Harold's heart ; and now he felt
that, perhaps, as she was not laughing and merry with
young Mr. Linden, she might possibly be thinking of
Harold himself.   Yet he did not go near her, for a
certain little resentment—a strange little mixture of
pride and bashfulness—prevented him, now that it
seemed she had been neglecting him of late.   But
just as Harold was about to leave the room, a pair
of plump little white arms were suddenly twisted
round him, and a merry, silvery voice exclaimed,
"Now I got you, now I have you at last, you trouble-

some one to catch!" Harold looked around suddenly, and there was Miss Linden's bright golden hair in a great mass blown into his face, and making him almost feel as blindfold as she herself was with the handkerchief about her eyes. When he gently released himself, he suddenly saw Athnie's face turned from them back to her writing again, but there was never so much as a smile of amusement on her countenance. Harold was leaving the room in confusion just as Miss Linden took the handkerchief from her eyes and discovered her mistake; but Athnie never so much as looked after him or said a word, or knew in truth that he was not still in Miss Linden's embrace. Another day she came into the store just as Harold was doing his best to smile at a really funny little story that Miss Linden was telling him, but Athnie only seemed to make a short hurried search for something near the door, and then went away before Miss Linden could call her back to tell her the little amusing thing also. Well, now, it seemed a sort of strangeness appeared to grow up between Harold and Athnie, and at last it came that she never went near the store at all, and whatever was wanted out of it Mrs. Brown would go and get.

Little Miss Linden—a merry, golden-haired little girl—would be often round to the store-office talking to Harold in a cheerful, laughing way of so many things, but it was only with an effort that he appeared to be gay and light-hearted in her presence, for his thoughts were constantly of Athnie, and wondering what was the cause of the change that had come over her, and thinking within himself could he, by any of his actions, be in any way responsible for it.

Harold would seem now to wear an air, not altogether of sadness, but he had a want of cheerfulness, and would be so pensive and forgetful that Mrs. Brown would ask if he were ill. Upon this Harold would try to be merry and would give a little laugh, that had a half mechanical ring about it, and he would say that people got so terribly serious as they got older. Then Mrs. Brown would perhaps give him a cup of tea, telling Athnie to get the sugar and put some in the cup. As she did so, Harold, appearing all the while to be only looking down at his saucer, but in reality only seeing the little hand that put the sugar in his tea, would feel an almost irresistible impulse to seize upon it, and cover it with kisses, and press it to his breast, squeezing it gently and lovingly, and kissing it again and again. But, instead, he would only look at her from the corner of his eye, and feel glad that she was not playing chess with young Mr. Linden, and sitting so close beside him as it always appeared to Harold.

Many a day went on like that, and when Harold would go back to his office in the store, he would feel such a want of cheerfulness that his face began to assume a settled cast of seriousness. So much so that travellers, who came to buy things out of the store, would speak of him in a whisper as being "a grumpy sort of a joker with not many pleasant words to throw away." But little Miss Linden would often come round to see him, and talk to him, and ask him all sorts of strange questions about the bush. Athnie, though, somehow never came near him, and in his restlessness he would every hour get up from his seat and go round to where she was in order that he might just see her only. It must be confessed, too, that he would feel lighter at heart when he would see her by herself, and not talking and playing chess with young Linden. In all candour we must also say that he would feel pleased to see her looking pensive and with a shade perhaps of melancholy : it somehow gave him a vague, comforting feeling that maybe after all she was thinking of him.

Thus he would come round very often, always on the pretence of wanting something from Mrs. Brown : he wanted some hot water to make ink, he wanted a broom to sweep out the store,—and then after awhile he would have to come back with the kettle and the brush, and his first glance would be to see where Athnie was. He would look at her and go near her in the hope that she would speak to him or even turn her eyes upon him. Once when sewing her thimble slipped from her finger and rolled along the floor. Harold pounced upon it before young Mr. Linden could do more than look up from the book he had been reading, and straightway he brought it to Athnie, feeling glad that he had this excuse for approaching her. She accepted it with thanks and

blushes, but then by some accident off rolled her
reel of cotton along the floor, and young Mr. Linden,
in his eagerness to secure it, half tore a leaf out of
his book. He however caught it before it stopped
rolling, and with a shortness of breath he brought it
to Athnie. Harold stood at the door looking on,
and he saw her accept the reel with a laugh as she
looked up, and said, "Oh, Mr. Linden, what a fine
cricketer you must be! Really, the way you fielded
my reel of cotton was something wonderful!"

Harold stayed no longer. He felt it so much that
she spoke so cheerfully to young Linden and never a
word to himself.

Chapter XXXII

"Rich the treasure,
  Sweet the pleasure,
Sweet is pleasure after pain."
  —*Alexander's Feast*—DRYDEN.

ONE day Harold walking by himself, sad and lonely, came across Athnie about half a mile away from the station, sitting under a large tree and reading a book. He could not resist the temptation to go and speak to her, to tell her how great was his love for her, and to ask her ever so penitently to forgive him if he had, unconsciously by word or action, done anything to displease her or give her pain.

Going up, he stood for a moment alongside of her, his heart almost in his mouth, and his breathing in short gasps. She did not seem to see him, or perhaps heed him, till he laid his hand gently on her shoulder, and said with a plaintive, almost beseeching voice, "Athnie!" Then she looked up at him with her beautiful, soulful eyes, in which there was some trace of sadness, and said, with a little nervous tremor in her voice, "Oh, Harold!"

After that, she sat for a moment looking down at her book, and playing nervously with the leaves of it—Harold stooping over her, his knees shaking and his heart beating so loudly that he could distinctly hear its throbbing. Then he sank down beside her on the short green grass, and his voice was full of the deepest emotion, and his eyes had the tear-drops standing in them, as he took her little soft hands and kissed them impulsively, saying, "Oh, Athnie, Athnie, Athnie! tell me, in the name of Heaven, how have I offended you? Tell me, I crave of you, and I will do any penance to atone for my fault. God knows how I have suffered all this time you have been distant with me. God knows (although I found it out all suddenly myself) how deeply, how passionately, earnestly, purely, madly, fondly, I love you. Athnie, I beseech you, let it not be hopelessly! Speak to me, my darling, my ideal, you whom I worship and look up to as the grandest and noblest of your sex—tell me, I entreat, if you do not love me—that you do not, at least, care for another! Ah, that thought—that you were lost to me for ever would, I think, drive me mad! Tell me, my dearest, sweetest girl, that if you do not love me yet—that there is hope, hope, hope!"

She appeared as if she were about to throw herself into his arms, but then, all suddenly it seemed, as if she resisted this, and flinging back her head and with something like an attempt at mockery, mingling with a pathetic sweetness in her voice, said, "Sir, how presuming you are! Do you know what I am? Do you know that I am the sole heiress of my Cousin Brown's station? Do you know that I am the only near relation he has in the world, and to me he has left everything? Do you know that he wishes me to marry young Mr. Linden, who has another £5,000 in his own right, and do you think I could displease my cousin, who is leaving me a station in his will? You should know, moreover, that you have neither house nor home, that you have not a situation in which you could support a wife, that you are penniless, save for the few pounds you earned since you came to my cousin's station, and those, I believe, you spent in books. Where, sir, are your prospects, and what advantages can you lay alongside of the fact that my cousin leaves me his station, on condition of my marrying young Mr. Linden? And now, sir, let me tell you that Mr. Linden, who is young, handsome, good-looking, accomplished, a scholar and a gentleman—possessed of a private fortune of his own, and to come into more after his father dies—let me tell you, sir, that he has proposed to me and I have——"

Here she suddenly stopped, and Harold clasped his hands, and there was a terrible look of anguish and overpowering misery in his face, as he burst out, " My God of Heaven, Athnie, you put the case with awful force, and Heaven help me! but the madness of my love did make me presuming. But when I had hopes that you might love me, I did not know that you were an heiress. I thought you were poor like myself, and I fondly hoped that with you to live for, and love, and labour for, I could put in an eternity on a desert island and feel I was the happiest of men. Now, God help me, I am the most miserable!"

Then turning to go, he said, with a great huskiness in his voice: "Though you have the justest cause for refusing my love, Athnie, believe all my best thoughts, all my deepest feelings, all my most earnest and heartfelt prayers will be that you may be ever happy. And while I have a memory, God knows the purest, noblest, grandest recollections of my life will be of you—you who have been the highest ideal to me, the very guiding star of my life. God bless, God bless you! and may no shadow of pain ever cross your life, my darling ; may a life-long happiness be your lot!"

But the poor fellow's heart was full to overflowing, and in the overpowering mastery of his emotions, he covered his face with his hands and burst forth with such a choking sob that it seemed as if his heart must break. Then all suddenly Athnie threw both arms about his neck, and her beautiful, silken hair fell in great folds about him, and her lustrous, tearful eyes looked into his, and she kissed him over and over again, and with tears and sobbing mingling with laughter, she said, "Oh, Harold, Harold, you did not let me finish what I was telling you. 'And I refused him,' I was about to say, and that because with all his advantages I did not love him, because I love another, and though he is poor and without house or home, I count my love for him against all the world. Yes, Harold, I am content to be poor with you, let it be even direst poverty, so long as our hearts be one!" She kissed him with a beautiful, touching fondness, and looking lovingly into his eyes added, with great earnestness, "Harold, I will always thank God that He has given me such a true, faithful, unselfish and loving man as you are. You dear, dear Harold!—I am yours, have been yours, and will be for ever!"

"Oh, my darling, darling angel!" he exclaimed, taking her on his knee, and folding his arms about her and pressing her to his heart, raining kisses on her face, and head, and neck: "My darling angel, it is I who have to thank God for the noblest, purest, and most lovable gift He has ever given to man! Always in my prayers will I thank Him for this."

Thus they sat wrapped in one another's embrace, looking into each other's eyes, and saying and repeating all the old loving terms which the sexes have used to one another since God at the creation gave each to each. Ah, there is no more beautiful thing in heaven or on earth than the deep and trustful love of a pure and good girl for a youth, noble and faithful, and worthy of such affection!

And thus they sat, the blissful minutes seeming

as but moments, and all around so deeply in har-mony with such love. The little birds of all varieties hopping and fluttering through the scented branches of the flower-decked trees, were telling and singing sweetly and melodiously to each their little tales of love. On the quiet lily-covered lagoon the ducks and wildfowl seemed to be quacking of love and love and love, and seemed to regard the two happy human beings sitting under the large tree on the bank as their friends, who would do them no harm nor hurt, but, bound and made happy by the same affection, wished them well.

Chapter XXXIII

"Round the sufferer's temples bind
Wreaths that endure affliction's heaviest shower,
And do not shrink from sorrow's keenest wind."
—WORDSWORTH.

THE same evening that the little love scene
occurred, which we described in the last chapter,
a very different scene took place in the store office.
Harold, always of a naturally straightforward and
candid nature, called Mr. Brownlow to the store,
as he had something important to tell him. When
he did tell him, Mr. Brownlow burst forth, "Good
heavens, boy, of all the cheekiest things that have
ever been mooted to me, this beats them all! Sir,
you must be a rogue, as well as a fool and an ass!
Let me tell you that Athnic Brown is my nearest
relation, and in the course of nature to her I must
leave everything. You must be a rascal then to
come pretending about love and all that idiotic
nonsense, only found in novels, when your aim is
to get into a nice station in time—a well-feathered
nest, eh? The dearest object of your heart, eh?
By gosh! your heart is set on my station and ready
cash!"

"Mr. Brownlow," said Harold, with such a desperate effort to act calmly that his voice had a strange, unnatural sound, "you have called me some hard names, you have accused me of the basest and most dishonourable of motives, but I bear no resentment against you for all that, for you have judged my case, as perhaps most of the world would judge such a case, when a very poor man dares to have hopes of marrying a rich woman—or at least one with such prospects as Athnie has. But it may seem the old cant, the old hypocrisy, if I were to say that I would never have dared to hope for her (though I could not help myself loving her) if I had known that her prospects were any better than my own. Now I have come to-night to tell you all, as in all honour I think it my duty to do."

"Ah, by the gosh!" roared Mr. Brownlow in great wrath, "but you got a fine sense of honour. Ah, the devil take it! but things have come to a pretty pass. The girl has got some liking for you, granted, but will your honour take advantage of that to get hold of her money, by the jumping Jupiter?"

"We love each other," said Harold quietly, "and no consideration of money ever entered our thoughts."

"Ho! by the hokey!" broke in Mr. Brownlow, with little regard to sentiment, "a romantic love, truly, but it's the sort that soon flies out the window, when the poverty that's close at hand creeps in the door."

"We feel that we could endure any poverty for

each other," Harold calmly answered, but the perspiration stood in great beads on his forehead.

"Well, then, by thunder! sir," burst out Mr. Brownlow, "but that's what your love will have to endure. But, sir," and he looked fixedly at Harold, as he laid a warning finger on his chest, "you have some sense of decency, I know, and, by gosh! let me lay this fact before you : if Athnie does not give you up, not one red cent of my money will she ever get."

"She would be all the dearer to me without it," said Harold in a low, earnest voice. And he added after a pause, "that is, if it were possible for her to be any dearer to me than she is."

"Dearer without it, be hanged !" hotly returned Mr. Brownlow. "It's only fools and madmen talk that way, or it might be also deep, cunning rogues."

But to this Harold answered not a word, though his heart was very sore. Mr. Brownlow went on fiercely, "Now this foolish girl has become attached to you, but if you have this honour you speak of, go away and let her get over this silliness. Otherwise you bring her to poverty like your own, for I'll cut off the pair of you, and be dashed to it all, whatever she may think of it now, she will, when it is too late, regret the folly of this affair. Would you be rascal enough to take advantage of this fancy she has for you, and bring her to want and misery, hardship and poverty, to live her life in struggle and wretchedness, you love-prating fool? If you

love her at all, the greatest proof of it you can show
is to leave her—to leave her to a home and comfort,
to all that she requires and all that she will ever
want, you dunderhead! Think she'll never cast
a thought on these things when it is too late? and
by Jupiter! though she may not say so in the future,
she will feel the terrible folly of what she's done,
and when love has sobered, think she'll thank you
for what you brought her to? Of course I could
turn you out this moment without ceremony about
it, but I want to drive home to this honour you're
prating about, how much you would be consulting
the girl's happiness by leaving her for ever, by having
no correspondence, no talk, no communication with
her, and by going and letting her know nothing
about it. Believe me, she will soon forget you, and
goodness only knows what fancy she ever took to
you the first day."

During Mr. Brownlow's long and forcible speech
the most utter misery was gnawing at Harold's
heart. It showed itself only too plainly in his face,
and Mr. Brownlow, rough in speech and exterior
as he was, could not help showing in his countenance
the pity he felt for him. He turned down the
kerosene lamp a little, and there was a dead silence
for several moments. Harold covered his face with
his hands and his heart was throbbing with the
most intense pain, and his brain in a strange whirl,
as if a sudden madness were about to seize him.

"God knows," he said at last in a choking voice,

"but poverty is not the greatest misery the poor have to suffer, but it is through it that they lose all that they ever loved and hoped for and all that made life worth living."

Mr. Brownlow, feeling that it might seem he was somewhat relenting, mustered his forces, and said, with a harsh voice, "Tut, tut ; this is all nonsense! You will soon get over all this."

With that he put out the light and Harold tumbled out of the room,.feeling in his heart and soul and brain a weight of sorrow and of pain such as the noble-hearted alone can suffer. He made his way to the little neatly-papered bedroom, and there he struck a match, and with a trembling hand lit the little lamp that stood on his table. Then, as he looked round the room, and saw on the walls the dear pictures that had been hung there by the dearest of little hands—all the other little things, too, the tidies and knicknacks—put there by the hands of her he loved, his feelings entirely overcame him, and falling on his knees he burst into piteous sobs that welled up from an overflowing heart, suffering, God only knows how much.

Before him on the table lay a little book ; it was one that Athnie had given him, and in which she had written her name. He kissed it tenderly. It was "The Encheiridion" of Epictetus, and the first place he opened it he read these words : "When Thales was asked what is most universal, he answered, 'Hope, for hope stays with those who have nothing else.'"

Then in Athnie's small, neat handwriting he read her own comment: "And was the only thing left in the box given by Epimetheus to Pandora, and has ever since been a bastion to human frailty and a beacon light to all those who have been cast down."

Then he put the book in his bosom, and, kneeling down, said his prayers, longer prayers than usual, and perhaps deeper and more earnest too, certainly in greater misery of heart than it might be he ever suffered before.

Chapter XXXIV

"Alone, alone, all, all alone."
—*The Ancient Mariner*—COLERIDGE.

NEXT morning good Mrs. Brown, not seeing Harold about anywhere, went to his window and, pushing it in, looked into the room. Then, to her great surprise, she saw that the bed had not been slept in.

"Oh, Athnie," she said to her daughter, who came up at that moment, "what can have become of Harold?"

A look of alarm spread itself over Athnie's face, and in great anxiety, she lifted the latch of the door and entered the room. Two letters were on the table—one addressed to Athnie herself and the other to Mr. Brownlow. The one addressed to herself she opened at once with trembling fingers. It was all blotched and tear-stained, and evidently written with a shaking hand. As soon as Athnie read the contents, she threw herself on to Harold's bed, and burst into loud and hysterical sobs. Her mother at once called Mr. Brownlow, who came directly to the scene, and was quickly made acquainted with the state of affairs. He made the best effort he could to scowl and look fiercely, as he

broke open the envelope of Harold's letter, and read
what was there written to him. It was a most
manly, straightforward letter, telling of his decision.

Mr. Brownlow could not help feeling the pathetic
forcefulness of all that was said to him, and the
nobleness and generosity in the writer's character.
Yes, he had gone, and as Mr. Brownlow turned over
the letter in his hands after he had read it, he somehow regretted it was so.   Then, in his characteristic
way, he left the room with loud growls, and saying
that the women were always the cause of the trouble
everywhere, and why they were ever made he could
not make out, unless it was to torment man's life,
like the sandflies and mosquitoes.

Meanwhile Athnie, with tearful eyes, was reading
aloud to her mother the letter which Harold had
left for herself.   Good Mrs. Brown would every now
and then wipe her eyes with the corner of her apron,
saying: "Ah, poor Harold! poor Harold!   And how
fond he was of you, Athnie, and how we will all
miss him ; oh, how we will all miss him !"

It was a most touching letter, in which he told, in
sorrow and humbleness, the cause of his going, deem-
ing it best for Athnie's happiness that he should do
so.   Not one word of blame to Mr. Brownlow for the
part he had taken in causing him to go.   And he
said it would be the constant aim and object of his
ambition to be worthy of the love between them—to
put forth all his best energies to attain a position in
life, and—it might seem perhaps a dream—a home

such as would bring her comfort, in which love would always be, and neither poverty nor want to mar its pleasures. The love she expressed for him he would ever and always think of, and the deep love in his heart for her would make him a better and a stronger man.

"Alas! alas!" he wrote in tear-stained letters, "the truest loves have the cruellest trials. My darling, I know and trust you—that you would share poverty with me; you would help me bear misfortune, anxiety, and care, and all the hard drudgery of life. And that is why I thought it better for your dear sake that I should leave you; for I could not bring you to the narrow circumstances of my own poor life—a life that will be in the future one of struggle and of effort worthy of the sweetest and fondest remembrances that ever for a moment fell to the lot of man."

[Here the letter was greatly blotched and incoherent, but where it could be read he said that the heaven above them only knew how much he would endure with pleasure for her dear sake, and telling her that his love was so great that he would gladly sacrifice himself a thousand times rather than see her suffer a moment's pain.]

"My darling, my darling," he concluded, "however unworthy of you I may be, I know the grief you will suffer in your pure, noble little heart, when you find out what has happened, and when you are reading this. I would to God that I could be permitted

S

to bear the burden for both, and that my going
would leave no sting of pain or sorrow with you;
that what you may feel might be lifted from your
heart and added to the overwhelming load of misery
that I already feel. As for myself, Athnie, think
what you have done for me. It was through you
and for you that I was lifted from the degraded
life into which I was fast sinking; it was by you
that I was made to feel the instinct of higher and
better things; and it is to you that I owe my education, my knowledge, my all. And you I must thank
day and night and always for having given me a
hope and an aim, and a higher and nobler ideal in
life. You I must look upon as my dear, good,
guardian angel; and my most heartfelt prayers will
be ever and always for your happiness. My
darling, my darling! God bless you a thousand
times!"

They were gloomy days on the station after this.
Athnie went about as one who had lost all cheerfulness and interest in life. She had indeed grown
much thinner, and was different in every respect to
what she had been a short time before. Good Mrs.
Brown would sit perhaps in a corner of the dining-
room, patching some old clothes belonging to Harold,
and saying maybe, "Ah, poor Harold, we all miss
him now, and likely some day he'll come back, and
it will be nice for him to find his clothes in order."

Mr. Brownlow, too, was different, and, as day after

day went on, he more and more felt Harold's loss. Every now and then, thinking of this, he would break out most suddenly that women were the cause of the trouble everywhere. Then he would often catch himself thinking and wondering where Harold was, till one day a traveller brought the news that he saw a young man answering Harold's description, carrying his swag in the direction of the new goldfields.

"By gosh, it must be him!" exclaimed Mr. Brownlow. "Gone to try his luck in the diggings then, eh? Did he have no idea of making his way back this way? No! Well, be dashed to him then, but he can dig his finger-nails off for all I care!"

Chapter XXXV

" οὐ γάρ πώ τις ἑὸν γόνον αὐτὸς ἀνέγνω."
—*The Odyssey.*

HAROLD with a breaking heart tramped along the road. From time to time a terrible longing would come over him to turn back and to see Athnie once more. It was only with a great effort that he resisted acting on such impulses; but the thought that he was leaving her was often more than he could bear. Day after day went on like this, and the same great misery was gnawing at his heart—the same deep regret that he had gone away without seeing Athnie, and the same constant desire to return and be with her again.

One evening, coming on towards sundown, he saw at a turn in the road a camp-fire in the distance. When he drew nearer, he saw to his great astonishment Ponsonby Oberon; but his surprise was still greater when on looking again he saw no other than the man who had years ago adopted him—the old merchant, Mr. Merton. Yet still greater wonders were in store for Harold, for he was no sooner seen by Ponsonby Oberon than that worthy man rushed out with both arms extended, and clasping the poor wanderer to his breast, called him his long-lost son.

"Ah," he exclaimed, as he threw his cap away and gave another hug to Harold, "it's a wise father that knows his own child, as the poet says."

Harold was too much astonished to utter a word, but with a look of great surprise in his face he turned to Mr. Merton with a mute appeal, which seemed to entreat for an explanation. Mr. Merton came up, took Harold by the hand, and kissing him affectionately, said, "Yes, Harold, my poor boy, he is indeed your long-lost father."

Overcome with wonderment, Harold went and sat down on a log, and rubbing his face with the sleeve of his shirt, seemed as one dazed and recovering from an impossible and incredible dream. He uttered not a word, but kept regarding Ponsonby Oberon and Mr. Merton with a stupefied, senseless stare that only showed too plainly that his mind was beginning to wander. Small surprise if it did, for the poor fellow had suffered so terribly both in mind and body during the last week that it was wonderful how he kept up so long. He had eaten hardly anything during that time, and sleeping even less, his mind in consequence became somewhat affected, and his nerves were all in shakes and tremor. Then these incredible surprises coming on him with such startling suddenness proved almost a climax to his strength, or rather perhaps to his weakness, for he was very ill both in mind and body.

Little more, indeed, it would take for him to break down altogether. Soon that came too, for the crack of a whip was heard up the road, and a loud and familiar voice was bellowing curses at no great distance away. Harold looked up with a wild stare, and to his final bewilderment he saw his late master, Mr. Brownlow. This was too much for him, and clapping his hand to his forehead he muttered, "My God, my God, what has come over me at all!" He sank down beside the log he had been sitting on, and then his senses seemed to leave him and many strange things came to him as in a dream.

He thought Ponsonby Oberon was bending over him, and it seemed as if he could hear him saying, "It is as the poet said, a little sleep, a little slumber, a little folding of the hands to sleep." His fancy seemed, he thought, to play him strange pranks, for the most grotesque scene of all was to see Mr. Brownlow sitting near him and taking his hand tenderly, hoping he was not very ill. And he thought too he asked Mr. Brownlow how Athnie was, and the strange answer he received was that women were the rulers of the world everywhere.

*   *   *   *   *

It was now twenty-three years ago since Ponsonby Oberon had left his wife. They were only married about nine months when they found out only too surely that their modes of life could never run together. Oberon, always a happy-go-lucky, careless sort of fellow, soon got through the few pounds he had when he married. Next he went into debt as far as he could get, and finally the pressure of his necessities caused him to run away, leaving to direst poverty a wife who was shortly to become a mother.

Oberon, after his escape from his creditors, took his way up into the bush—that refuge of the pariah, the spendthrift, and the ne'er-do-weel—and there he got employment droving. The first five pounds he earned he sent at once to his wife's address. But after a time an envelope came to him from the Dead-Letter Office returning his five-pound note, as well as his affectionate letter to his wife. Then Oberon having by this time earned another £5 hastened off to see what had become of his wife. He was in a great state of excitement all the while, and he made enquiries about everywhere in such a wild, erratic manner, quoting poets and throwing his cap off here and there, that people thought he was a lunatic at large. However the few pounds did not last Oberon long ; he had to go back once more to the bush, and never again did he see his wife, or hear what had become of her.

When Oberon left her she changed her name to Effermere—her grandfather's name. She somehow found her way down to Sydney, and there she got odd jobs of washing clothes and scrubbing floors and such-like. Then Harold was born, and that was the hardest trial of all, for on that day there was not a bite or sup in the place, and there seemed no prospect for the poor woman but to perish with her babe by starvation and want. Truly she had come to a terrible state of misery and suffering, and it would be hard to conjecture what the miserable end would have been, had not God in His mercy sent good Mrs. Merton to the relief. The reader already knows the rest.

Now it is a most wonderful thing how strange chances do sometimes come to pass: perhaps it is the will of Heaven that it should be so. Well, when Ponsonby Oberon delivered Mr. Brownlow's cattle to the agents he went down to the office to be settled up with. There he was introduced to a fine-looking old gentleman, who had come to invest some money in station property, and who was told Ponsonby Oberon would be able to give him full information about the run he was making terms for. They were not talking long when Oberon, in his wild way of touching on everything, mentioned the name of Harold Effermere. Thereupon the old gentleman jumped to his legs, saying hurriedly, "What, Harold Effermere! Did you ever hear him speak of me? He was my adopted son."

"By Heavens!" exclaimed Oberon, "are you the same Mr. Merton? Shake hands again. Did I ever hear him speak of you? Ah, many a time and oft, as the poet said, and always with the deepest gratitude and the greatest praise."

From that it led to old Mr. Merton telling the story of Harold's childhood; how Mrs. Merton had found mother and child in dreadful poverty, and how Mr. Merton himself came to adopt the boy. Then he told the story of Harold's mother; her desertion by her husband, with whom she only lived a few months, and finally that he was a drover of the name of Ponsonby Oberon.

Upon this Oberon exclaimed with the wildest gestures, "What is this I hear at all! After many years, as the poet said, the news has come at last. Know you not, sir, that I am the same Ponsonby Oberon? After the fitful fever of many years, as the poet said, I now know all. So Harold Effermere is my son! My Heaven, but of all the strange things that ever came to pass in God's unlimited creation, as the poet said, this surpasses them all—surpasses all understanding, surpasses all that might be dreamt of or imagined."

Then he got up and walked about the room, pulling his hair and going on in a strange frenzy with a multitude of misquotations, and a wild, mad, fiery gleam in his eye, and the look of a man generally who had taken a final farewell of his poor chaotic senses.

Well, we need not say any more about Ponsonby Oberon's behaviour on that occasion. It was highly characteristic of the man, and might perhaps, from a knowledge of his peculiarities, be better imagined than described. In short, then, Ponsonby Oberon received from Mr. Merton a full account of Harold's childhood and boyhood days, and in return Oberon told Mr. Merton the full history of the later career of the wanderer. Ponsonby Oberon told all after his own style of narration, which was a rich mosaic

work of misquotations. It happened that the station
Mr. Merton was about to purchase was situated at
no great distance from Mr. Brownlow's place, and
was a large straggling run with a neglected herd,
fully two-thirds of which were unbranded. It was
this fact that induced Mr. Merton to purchase the
station—for he was getting it on very low terms—
taking a book muster, and of course would not have
to pay for any of the unbranded cattle.

Now Mr. Merton, whatever his hard business principles might be, had a good heart, and somehow the
feeling clung to him that, though Harold was no
relation or connection of his, still, for the sake of the
old associations, he felt it almost a duty that he owed
the young wanderer a helping hand, should he be
deserving of it. His object then in going up into
the bush was to inspect and take delivery of his new
purchase, and to give the management of it to
Harold, should he have sufficient knowledge of stock
and station affairs to take charge of a cattle run.

Chapter XXXVI

"All that is pure, and sweet, and beautiful
Is born of pain."
—*The Two Goblets.*—Geo. Essex Evans.

POOR Harold was very ill all that night, and the next day. They made a bed for him in the bottom of the wagonette, and continued their journey, Mr. Brownlow returning with them. It seemed strange that he should be turning back now, as he told Mr. Merton and Ponsonby Oberon that he was just on his way to purchase a lot of bulls. It seemed strange also that he should want the bulls, for it was only a short time before that he had bought a mob—sufficient to do him for the next twelve months. However, on they went, Mr. Brownlow riding alongside of the wagonette, and Harold every now and then looking out at him with a strange, puzzled stare, that seemed to question his presence in such a place.

Ponsonby Oberon rode in the buggy with Mr. Merton. From time to time he would look back at Harold, and say, "So, my son, you were about once more to become a wanderer on the face of the earth, as the poet said. Ah, I know full well the reason," he would whisper to Mr. Merton, at the same time taking a cautious glance around to see where Mr.

Brownlow was. "The reason is, that old master of mine is a regular Turk to live with. Only I have had the patience of a saint, for all these years I could never have got along with him at all. And as for himself and Harold running in double harness, why it is, as the poet said, 'Crabbed age and youth cannot live together.'"

Harold remained very ill all through; and when they arrived at Mr. Brownlow's station very late one night, he was taken from the wagonette and put straight to bed, in the old familiar little room, which was connected with some of the saddest and sweetest memories of his life.

Presently good Mrs. Brown came in, bringing a cup of soup, which she laid down beside him, and then taking his thin, wasted hand, said affectionately, "Poor, poor Harold; I would have hardly known you. Oh, how ill and weary you are looking!"

Harold turned his eyes gratefully towards her, and smiling sadly, said, "And Athnic, how is she? Dear, dear little Athnic, I could never live without her; and oh, Mrs. Brown, I can never tell you how much it cost me to go away, and how much I have suffered since. And why and how I am here now I cannot tell, for so many strange things have happened lately, that I sometimes think it is one long dream."

"Ah," said Mrs. Brown, in her good, motherly, affectionate way; "you must rest now, Harold; you must not think about anything, but get well again as soon as you can. Here, take this soup, and

then have a long sleep, like a good, dear fellow.
Things will be better with you by-and-by."

Harold obeyed like a little child, and after that he
laid over on his pillow, and smiling, looked up at the
ceiling, and then at Athnie's dear little pictures on
the wall, and at all the other sweet, familiar little
things that were to him as dear as life. Then kind
Mrs. Brown settled the pillow under his head, and
said to him, "Harold, you will now go to sleep,
won't you?" And he answered obediently that he
would. Then she held out her hand to him to say
"Good-night"; and the returned wanderer took her
good, motherly hand between his own wasted palms,
and said—two tears running down his worn cheeks—
"Good-night, Mrs. Brown, and God bless you; and
dear Athnie, too—always and always." Then Mrs.
Brown took away the light, and Harold, with the
prayers of his childhood on his lips, closed his eyes,
and as a weary infant went to sleep.

After a while, Mr. Merton and Mr. Brownlow came
into the room—very quietly too, so as not to disturb
the sleeper. They lit a small bedroom lamp, and
turned down the shade.

"Poor fellow," said Mr. Merton; "he is sleeping
very quietly now, and looks very much better than
I have seen since his illness. So this is all true
that you tell me about him?"

"True!" echoed Mr. Brownlow. "By gosh, sir,
he's a trump. I can tell you I'm no easy man to
deal with, besides; but for all the abuse I slung at

him, I never had an impudent word from him. He's
always done his duty to the letter, and, by hokey, he
would take such pains to learn everything that was
taught him, that with all the curses that I used to
crowd on to him, I could not help but liking him.
Confound him, I don't know why! You'd think he
was born among cattle to see the way he picked up
all about them ; and it was the same with everything
else."

"Well, you cannot know how pleased I am to hear
all that," said Mr. Merton. "At school he had the
reputation of being a wild boy, with no taste nor
desire for study ; and certainly when he came home
he showed the fruits of it, for he knew nothing.
Now you tell me he has tried to remedy the results
of his own neglect at school."

"Why, he had not a spare minute but he was at
his books," said Mr. Brownlow. "I know I often
wanted to get a slant at him to give him a regular
broadside, be gosh, for going reading when he should
be at my work; but the fact is, I must admit, that
he had a time for both. Not that I approve of too
much learning at all, myself. No, no; I think it
presses on to a man's brain-pan, and squelches
foolery and idiocy out of him, like Ponsonby Oberon,
who's got so much learning that he can quote a poet
for anything ; but for all that he's a cursed natural-
born fool, as you can see for yourself."

"Well, well," said Mr. Merton ; "now that we've
talked over this matter, and seen that Harold is

right and sleeping quietly, let us also get to bed ourselves."

With these words they were leaving the room, when they were met at the door by Ponsonby Oberon, who was coming into Harold's room with a cup of strong tea in one hand, and a lump of buttered toast on a plate in the other.

"Where are you going to with that?" asked Mr. Brownlow, catching Oberon by the shoulders, and turning him out of the room, the door of which he quietly closed.

To this question Ponsonby Oberon answered, his eyes getting to blaze up, "Is there any need to ask? Can't you see that I am going to succour the distressed, as the good father attends to the wants of his offspring, so the poet said. I have made some toast for Harold with my own hands, and some good strong tea, that will make him feel as fresh as a sea breeze."

"Hear now, by the hokey," broke in Mr. Brownlow; "just turn back with the whole thing at once. Strong tea to a fellow that wants sleep and rest, and then to wake him up at this time of night to take it, too! By the gosh, Ponsonby, but you're getting more and more of a fool every day. Dash my wig, do you want to keep him awake all night, you confounded batter-brained idiot?"

Ponsonby Oberon laid down the tea and toast with such haste that the one was spilt, and the other rolled over on the floor. Then he pulled off his cap, which he seemed to wear almost day and night, and threw it with all the force he could muster against the wall of the house. Mr. Merton thought that the excited drover was preparing to fight, so he laid his hand on him with a soothing touch, and said, " Come, come now, Mr. Oberon, calm yourself, will you ? Really, though Mr. Brownlow used rather forcible language——"

" I have the steady calmness of a haloed saint, as the poet said," broke in Oberon, and he went on in such grand heroics that Mr. Merton thought he must be drunk. But Mr. Brownlow seemed to take no notice of him, and explained that it was only Pon-sonby Oberon's peculiar form of madness that made him go on like that. " The madness," he said, " of a natural-born fool." Then he ordered Oberon off to bed, and told him not to come disturbing Harold any more that night.

" I obey," exclaimed Oberon, as he walked off with a wild gesture; " that obedience which, as the poet said, has always been the bane of my genius."

Chapter XXXVII

Love—in a hut, with water and a crust,
Is—Love, forgive us !—cinders, ashes, dust.
—Lamia—KEATS.

AFTER what we have told in the last chapter, two or three days passed away, and Harold was getting gradually better, and regaining his strength. But he saw nothing of Athnie during that time, and he often wondered and wondered what could be the cause. Once when he had been asleep he woke up very suddenly, and as he did so, he thought he saw the flutter of a white dress, as it vanished out at the door. But when he came to think over it, he knew he must be mistaken, for he heard no footfall, and he saw nothing further. He turned his head around and his eyes fell on some delicacy, which had been prepared for him and left on the table beside him.

"God bless good Mrs. Brown," he exclaimed, at the sight of this; "she is always doing me all sorts of little kindnesses whilst I am asleep."

That evening he was able to get up and walk about a little. A small slab and bark-roofed dairy was the nearest house to him as he went out from

T

his own room. Seeing the door of this building open, he went over and walked in. How great was his surprise and delight to see Athnie there. She was all alone, and did not see him, for her back was turned towards the door, and she was bending over a milk-dish—carefully skimming off the cream. Gently he walked over towards her, and she did not hear him. He laid his hand softly on her shoulder, and said, in a quivering voice, "My darling Athnie."

She dropped the skimmer from her hand, and, trembling and much agitated, looked up at him with bashful eyes—the blood coming and going in her cheeks all the while. He strove to take her in his arms, but she put out her hand, and with a gesture kept him off.

"I am glad to see you are getting better," said she; "you have been very ill."

She was trembling all the while, and her voice seemed to choke her.

"I believe I have been ill," said Harold, with a far away tone in his voice. "Something appears to have been the matter with me. I feel dazed and stupid now, and there are so many things seem to me as a dream—a terrible dream and nightmare they appear to have been, but at times, and here and there, a vision of sweeter things." The sad expression on his face touched her woman's heart, and she said, in a voice full of tenderness and pity, "Poor Harold." And thus her love had overcome her pride, and the next moment they were in one

another's arms, and Harold felt that the happiness of
that moment compensated for all the misery he had
suffered. After a while, he looked at her pleadingly,
and said, " My darling, you have been distant with
me."

"Oh Harold," she replied, in her sweet, loving
voice, " I thought you could have never really loved
me, or you would not have gone away without me."

" My sweetest," he said tenderly, " it was the very
greatness of my love for you that made me go
away."

" Ah, but without me, Harold," she urged, " without
me."

" My dearest," he said, " could you be content with
a poor man's lot, in a boundary rider's hut ? "

She turned her pure, trusting eyes on him, and
said, " And why not, my Harold, dear? the greatest
happiness is often in the humblest cot."

" Ah, but consider it, Athnie; consider what it
would mean."

" I *have* considered it, Harold," said she, with deep
earnestness, "and I know with you I should be
happy, if it were only a sheet of bark we had to live
under."

He could not refrain from clasping her to his heart
again, and exclaiming, " Oh, my darling, I never
thought your love for me could be like this." He
kissed her again and again, and at last she broke
away from him, and laughing, said, " You'll have to
help me skim these dishes now. You bad boy, you

have caused me to waste so much valuable time, that you must now try and make up for it."

' Let me do it all, Athnie," said he eagerly, as he took up a skimmer, and proceeded, in a very clumsy and inexperienced manner, to take the cream off the dishes.

ₑ Ah, but you mustn't dip down like that," said Athnie, standing over him, and giving him a playful box on the ear. "You dear, foolish, stupid, awkward fellow, you are taking up the thick milk, as well as the cream."

She attempted to take the skimmer from him, but he seized her hand, and pressed it so that she cried out, "Harold, Harold!" Then he kissed the little hand ever so tenderly, and said he could eat it. And for that she again boxed his ears, and playfully hunted him out of the dairy altogether.

Well, all this is very foolish no doubt—very foolish to us old fellows, who cannot understand the sweet foolery of love, and all the delicious nonsense which overflows between the young hearts of boys and girls.

Chapter XXXVIII

" For rum and everlasting 'baccy lusting,
   And altogether filthy and disgusting."
          —*A Piccaniny*—J. BRUNTON STEPHENS.

" WHY here you are, my son, 'full of life and
youthful vigour,' as the poet said. Be gosh,
only yesterday evening I was looking for you everywhere. I wanted to give you a piece of paternal
advice on things in general, for, as the poet said,
' Train up a boy in the way he should go, and when
he is old he will not depart from it.' "

This was the morning after the little affair of the
last chapter, and, needless to say, the speaker was
Ponsonby Oberon, and his characteristic speech was
addressed to Harold, who was just returning from a
morning walk, and was feeling happier and better
and stronger than he had done for a long time

Ponsonby Oberon clapped Harold two or three
times on the back, and continued,—

" Now, my boy, your fortune is made if you only
have the grit and tact of your father. As the poet
said, a chance comes to every man at least once in a
life time, Yours has now come, and if it is a case of

'like father like son,' as the poet said, you will make the most of your opportunity, and, Harold, be a credit to me."

Harold looked at him in some surprise. Oberon, giving him an occasional enthusiastic clap on the back, went on,—

"Yes, my son, you are to get the management of this new place that Mr. Merton has bought; that is, of course, if you prove up to the high water-mark of his expectations, as the poet said. And now I have to give you the advice of an old dog of the roads, and that is, a little judicious flattery covers a multitude of sins, as the poet said. The love of praise is the weak point of every man; and now, my son, Mr. Merton is the man you must give a broadside to in that quarter. You must hold by the talent you inherited from me, the advantage which my genius obtained for you."

"In that you are mistaken in me," said Harold quietly, "for I will flatter no man to obtain a favour for myself, and what is more, I will compliment no man who has done me a good turn."

"Ah, the same old conscience that troubled you when we were travelling on the game," exclaimed Oberon impatiently.

He was prevented from going on farther, and warming up to his subject, for just then the bell rang for breakfast, and Mr. Brownlow's great loud voice called out at the same time,—

"Come here, you two fellows; let us get along

with our tucker, for we have no time to spare if we are to get to the ' Yellow Water-hole ' to-day."

" Yes, yes," said Oberon to Harold, " we are all making a start for Mr. Merton's new place to-day, and all going well, should get there the day after to-morrow. But what old Brownlow wants coming with us for, dash me if I know, for, as the poet said, he will be more a hindrance than a help, and he will be croaking like a bull frog all the while."

This last sentence he uttered in a very low and cautious tone, taking good care, of course, that his employer did not catch any of it.

However, after breakfast off they started, Mr. Merton and Mr. Brownlow in the buggy, and Harold and Ponsonby Oberon riding on horseback. In short, then, towards the evening of the third day, the party arrived within sight of the station they were about to take possession of. As they drew nearer a crowd of hungry-looking blacks' dogs ran out to yelp at them. The homestead itself was situated in a semicircle of native humpies and gumpas, which were composed of grass and boughs, some of them being partially plastered over with mud. Out of each of these vile dwellings came forth from one to half-a-dozen foul-smelling, dirty, rag-clothed Aborigines. There were males and females; some were old, and others appeared young, but all looked as if they belonged to some wretched lazar-house, where only the most nauseous and terrible diseases were dealt with. Ah, yes, they were indeed a poor, miser-

able, pitiable, disgusting lot, as they swarmed around
the buggy, asking, in broken English, " Where come
from ? " " Which way come up ? " " You got 'em
terbacca ? " and such like. Every now and then
some old black fellow or Jin would throw a stick at
the yellow barking curs all around. From time to
time, too, the miserable, starving dogs would take to
fighting amongst themselves, and then there would
be such noise as was never heard before—black
fellows cursing and swearing in a mixture of English
and their own tongue ; decrepit-looking old Jins
jabbering and screaming away, and dealing out blows
here and there on the groups of snapping, yelling
dingoes that seemed to be without limit. Ponsonby
Oberon exclaimed,—

" It is, as the poet said, ' chaos and confusion all
embroiled, and discord with a thousand various
sounds.' "

He had scarcely uttered the words when some
yelping dingoes nipped his horse's heels, and straightway the animal gave a kick up and a plunge, and
poor Oberon was laid over in the filth and ashes of a
black fellow's camp. Immediately half a dozen Jins
gathered around him, wiping the dust and ashes off
him, and sympathising with him after their manner
in their own poor kindness of heart.

" Poor fellow, you," they said, slapping him with
greasy hands, which left more dirt than they wiped
off; " poor fellow, you ; too much a stupid cobra.
Can't savvy which way ridem buck a jumpa."

Oberon had been smoking at the time of his fall, and his beautiful meerschaum was now in the mouth of a grey-headed, greasy, old black fellow, who came up smoking it, and asked if he might keep it for his honesty. Ponsonby Oberon, in his confusion and wild excitement, snapped the pipe from the black fellow and put it in his pocket. Then, thinking over what he did, he took it out again and threw it off as far as he could heave it. Immediately there was a wild scramble of Jins and black fellows to get the "budgery fellow pipo, cranky fellow, white fellow, throw away."

Mr. Merton was now laughing till the tears streamed down his cheeks. A short time before he had been calling out, in the most utter disgust,—

"My God, my God, what sort of a place is this I have bought at all?"

Ponsonby Oberon's horse was now careering down the road, followed by half-a-dozen yelping dogs, and Harold racing as fast as his horse could go to try and catch the runaway.

"Here, come, come," said Mr. Brownlow impatiently, in a loud, gruff voice, "get up in the buggy, Ponsonby. Nature has made a natural-born fool of you enough without you making matters any worse."

Oberon, with much slapping of his chest and wild gesticulation, obeyed, quoting poets and thundering wrath all the while. The buggy went on a little farther, and then stopped at a little low slab hut, roughly thatched with coarse grass, the only building

that had even the remotest pretensions to the name
of house.   Here there were also crowds of blacks, and
the place all round was strewn with bullocks' bones,
dirt, and rubbish of the most evil-smelling varieties.
There was no sign of a white man to be seen anywhere, and, excepting for a few pots and pans and
dirty cooking utensils here and there, the place might
be taken for a blacks' camp.

"Is there any one at home?" shouted Mr.
Brownlow.

No answer.

"Is there any one at home here?" repeated Mr.
Brownlow, in a loud and terrible voice.

Immediately there was a shuffling of feet and jabbering inside the hut. Then the door opened, and
a woebegone looking man came out and stood blink-
ing stupidly in the light of the setting sun.

Chapter XXXIX

"And the cattle we hunt, they are racing in front,
  With a roar like the thunder of waves.
  —*Song of the Cattle Hunters*—HENRY KENDALL.

YES, a woebegone looking man he certainly appeared to be. He shaded his eyes with his hands, and looking up with a puzzled stare, said, "Oh, you're the gentleman come to take delivery of the station. Get down, get down, turn your horses out, and come and have some supper. I got no cook or stockman here just at present. Knocking along the best way I can. Things are a bit rough, as you may see, but I suppose you're bushmen, and don't mind that."

"Ah, by Heaven!" said Ponsonby Oberon, slapping his chest, "we're bushmen, but there is even a limit to endurance, as the poet said." Then turning to Mr. Merton and Mr. Brownlow, he continued, "Let us go and camp down at the creek. Why, this cursed cabooche is only a blacks' camp at large."

Mr. Merton, though not admiring the way the suggestion was put, still felt it was the best thing they could do. So he said politely, "As you have no cook, and there is a big party of us, I think it would be the best if we rigged our tents down by the water-hole. You see otherwise we would be putting you to a lot of trouble."

"Well, yes," said the man, "perhaps, now, it would be the best. You see things, as I say, are a bit rough here, and, anyhow, I'm run ashore for tucker."

Mr. Brownlow, who was driving, touched up the horses, saying, "Well, let us go and get turned out, then."

"I never thought, Brownlow," said Mr. Merton, "that that man could come down so low and be such a wreck. I know his family, and they are highly respectable. He has one brother a leading barrister, and another a doctor with a wide practice, and there is a sister of his a leader of fashion."

"There is a black sheep and a ne'er-do-weel in every family," said Mr. Brownlow gruffly.

"Your ne'er-do-weel, after all, is only genius run to seed," said Ponsonby Oberon, standing in the back of the buggy and clapping his chest.

"Ah, and by gosh, man, what sort of a fellow is a natural-born fool run very much to poetry and to seed?" said Mr. Brownlow, as he turned round and looked at Oberon. "What is the difference now, I ask?"

"By Heaven, sir!" exclaimed Ponsonby Oberon, throwing his cap down in the bottom of the buggy, "if you had asked what is the difference between a learned man like myself and an uneducated man, I could have answered you in the words of the philosopher and poet, the same difference there is between a live man and a dead one."

With these words he jumped out of the buggy and took his horse from Harold, who had just come up leading the animal by a broken bridle.

"Well, we'll camp here," said Mr. Brownlow, pulling up the horses beside a lily-covered lagoon. "And I have to remark that it's a nice place for any fellow who's been rolling in the blacks' camp to jump in and knock some of the muck and stink off himself."

But Ponsonby Oberon did not hear this, and so there was no reply to the remark.

We need not be too lengthy at this point. Next morning the man in charge of the station came down, and Mr. Merton made known to him that he wished to be shown over the run, as he wanted to see the country, cattle, horses, and anything connected with the place. Horses were got up and off they started. After travelling for an hour or so they got amongst the cattle, but they were so wild that it was as much as Harold, Oberon, and Mr. Brownlow could do to round them up and steady them. Mr. Merton, who was no horseman, did not go out of a canter. When he came to where the cattle were rounded up, Ponsonby Oberon shouted out, " By Heaven, sir ! this herd has gone to want and wreck with a vengeance, as the poet said. They're as wild as March hares, and there is only an odd one here and there that's branded. What the neighbours have been doing that they didn't soch their stamp on to them is a thing that knocks me into ' pye.' "

Mr. Merton looked at them and rode round them, saying, " It's only too true ; there are far more unbranded than otherwise."

Mr. Brownlow, with a laugh and a curse, uttered the grim and suggestive joke, that it was like his confounded luck that this unbranded herd weren't a bit nearer to him.

Just then something again startled the mob, and they split into a dozen lots and rushed in all directions through the thick Gydia scrub. All that day they had the same experience, both cattle and horses were as wild almost as they would be in their natural state, and for the most part there was only a percentage of them branded up.

In the evening, as they were riding back, Mr. Merton and Mr. Brownlow dropped some distance behind the others. " Well," said the former, " what do you think of it all, Brownlow ? "

" Think of it ! " shouted Mr. Brownlow with a curse. " Be gosh, Merton, it would take a dozen heroes two years, working day and night, to straighten up this herd. They are utterly gone to pot altogether. It would take a good man on a trained race horse to catch some of the mobs, and when he does, he might as well try to hold the wind as keep them. Why, man, there is not so much as a yard on the place that would hold a pet calf. A man would have to work like a giant and a bullock to go anywhere near putting this station right. Dash my wig, sir, how did this man ever come to get charge of the place at all, and what sort of asses of owners must they be, that they did not make him double quick march long ago."

"He was looking after the place for two rich cousins of his, who knew nothing whatsoever about pastoral affairs," said Mr. Merton. "They got disgusted with their sinking fund at last, and put the place up to auction, and sold it for whatever it would fetch. I had been told by a very reliable authority that there were six times more cattle on the place than showed in the books, and as it was sold on a book muster, I considered that I had a great bargain."

"Ah, well, it's most likely it will turn out a dear bargain for you in the long run," said Mr. Brownlow, with brutal candour. "That's what you townsmen get for not sticking to what you understand."

Mr. Merton rode along for some distance after this with his head down and feeling very much dispirited. At last he looked up suddenly and said, "Brownlow, as an old and experienced bushman, what would you advise me to do?"

"Advise you to do," repeated Mr. Brownlow, with a jeering laugh; "why, sir, I would advise you to try and find bigger fools than yourself, and get them to buy your pig in a poke, as the saying is."

Mr. Merton was silent again for a while. He naturally felt the bluff counsel of the rough old squatter. At last he said, with some decision, "No,

Brownlow, I'll give it a trial, anyhow, before I put the place in the market again."

"Well, you got stacks of money, Merton," said Mr. Brownlow, "and of course you can please yourself in the choice of a hobby ; but I should think, be gosh, something in the way of a model farm in the suburbs of a town would be more in your line. But, man, if you ever do get this herd straightened up, what will the most of them be but stags and scally-wags."

"Well, I'll give Harold a chance to do something with the place," said Mr. Merton.

"It will be your last chance," replied Mr. Brownlow ; "he'll do the best he can, that you may depend on."

Just then Harold dropped back, and Mr. Brownlow shouted to him, in his loud, gruff voice, "By gosh, me shaver, this is a nice thing Mr. Merton is going to do for you—going to give you a cheque book and a free hand to run this station to the last degree of destruction. Ah, by Jupiter, me boy, won't you have a fine time of it—won't you make things hum over in the little township ? You'll turn artist, too, and paint it red."

Mr. Merton turned to Harold and said, "Yes, it is all true. I am going to give you full charge of this place : you'll have a cheque book, as Mr. Brownlow says, and an account in the bank as well, and you will do the best you can in my interests, will you not ? "

"Ah, that I will, Mr. Merton," said Harold earnestly; "that I will, sir, and it will not be my fault if things are not to your satisfaction. Mr. Merton, I have to thank you again and again for your very great kindness to me."

Chapter XL

" Sed res docuit id verum esse quod in carminibus Appius ait,
' Fabrum esse suae quemque fortunae.' "
—PSEUDO-SALLUST.

WELL, good reader, we suppose you would like to know how Harold got on in the heavy duties which he had undertaken. As you are anxious to know them, perhaps it might be as well if we just give you a brief summary of what he did. Be it remembered in the first place, then, that it is just a year and ten months since he took charge of Mr. Merton's station, and now we will tell you in a few words what he accomplished in that time. Mr. Merton, as he said, gave Harold a free hand, and placed ample funds at his disposal to work and manage the place.

The first thing the new manager did was to set half a dozen good, capable men to work making a proper stockyard. They did not lose much time over the work, as they were to get a bonus if they had it completed by a certain date. When the yard was finished, he sent the men to make three other branding places on different parts of the run where the cattle were thickest, and after that he had large tailing yards made all over the station, and on the back creeks and places where they were most required. But in the meantime, and immediately after the first yard was finished, the real business for Harold commenced. He succeeded in getting three or four good stockmen, and these, with seven black boys, composed his mustering staff.

Day after day Harold and his party went out, coming in late in the evenings with great bellowing mobs of cattle, which would often break and rush in all directions when it came to yarding them up. But they used generally to manage to get them all in after a lot of trouble and chasing of obstinate runaways. Then next morning, very early, they would draft the calves from the cows, and after breakfast they would be branding for the remainder of the day. Such calves as they were too: some of them would be three and four years old, and in a great number of cases the calf and its mother would be branded the same day. There were even instances where three generations of clean skins were branded at the one time.

As soon as one mob was branded no time would be lost in going out to get in another. But the getting them—that was the trouble. Many and many a time Harold came out of the thick Mulga scrub with hardly a rag of clothes on him. He might perhaps have the collar of his shirt or the waistband of his trousers, but that would be about all—the bristling scrub could account for all the rest. Once he was charged by a wild bull, and was turned over, horse and all. It was a miracle that he was not killed, but as it was he did not recover for several days. On several occasions the horse he had been riding was severely horned. Once going at a terrible pace through the timber, the animal he was riding went into a hole, and turning a complete somersault broke its neck, and coming over on Harold's leg at the same time, pinned him to the ground. There he might have died, had not fortunately one of the stockmen come that way and released him from his position. He had to be brought home in a cart and suffered terribly for several days.

One day a horse was brought in that none of the stockmen would ride. It was a splendid-looking animal, but had all the vices of the devil. "Very well," said Harold, as the men one and all refused to have anything to do with the brute; "very well," I will not ask any of you to do anything of this sort that I cannot do myself." With these words he put his own bridle on the animal, which had to be held by two strong men to get it saddled up. The girths were hardly tightened when the brute broke away, and with terrible squeals, roars and grunts, plunged and bucked about the yard in a most terrific manner.

The stockmen all ranged themselves on the top rail of the fence, and had their own remarks to make, such as, "By jingo, he's a corker; I knew him when he smashed Sam Hennis's leg." "I remember when he stove a nigger's skull in," and a third told how he got rid of a crack rider and was a month in the bush with the saddle on. They all agreed that the boss was a "pluckton" as they said, but were afraid that he would have more than he could deal with this time.

They were mistaken. Harold rode the horse without the least difficulty, despite all its efforts to get rid of him. But when the rails were let down, the mad brute plunged out through the opening, and being badly mouthed tore off, bucking, plunging and bolting at a most ungovernable rate. As the animal raced off at a furious pace for the scrub, the men sitting on the stockyard exclaimed almost with one voice, "God Almighty, he'll be killed in the timber!" Next moment they saw the vicious animal dart into the scrub, then seemed to plunge over a mass of dead trees, and giving a terrible buck reared over, crushing Harold on a heap of falling branches and decaying logs.

The men carried him to the house, and after a while, opening his eyes, he looked at them and said, "The accident is a bit of bad luck; but, boys, all of you go and camp out on Myrtle Creek to-day, and muster all the unbranded cattle there, and hold them in the big tailing yard up the creek. I will meet you the day after to-morrow."

The men went out, saying, "More likely it will be the week after to-morrow after the smashing up he has got."

But Harold, though terribly bruised, kept to his word, and towards the evening of the third day they saw him, to their great surprise, coming across the plain. But their astonishment was, indeed, many times greater, when they saw that he was mounted on the animal that had dealt so foully with him only three days before.

We just give that little incident down as an instance of Harold's varied experiences. We now hasten to matters of more importance.

In nine months all the yards were made, and before the year was out there was not an unbranded calf on the place over six months old. After that Harold mustered all the stags on the station, some fifteen hundred in round numbers, and he sent them off to the boiling down, where, although they only netted twelve and sixpence per head, still they more than paid for all the improvements he had put up. Then he sent away all the marketable bullocks that were fat to the Sydney market, and realized splendid results. Next he sold 4,000 cull cattle at an average of thirty shillings a head, and then he spayed all the worst of the breeders that were left, and weaned and herded all his young cattle. After that he got up a splendid lot of well-bred bulls, and thus made a great move towards the future improvement of the herd.

As for the horses, he sold them all off excepting about 150 of the best, and these he kept in two horse paddocks, and always had them quiet and convenient.

But to our lady readers all this will have little

interest. They will no doubt be asking how about his relationship with Athnie all this time. Well, we shall have much pleasure in saying just a few words on that point. Harold had a private interview with Mr. Brownlow some time after taking charge of the station. What he said we do not know exactly, but the sturdy old squatter was heard to exclaim, "Oh, dash your buttons for a pair of fools! I won't trouble myself any more about the affair. Yes, you can come over here as often as you like, but mind, be gosh, that you don't collar any of my calves when you're going back. You got the name of being dead nuts on anything that's not branded, and now that you got Mr. Merton's herd cleaned up, you'll be wanting to keep your hand in on mine."

Harold took Mr. Brownlow's hand saying, "Sir, let me thank you ever so much for your kindness. You do not know how happy you have made me."

"Oh, be off with you," burst out Mr. Brownlow, in his gruff way. "Dash my wig, but you're a fool—be gosh, you are."

Well, after that Harold would be over as often as he could spare the time, and he would take the old walks with Athnie—the old delicious rambles by the river bank—but what they said to each other on those occasions it is not for us to repeat. Sometimes Mr. Brownlow would look out, and seeing them together would exclaim, "By gosh, to think that that fellow should have such a reputation as a manager, and being a level-headed fellow and all that, when I see him acting the fool before my very eyes."

Mr. Brownlow used often to make that remark, and before Ponsonby Oberon went away with the fats, the reply would always be, "'*Acting* the fool,' you say, my master! But know you not what the poet says, 'It takes a wise man to act the fool. Harold is a true son of a worthy father, in fact, like father like son, and acting well his part where all the honour lies, as the poet said."   With that he would slap his chest with both hands and look proudly at Mr. Brownlow, who would return the look with a dreadful scowl and burst out, "You cackling poet-quoting idiot! Talk about acting the fool ; I tell you, sir, that no one can do the part of a fool properly but the natural-born fool himself."

Chapter XLI

"But ne'er on lovelier bride than thine
   Looked these delighted eyes of mine ;
And ne'er in happier bridal bower
   Than hers smiled rose and orange-flower."
              —FITZ-GREENE HALLECK.

THESE little chronicles are now fast drawing to a close, but there is one happy scene we must not forget to mention before saying "farewell."

It was a most beautiful day in the end of April—beautiful in every respect. The sky was clear, the air was cool, and the strange, sweet odour of the wild flowers floated in the zephyr. On the shady side of the garden the dew still glittered on the blushing rosebuds, and the sweet young grass matted the country all around with an emerald carpet, fresh and clean and beautiful. Perched on the giant eucalypt, the melodious magpie warbled his sweetest notes, deep, joyous and clear. On the smaller bushes great varieties of curious little, hopping, fluttering birds twittered and screeched, whistled and cooed, a marvellous medley of songs. Great gorgeous butterflies came fluttering lazily along on perfumed wings, and tasting daintily of every flower, floating backwards and forwards, hovering over plant and bush, lighting now for a moment, and opening and shutting their great vari-coloured wings, as they drank in the honey from the flowers. In short, we may say a delicious scene, and one to make glad the heart of any man who was not altogether devoid of the sense of appreciating the highest poetry of all—the poetry of Nature, and the deep, sweet sense of the beautiful and the sublime.

Here then we have to describe another scene.

In the middle of the garden a great marquee was erected, whilst all about the enclosure there were smaller tents. All suddenly from one of these we hear a familiar voice calling out in excited tones, "By the hokey, Lenden, old man, what have you done with my other boot? Here I am the proud father of a worthy and happy son, and am I to go to his marriage in a few minutes' time with only one boot on? It is not as if I was about to lose a son, as the poet said, but I am to gain a daughter. Come, disgorge the boot, for there's not a moment to spare."

Ponsonby Oberon was going about from tent to tent blaming every one in turn for having taken his boot.

Presently Mr. Brownlow came along and called out, "What's this devil of a racket you're kicking up here for a mad fool? And what the deuce have you been throwing the bed-clothes about like this for? And here's a pillow-slip laying in the dirt, and, by gosh, if there's not a boot in it!"

Ponsonby Oberon slapped his chest with great vigour, and, coming over, exclaimed, "By heaven, sir, it is, as the poet said, by losing we are rendered sager. I mind me now I put it in the pillow-case myself last night just to have a playful whack at young Mr. Lenden. Ah, all is not lost that's carefully put away!"

"Carefully put away!" echoed Mr. Brownlow. "By Jupiter, sir, you want carefully putting away in a lunatic asylum yourself. Here are these two fools, who are going to try whether marriage is a failure or not, just waiting to be hitched, and you fooling round this way at the last moment."

In spite of Mr. Brownlow's contempt for love and marriage, and all that relates to the married state, there was a look almost of happiness on his rugged old face as he walked up to the clergyman with Athnic on his arm; for he was to give the bride away. And Harold, how did he look? Well, in the words of his erratic father, he "seemed as if he breathed happiness at every pore, and wished an eternal peace and goodwill to all mankind, as the poet said."

Where did the clergyman come from? He came all the way out to the station, over a hundred miles, purposely to perform the ceremony that would make two happy, and both as one.

Mr. Brownlow's house was not large enough to give accommodation for all the guests who were invited, so small tents were rigged in the different parts of the garden, and there the bachelors found pleasant quarters. And a jolly time they made of it, too, the night before the wedding. Truth to tell, most of them had drunk more than one glass of whisky, and they felt so happy and merry that they were singing, playing, and dancing more than half the night. But, with the exception of Ponsonby Oberon, it was only the gay young bachelors, like young Lenden, who were carrying on in this way. In the house slept Mr. Merton, who came all the way up from Sydney to see his station, and be present at the wedding. Old Mr. Lenden and his wife and family were there also, and Miss Lenden acted as bridesmaid, and, we believe, captured the heart of a good-looking young squatter, who lately came up to that part to live.

Well, it was all very pleasant, and all were very merry and happy. Perhaps young Mr. Lenden showed a slight trace of sadness just at the time the marriage was to take place, but he acted his part of "best man," so Ponsonby Oberon said, "as if to the manner born;" and he kissed the bride too, and, with something of a tremor in his voice, wished her a life-long happiness. Then, turning to Harold, he earnestly wished him the same, and, shaking hands with him, offered his congratulations, and added, with a playful little smile, "Harold, old man, this is one of those cases where the 'best man' did not win."

And the breakfast in the big marquee! Ah, that

was another most pleasant affair. And the speech-making! Well, there was never such a variety of rhetoric since the world commenced. Mr. Brownlow stood up and gave vent to a remarkable piece of oratory. He had, perhaps for the first time in his life, taken just one glass of whisky too much, and it was marvellous how it altered the whole character of the man; so much so that Ponsonby Oberon, who came after, said that though he knew his worthy old master for a long time, he "only now for the first time found out that there was nothing of the bear about him, but the skin, as the poet said."

To which Mr. Brownlow interjected with some vigour, "Be gosh, Ponsonby, it did not take me as long to find out that there was nothing of the fool about you, but the head."

But the real speech of the occasion was made by Mr. Merton, who dwelt eloquently on Harold's success as a station manager, and the splendid results his ability, his industry, and his courage brought about. Mr. Merton's style was perhaps somewhat lofty and rhetoric, but, after he had gone on for some time in Harold's praise, he said, "You all know the history of my investment in station property. You all know the sort of a place I purchased, what a hopeless, tangled, neglected station it was; the cattle running as wild and uncared for as the buffaloes of the American prairies, and the horses as free and untamed as the mustangs of the pampas. That was a state of things that meant a sea of work to rectify, and the man who was to do it must be possessed of mental and physical energies, such as few managers of our time can lay claim to.

" I confess when I saw the place myself, and saw the cattle and horses, or rather caught a passing glimpse of them—I confess, my friends, I felt that I had once for certain made a serious mistake. My friend Mr. Brownlow did not encourage me to take a more hopeful view ; advised me, in fact, to get rid of the place as soon as possible, and to make the most of a bad bargain by considering the first loss the best, and to sell the place before I incurred a greater. By some strange obstinacy on my part, ladies and gentlemen, I did not take that advice, though it was the opinion of one of the oldest and most experienced pastoralists of this Colony. That advice, my friends, would probably be the soundest that could be given under ordinary management, but I was fortunate in securing one to look after my interests, who carried out and so thoroughly accomplished his great work as to exceed my most sanguine expectations.

"At this moment, ladies and gentlemen, the station has not only repaid with good interest all that it has ever cost me, but it has yielded a few thousands besides. You all know (pointing to the bridegroom) to whom I owe all this, and proud and delighted I am to be here on this happy occasion to speak about it. You all, no doubt, feel that to one who has been such a good, true, faithful, and laborious servant I owe something more than mere thanks and praise besides his salary, for this has truly been a labourer more than worthy of his hire. If that be your thoughts, you think justly, and I myself will not be one of the last to take a less liberal view. Therefore, I think I can make no more suitable and substantial wedding offering than to take my young friend in as an equal partner in the property which he has so well, so ably, and so systematically managed and conducted."

With these words he sat down amidst great applause ; and Harold, too overcome to express his feelings, could only at first tearfully declare his thanks and gratitude. But after a while, gradually gaining the mastery of his emotions, he spoke slowly at first, but as he went on, growing stronger, more confident and more eloquent, till at last his ideas and feelings came forth in one grand unbroken stream of words.

"As for myself," he concluded, " I take no credit for what I have done. My good and generous employer has been pleased to accord me the highest praise for it, yet the feeling remains with me that I have done no more than my duty, and I hope, with God's help and blessing, I shall never do less. It is, of course, a well-worn truism that we all have our duties to perform ; let us but endeavour to carry them out to the best of our power, though in my own humble efforts I often feel how much I fall short of my aim, however earnest and hopefully resolved it might be. But, my good friends; ladies and gentlemen, whatever little I may have done in my good master's service, and in improving my own poor state, I owe to the gentle guiding hand of one who is and has been to me the dearest blessing of my life. Whatever little I possess of knowledge, of learning, of goodness, or charity, or of better things, I owe to that same dear one, and it will be now the further duty of my life to make *her* life as peaceful, as happy, and as free from cares as ever did man truly devoted to one he loves beyond all things, to whom, through the goodness of God, he owes the noblest, grandest, sweetest happiness of his life."

Chapter XLII

"After many years"—H. C. KENDALL.
"Still in thy right hand carry gentle peace,
To silence envious tongues. Be just, and fear not ;
Let all the ends thou aim'st at be thy country's,
Thy God's, and truth's."
—*King Henry VIII.*—SHAKESPEARE.

I T is years long after, and though the curtain
has long ago dropped, we stand before it for
the last time to say a few words concerning the
characters, who are now hidden from view.

Harold has now grown a rich man, a very rich
man, some say a millionaire, but we can hardly
think so yet. Long ago he was appointed a
Justice of the Peace, and took the trouble to at
once make himself well acquainted with his
"Magistrate's Guide," and to serve out justice
kindly yet impartially. All he says and does
has force and wisdom, and thus it is his opinion
is constantly looked up to and asked for, and his
word has weight.

In learning and knowledge too, what a field he
has travelled over since last we saw him. There
is not a standard work of value, scientific, classical,
mathematic or philosophic, that he has not found

X

time to make himself acquainted with, and with
his marvellous memory to retain and extract the
pith and marrow therefrom. Thus his classical
learning has given him refinement, culture, and
poetic taste; his mathematics have made him calculating, methodical, exact and logical, whilst the
scientific and philosophic have broadened and deep-
ened his mind, making him tolerant and kindly
towards all religions and creeds, and at the same
time causing him to feel not anger, but pity and
sorrow, for the narrow-minded sectarian bigotry to
be found within so many professed followers of
Christ.

He is a high authority on political economy, and
it may be perhaps for that reason, as well as his
practical knowledge of governmental affairs, that he
has been so often asked to stand as member for
the district. But so far he has always declined
the honour, though lately they have been touching
him on his weak point, and telling him that it is
his certain duty that he should give some portion
of his knowledge and abilities towards the service
of his country. It is this word duty that is making him think over the matter. At the same time
there is a large section of the people who say they
will return him at the next election in spite of
himself. At present he takes the chair at all district meetings; he is a ready and masterful
speaker, and on more than one occasion has been
deputed by the people of the district to go down

and interview the minister on certain important local matters. Yet withal, he is a plain, simple man, with no vanity or pride about him, and seeming always to be perfectly unconscious of his merits. And, moreover, he is good-tempered, cheerful, obliging, having no foes, and in fact the idol of all who know him.

His wife is not less popular, and their two little children are the admired of the district. Such pretty, well-mannered, good-natured, loving little things they are; bright and intelligent also, but withal full of that beautiful, touching simplicity, which is the sweetest charm of childhood.

Mr. Brownlow lives on his own station, and for a man of his age it is wonderful how he gets about. He constantly visits Athnie and Harold, finds fault with everything, and never seems to be so happy as when he is growling to the best of his ability. Nevertheless, the two little children are always delighted to see him, and when they hear the dogs barking on his arrival, they run to the door, and clapping their little hands, call out, "O, mamma, here's the goody man that always brings the lollies." Then they will run out to meet him, and if he sees no one looking he will take up the two little things and kiss them, and stroke down their bright little curly heads, calling them all sorts of endearing names. When they think there has been enough of this, they will break out quite suddenly, " Did oo bring any lollies dit time ? "

Mr. Brownlow will answer, " You hungry little savages of sweet tooths, how well you never forget them." With that he will put his hand in his pocket and pulling out a handful of sweetmeats nearly choke the children with them. " There you are now," he will say. " You little grinding machines, it's like feeding a pair of corn crackers to see the way you can munch."

But he does not like to be caught doing these things, and he will say to Athnie that " Youngsters are the plague of life ; they are always howling and screeching and going on in such a way as if they liked it."

Mrs. Brown lives with her daughter. She is now a fine, stout old woman ; more good-natured than ever if that were possible. She often likes to talk with Athnie and Harold about old times, and to laugh and cry over them again. Such a good, dear, lovable old woman she is that one is made cheerful and happy by only just seeing her.

But what about Ponsonby Oberon ? Yes, certainly, he must not be forgotten. Well, some time ago, he came across Hain Friswell's *Familar Quotations*, and the book so charmed him that he stole it. He now makes it his constant study, and in fact speaks in quotations. There is nothing that he delights more in, than to rattle a few of them about Mr. Brownlow's ears. And Mr. Brownlow will get in a terrible rage and shout out, " Dash my wig, Ponsonby, you natural-born fool, I thought I knew all the old rubbish you'd picked up from those cursed potes, but lately you seem to have gathered a whole stack of new ones, and be gosh, man, you are headlong on the road to destruction now !"

Then Ponsonby Oberon would slap his chest with great vigour and say, "Ah, sir, you well might ask with the poet, whence is my learning or hath I toiled over books, consumed the midnight oil. My learning is without limit, sir ; and as you know I can throw a light on any subject, and, as the poet said, 'adorn everything I touch.' But what am I saying ; is it not throwing pearls before swine? Is it not wasting one's sweetness in the desert air, a man of my talent here in the bush, as the poet says?"

Butler & Tanner, The Selwood Printing Works, Frome, and London.

www.ingramcontent.com/pod-product-compliance
Lightning Source LLC
Chambersburg PA
CBHW031031120726
47905CB00007B/2130